J. B. KEATS

HE CAN SEE HEAVEN

THE HIEROPHANT

Printed in the United States of America

First Printing, 2015

ISBN 978-0-9904489-0-7

Nonester Press
4216 Aralia Road
Pasadena, CA 91001

jbkeats.com

HE CAN SEE HEAVEN

For Molly

ACKNOWLEDGEMENTS

To write a first novel at twilight calls for a pinch of courage, a dollop of arrogance, and at least some measure of foolery, but central to the recipe is the coaching, council, and cheer of good people.

Thanks most to the young woman who edits my spirit as well as my prose, Shea Lynn Keats. Her tuition replaced formal instruction as did catalytic lessons from her mentors, Peter Greene and Perry Meisel. For spiritual acumen I consulted the only holy man I know and then the most moral, Drs. Joe Gent and Jamie McLaughlin. Similarly were recalled the still voices of John Berle Keats, Sister Maria Teresa Ferenzi, and Grand Knight Daniel T. Brahaney. Perhaps the most salient counsel came from my everyman, the Arkansas Bard, Jeffery French. Thanks especially to my love and champion, the kind spirit who gives comfort and hope through my trial, Debra Crowningshield Fallon. To a score and more of friends, family, and acquaintances who endured the first drafts, I'm particularly grateful. Kudos also for the professional services of Ryan Evans, Brittany Farmer, Ian Harper, Ruth Lehrdal, Kimberly Martin, and Scarlett Rugers.

Finally, to the New Testament scholars and other cited authors, I'm indebted for their gift of knowledge, the only treasure less precious than time. Their analyses and insight give hope that the mysteries of the magnificent Jesus of Nazareth might someday be explained.

AUTHOR'S NOTE

This work was provoked by the notion that far less is known about Jesus of Nazareth than his first followers tried to tell and that much of his message has been lost or changed by time and human nature. It represents a fancy founded in fact, a hypothesis anchored to history, and a hope that someday we might learn more about the man-god we call Jesus Christ.

The historical figures and events depicted here are as authentic as could be constructed, with most characters and happenings factual, some interpolated, and a few manufactured. Following the text are appendices of pertinent persons and concepts as well as a list of related readings.

A corollary of this novel reminds us that history, defined as the record *written* by humans who've gone before us, is an imperfect means of viewing the past, but that besides the archaeological evidence, it's all we have. Therefore we must strive to discover and preserve its most accurate sources. Those sources should be, as best we can make them, free from the mistakes and bias of those who created, copied, or translated them— whether with charcoal, chisel, reed, quill, printing press, PC, or smartphone. In most cases that means acquiring the original documents, or at least the oldest we can find.

BOOK ONE
THE QUELLE

1

ASHLEY ROBBINS

Monday, 12 January, 12:56 A.M.
San Nicolas Viewpoint
Granada
Spain

The cold drizzle fell obliquely, soaking her leggings from behind. From there the chill seeped in and she began to shiver. Ashley was afraid, as afraid as she'd ever been. She trusted the man she was to meet—at least enough to wait for him as he'd asked, by herself at the center of the ancient lookout—but he said he'd be there by eleven-thirty, midnight at the latest, and it was almost one.

Many times she'd gawked at the viewpoint's sweeping panorama, gazing across at the Moors' mighty palace set against the snowy Sierra and then down on the Darra valley and its Arab quarter nestled under the trees. Always bustling and merry for its kaleidoscopic sunsets, the stately church plaza is the favorite vantage of natives and tourists alike. But the lovers and travelers were long gone and the misty black night made the lookout macabre, turning the church's bell tower into a ghoulish giant and its cherubs into gargoyles. Alone and trembling in the dank winter shower, Ashley fought waves of dread as she drew her cellphone. The professor answered on the first ring.

"Miss Robbins. Do you have them? Do you have the scrolls?"

"He didn't show, Professor. Ten minutes more, and I'm leaving," she declared.

"You'll do no such thing. The Turk will honour our bargain. You must wait all night if you have to... Did you evade Mister Barefoot?"

"I snuck out," Ashley replied, "like you wanted."

"He'll be there, Miss Robbins. I'm sure of it."

"But Professor," she objected.

He hung up.

Just then she heard fast footsteps coming up the nearby alleyway. Ashley turned to see a small man emerge and head straight for her. She recognized him easily as the silhouette grew larger, even with the Fedora folded down. The man was hugging himself, both arms across the chest, and as he came to her she could see that he was clutching a thick bulge beneath his unbuttoned overcoat.

As the rain mixed with sleet she extended the handle of her umbrella to offer shelter. The man crowded close, shouting up to the much taller woman. "What you ask for, they are here!" he barked as he looked to the bulge and squeezed. "Money you have?"

His broken Spanish was hard to understand, the steaming breath repulsive. She picked up her briefcase, struggling to open it with one hand.

He frowned as she fumbled. "You show money, now."

Ashley passed the umbrella to the little man and he drew the handle to him, one arm still clasped against his chest. She felt the icy rain on her neck and leaned in to open the briefcase. He ogled the cash and then reached to his waist, letting go of the coat and the bulge beneath. Her eyes ballooned when she saw the rolled newspapers at their feet, and then looked to his in panic.

The instrument entered below her navel, razor edge up. It made one swift incision from there to the breastbone. Ashley's gasp was short and muted. The man reached into the cavity, spilled her entrails to the stones, and then let the body go. Shedding the remaining papers over the carcass, he quick-stepped toward the alley tilting the umbrella into the rain with briefcase firm in hand.

The blood trail washed away as it fell.

2

ELLEN SHEA

Thursday, 7 May, 1:12 P.M.
Antechamber, Main Reading Room
New York Public Library, Manhattan Branch
42nd Street and Fifth Avenue, New York City
USA

Ellen had been to the library at least twenty times. Number five train to Grand Central Station, up the steel stairs, one block to the crosswalk, and then along Fifth to the main entrance. It took one swipe on her Metro pass, at noontime, thirty minutes max, but the transit union chose that Thursday for their slowdown, and that's just what it was. She jaywalked 42nd Street, jogged down Fifth, rushed between the stone lions into Astor Hall and two-stepped all four flights, at last stumbling breathless into the foyer of the cavernous reading room.

She'd Googled the professor and had an idea of what he looked like but couldn't identify him among the widely scattered patrons. Ellen worked her way down the central aisle, leaning in on her fingertips at each oblong table, examining the men's faces and catching odd looks in return. She worried that she'd missed him, yet the gold clock said she was only seven minutes late. *Would he have gone so soon?* she wondered. *You're supposed to wait twenty minutes for a full professor, but how long would one wait for you?* She returned to the foyer to survey the great hall, frustrated and afraid she'd blown her chance.

Arching tall and with eyes yawning, Ellen scanned the huge space. "Goddammit," she half-whispered.

A British baritone came from behind. "It couldn't be Miss Shea, Mateo. An educated woman would never curse aloud in a public place, especially not in a library."

She turned to see the professor's dry smile. "Professor Parkinson?"

Tall, gaunt, pale, and freckled, in frayed tweed jacket, high collar and wrinkled bow tie, the middle aged scholar took a short step forward. His uncombed pewter hair, smudged goggle-bifocals, and stooping posture seemed a caricature from her grandfather's time—a shabby Sherlock Holmes—the only things missing were the goofy hat and Baskerville pipe. He'd squinted intensely as he made the quip, his bulbous nose quivering like a rabbit's. *A tic,* she wondered, *or an intentional distraction?*

His young companion, standing beside and just behind, was the professor's reverse. A shorter, chiseled man in a striped business suit and mirrored blue sunglasses, he was stout but trim and wore a blank façade matching his military manner. The tar black hair was cleaved precisely at mid-scalp and braided tightly in back, its tapered tail bisecting the shoulder blades. The skin was rose-copper, stretched between high cheekbones and a bold jaw. He stood at attention and spoke not at all.

Native American? Ellen guessed. *Wish I could see the eyes...*

They found a vacant table in the far reaches of the quiet side and sat across as the younger man stood vigilant, braced against the wainscot behind the professor. Rigid and robotic with hands clasped behind, his empty face oscillated, scouring the room with symmetric rotations. The Secret Service style struck her as out of place in the library, almost comical, and it was distracting, but she waited for the academic to speak, primly posed with lips pursed and hands in her lap.

Finally, after tossing one gangly leg over the other, putting hands to pockets and lounging back, the professor looked to her. "Well, Miss Shea, Monsignor Brahaney tells me you're the best the Fordham Antiquities Department has produced in decades. Apparently promptness is not one of his criteria."

"I apolo-"

He cut her off. "Apollo is a god, not an excuse, so don't bother, young lady. Brahaney says you're a linguist, that you're familiar with Granada, and that your knowledge of the Byzantines is considerable. It seems hard to believe: an astute intellectual in such a young, and should I say, *polished* package. Is the priest correct or merely exaggerating? The old toad's always overstating his case."

"Well," she began to answer.

Again he interrupted, this time squinting and with the snout in spasm. "'Well' is a state of health or source of water, Miss Shea. Can you speak the King's English, or only swear?"

That was all her Gaelic spine would bear. His clumsy attempts at intimidation had offended her to the quick, and as Ellen smiled at his smugness, she prepared her retort. Bending steeply toward the man with elbows anchored on the table's edge and index fingers to her lips as if to comply with the QUIET signs, her intent was to make Parkinson lean in likewise, which is just what he did. The android in the pinstriped suit, by then in parade-rest position, flexed his brow.

Ellen's eyes pithed Parkinson's. "Now hear this, Professor *Smart-ass*," she said in a harsh whisper. "I hustled down here between classes as a courtesy to Monsignor Brahaney, not to please you. You said on the phone there was a job to be had, and I could use the money—badly if you need to know—but I'll be damned if

I have to put up with your English ego to get it. I cut my teeth around four wise-ass brothers, every one as crass as you, and my tongue is quicker than yours'll ever be." She let the venom diffuse. "Now, are you interested in my credentials, or not?"

The professor recoiled, palms deflecting and bullet eyes gaping, and then went suddenly civil. "Go on, Miss Shea, pray tell."

Ellen resumed her posture, hands Geisha-style. "Thank you. You know about my undergraduate work: degrees in Antiquities and World Languages. I grew up speaking French with my father and Spanish with my grandmother, spent my summers in Tangier, and published my first peer-reviewed paper in high school. My Arabic is near native and I can read all of the old Greek and Latin. I did four semesters at the University of Granada and have their degree as well. It's my last post-grad year with Monsignor Brahaney, with only the dissertation to go... You're overstating my Imperial expertise. I wrote a few sappy papers to impress my profs, but the Roman historians bored me—far too predictable and way past arrogant—even for men. My real interest is the Spanish Moors, the Nasrids in particular. That said, I'm forthright and hard working. If the job *can* be done and if you pay well enough, what you require will happen." This time she leaned in only slightly. "Now, sir, what else would you like to know?"

Ellen had to wait for his reply.

"My! You certainly are forthright, as you say. I shall be frank as well, but must request your complete confidence."

She agreed with a blink. Seeing that, he wagged his finger. "If you should betray my trust, young woman, I should have to—"

There he goes again, she thought. *Now it's my turn to interrupt.*

"Professor Parkinson, please. Don't speak to me as if I were one of your whiny clerks. I'll keep your secrets, but this won't work unless we're on the same page."

Only the tip of his nose quivered. "Quite so, Miss Shea. Shall we adjourn to the privacy of my automobile and continue our discussion? We can drop you at Rose Hill when we're done."

3

PAUL P. PARKINSON

Thursday, 7 May, 2:15 P.M.
Curb Lane
Park Avenue, Manhattan, New York City
USA

A stretch Cadillac with ambassador's plates eased up to the sidewalk. The professor's peculiar companion tended their door before taking his seat up front. Without looking, he closed the glass partition as the driver merged into traffic. Creeping up the curb lane in the afternoon clog, Parkinson outlined his proposition to Ellen.

"Last year, a clearly legible parchment fragment, about twenty-five centimeters square, was offered to us by a Manhattan antiquities dealer. He was pedaling it as Gnostic[a], but straightaway we knew it was more: Koine Greek on Anatolian calfskin, dated by our laboratory to the second century and telling of a prophet yet to come, a herald of end-times called 'the Hierophant.' We'd never seen anything like it. It's early Christian, part of a Quelle[b] parable we think, referenced in Eusebius'[1] history of Papias[2], but unlike any surviving text."

The professor continued. "Last fall, a second piece, a short but intact scroll, came to my colleagues at Johns Hopkins and they called me down for an opinion. It was another unknown sayings passage, but in Aramaic. Like our piece, it was intricate, poetic, and plainly beautiful, but what shocked me was the skin—more than similar to our piece—the same texture and identical in shade. The Hopkins people were good enough to share a sample from the margin and we've confirmed that it's from the same lot as our Greek piece. The chemistry and microscopy were perfect matches, without doubt from the same Christian craftsman."

Ellen hid her excitement behind a straight face. "What did they think of your parchment?" she asked.

Parkinson peeked out the window. "There was no need to mention it, Miss Shea. They didn't ask."

"Oh," she said as she wondered. *A professor without scruples?*

"Mateo traced both pieces back to Spain," he said, "to Granada. The Moroccan dealer who handled the Hopkins' piece acquired it in the bazaar, but he couldn't remember where, and we *cannot* locate the shop. The New York scrap came from a bodega in Almeria, but the manager said he purchased it in the same place. His description of the store and its owner was identical to the Moroccan's but his memory of its location was just as weak. Like the other man, he got lost in the maze of crooked little lanes when we took him there. We think we've searched every dingy shop in that part of the city, but have nothing to show for it. Mateo and I spent the whole bloody winter over there, my entire sabbatical, for naught. We require a fluent, knowledgeable, aggressive investigator with a low profile and some new ideas."

"Who's Mateo?" she asked.

He fingered the man in the front passenger seat. "My well-dressed associate, there: a genuine 'noble savage,' with an intricate brain." Parkinson ignored Ellen's sour face. "The priest tells me you're to sit for exams next week. We'd like you to come to work for us immediately thereafter. How does it sound, Miss Shea?"

Ellen tried for tranquil. It was a dream assignment, something she couldn't have hoped for until she was a scholar in her own right. The truth was that she'd have done it for air fare, but the young woman had her grandfather's instinct for a gamble and sensed she was holding a flush, so she played it.

"Well, it's interesting, Professor, certainly something I could handle," she said. "I lived in Granada's Albaicin neighborhood, opposite the Alhambra palace, a few blocks above the bazaar, and I know those 'little lanes' very well. No offense intended, but with your retro-looks and prickly manners?" She smiled. "You weren't getting straight answers from the shopkeepers. Most are North African, worldly but sweet. You have to know how to stroke them, gently, how to share a pipe and lead them to the bargain, just as they would with you. They prefer French to Arabic, and certainly not English or Spanish."

She continued. "As for the artifacts, Koine's easy for me, but I'd have trouble even identifying Aramaic. It looks like the old Hebrew, doesn't it?"

"Correct, my dear," Parkinson answered, "but the artifacts were together. If you find documents in one script, you'll find the other. There are dependable techniques to identify the parchment, and we've made them portable."

She looked out the window and spoke with a hint of whine. "I was really looking forward to going home for a while, Professor. I never miss my granddad's Memorial Day. He roasts a pig and has half the town over. I haven't seen him or my brothers since Christmas, and it'll break his heart if I'm not there." She sighed. "Besides, Granada can be terribly hot in the summer, and lousy with Americans. It would have to be worth my while... I'm not sure."

"Indeed, Miss Shea? I'll be frank. Currently, you're our only qualified candidate, and be assured, we'll make it very much worth your while. Of course, should you acquire more objects, there will be a finder's fee. Let's say, one thousand dollars per scroll."

Ellen stalled for time to think. "The library must have a bigger budget than we do. It would take us a year to get something like this approved, and they'd underfund it by half."

"Oh no, this isn't an NYPL venture. I've been engaged by a private party to supervise this project and we have no restrictions save time. I don't have to tell you what a furor there would be if we proved that 'Quelle' documents still exist. Such a find would be bigger than Codex Siniaticus[c], Nag Hammadi[d], and the Dead Sea Scrolls[e] put together. Indeed, Miss Shea, I'd wager that it would be the greatest biblical discovery of all times. It would mean instant tenure for you at any university.

"To be honest, I never believed in Quelle, at least not a *written* Quelle," he said, shaking his head. "Too simple, you know—a new record of what Jesus[3] said and did, from direct observers, chronicled within a few years of his death, predating accepted scriptures and uncorrupted by the early Church? And this new apocalyptic prophet, 'the Hierophant?' ... It's just too fantastic. I'm sure you know how the churches would regard such a find—the Quelle would trump the New Testament and threaten their very existence—they'd do anything to have such scrolls, and short of that, to destroy them."

Ellen glanced down on the river as they crossed into the Bronx, ashamed of her total ignorance about this "Quelle" subject. Wary of revealing her naiveté, she looked to Parkinson and nodded, puzzled but comfortable with her deceit. This was clearly a negotiation.

"Threaten their existence?" she questioned. "Aren't you exaggerating, Professor?"

"Not at all, young lady. Christianity is like other canonical religions. Whether it's the Qur'an, Book of Mormon, Dianetics, Mein Kampf, or in this case, the New Testament, they're defined by their texts. Should we find the Quelle—the first record of what Jesus said and did—eyewitness accounts and unaltered quotations, lost for nineteen centuries and more factual than the Bible?" He raised one eyebrow. "It will shake their foundations. They'll reject it out of hand and attack."

Again she nodded as if to understand. "If you succeed, Professor, if you do find this 'Quelle', would it shake *your* beliefs?"

"My beliefs, Miss Shea?" He giggled. "No, I think not. My beliefs are quite firm."

Parkinson pivoted. "We've taken the liberty to arrange a first-class sleeper on Air Iberia, the evening of your last exam—Tuesday, according to the priest. This automobile will be in front of your building at 5:00 P.M. and will carry you to the airport. Mateo will meet you in Granada and escort you to a residence hotel near the bazaar. You'll find tools of your trade there as well as currency, two credit cards, one Europhone, and five cashier's checks on Banco España. Guard the checks, Miss Shea. They're as good as bullion. We expect you to keep proper records, of course, but impose no limit on expenses. Mateo will be close by at all times. His number and mine will be quick-keyed on the cellphone."

Parkinson paused to be certain she was following. "If you find something and need help assessing it, use the camera on your phone. And Miss Shea, if you feel confident, you are to purchase on the spot. Call me if you can, but carry cash and a bank check at all times. From what I've observed, we needn't be concerned about your gullibility."

Ellen had trouble encompassing it all. "Thank you, Professor. All that's premature, but tell me, what's the most you're willing to pay for the scrolls, apiece?"

He opened his arms and shrugged. "Consult me if you have the opportunity, but if not, make your best bargain. There's no limit on the account."

Fordham's brick perimeter appeared. She glanced toward the gate and then snapped back, engaging

Parkinson's little eyes. "Okay," she said. "I'm interested, but I'll have to talk with Monsignor Brahaney. I wouldn't think of taking a job like this without consulting him. Assuming you check out, when will I see your parchments?"

Parkinson puckered. "Report to the faculty door on Sunday, Miss Shea. Let's say, one o'clock? We'll review them and teach you how to verify the parchment."

He offered his business card as the limousine coasted up to the curb. Ellen snatched it and popped out with the car still moving, holding the door wide before Mateo could tend it and blocking him as she peered down at Parkinson.

"One o'clock Sunday then, assuming Monsignor gives a good reference," she said. "We can discuss my salary. And Professor, you've understated the value of the scrolls considerably, as I'm sure you know, so if I am lucky enough to find more, I think *ten* thousand apiece would be fair." She winked. "Don't you agree?"

The professor's pockmarked nose quaked as he nodded.

Ellen about-faced and let a grin escape. Shouting over her shoulder, she quick-stepped away. "Good day, gentlemen!"

The men looked to each other, gaping.

4

MONSIGNOR BRAHANEY

Saturday, 9 May, 4:10 P.M.
Faculty Rectory, Fordham University
Rose Hill Campus
Bronx, New York City
USA

Ellen heard all of her classmates' stories about Monsignor Brahaney, most of them two or three times. Rumor said the cantankerous priest was no less than eighty years old, and most thought eighty-five was more like it, but none would have dared to ask. The Jesuit's vigor and salty exuberance pegged him at half that age. His favorite classroom stunt was to challenge contrary young men to one-armed pushups on top of his desk, the loser to pay in single-malt. The result was more rectory whiskey than the priests could swig. The few feisty women he encountered had no such opportunity—in its place came polite rebuke. He ruled his archaeology department like a shogun, but in a style that allowed initiative and independence such that all were respectful and most content with their spirited mentor.

She knew of the legends as well. The monsignor was the youngest of five, they said, orphaned when his immigrant mother died with the sixth in a botched tenement delivery. Gone to sea at fourteen, a tanker sank beneath him in the merchant marine, and one year later, a warship off Okinawa. He'd been a brawler in the Navy, an undisciplined hellion who spent as much time in the brig as at sea.

But Ellen learned of the monsignor's spiritual transformation from the priest himself. He told of his recruitment into Loyola's holy army by a Jesuit who knocked him to a Bowery sidewalk when the drunken Brahaney mocked him. According to the monsignor, his conversion was swift and complete, making reason his guide and the Jesuit brotherhood his home. He credited an elder teacher with launching his academic career, begun during penance in Chiapas. It was there he fell in love with archaeology, he told Ellen, making treks to the Mayan ruins and discovering a new site along the way. After returning to the U.S., Brahaney rose quickly in the John Carroll and Fordham faculties, and still a young man, carried himself and his chairman to academic celebrity with a Coptic discovery in Sudan. The monsignor was everywhere regarded as dean of deans when it came to Christian artifacts, and he could navigate the Holy Land blindfolded. Even the Israeli antiquarians believed him. His thorny veneer didn't bother Ellen—she knew it was a practiced put-on, affording the distance he needed to work and reflect.

Ellen chose Fordham's program for its reputation of turning out the best field scholars, tutored by Brahaney in alacrity and grit. Several had become department chairs at other universities, and that was her long term goal. And she was aware of her special status—Ellen was the monsignor's all-time favorite, ever since that afternoon seven years before when she demanded his attention during the opening lecture of his Comparative Religion class. He'd barely begun when Ellen, seated in the top row of the small amphitheater, raised her hand. At first the monsignor ignored her, causing an ever more vigorous wave.

Finally annoyed by the distraction, he pointed up. "Yes, you there! What is it, for heaven's sake?"

Ellen stood with a smile. "Thank you," she said. "No offense, Monsignor, but how can we expect a Catholic priest to be objective about religions? It would be like having a eunuch lecture us on the Kama Sutra."

The priest gaped along with the students. "Sit down, Miss ...?"

"Shea, sir, Ellen Shea."

"Sit down, Miss Shea, and you'll see just how objective *this* priest can be!"

He would have owed her the liquor.

The teacher was as professional with Ellen as any student he'd shepherded, but both knew that theirs was a special connection. Her call to his chambers that Saturday was risky, nonetheless—all knew that his private sanctum was verboten to visitors and phone calls alike.

With the rectory's phone in hand, Brahaney's young colleague swallowed hard as he knocked on the senior priest's door, at first lightly and then with force. There was no response, causing him to bend full from the waist and shout upside-down through the louvers, a trick he'd used once before. The flexible novice was folded like a jackknife, his bushy hair brushing the hardwood as he peered through the slats.

"Monsignor! Sir! Excuse my intrusion!" he shouted. "A young woman has been calling for you, constantly. She will not be denied. Monsignor. Monsignor!"

Frowning deep, in a tattered open robe with his package dangling and a chipped whiskey tumbler in hand, a thin, barefoot old man silently opened the door and was greeted by the young cleric's rump. He scowled as he pondered on it, but then reversed to a smile. "That would be Ellie!" he declared.

The young priest bolted upright. "Why yes sir, a Miss Ellen Shea, sir."

Brahaney snatched the receiver. "Ellie?"

"Yes, Monsignor. I'm sorry to disturb you. Please forgive me."

"I figured it was you," he said. "You're the only one who's got the balls to call me here. What is it?"

"I was asked down to the Public Library by a Columbia professor, Paul Parkinson. He says you gave him my name, and he's offering a summer job. I have to decide before I see you on Monday and need to know if he's legit."

"In the chapel," Brahaney responded, his voice suddenly soft. "Thirty minutes."

5

SAINT PETER

Saturday, 9 May, 4:45 P.M.
Front Pew, Fordham University Church
Rose Hill Campus
Bronx, New York City
USA

Why they always had to meet in the university's chapel was a mystery to Ellen—the theatrical atmosphere, perhaps—the old priest thrived on melodrama. Gothic and cave-quiet, its architecture and bells are supposed to have inspired Poe's morbid poetry. Piney incense lingers there and man-sized candles flank the altar, casting an eternal twilight across the tiger-oak pews. Its walls are stained glass, a gift from Philippe, King of France, portraying the four Evangelists alongside Peter and Paul. The French artisans' depiction of the larger-than-life saints is psychedelic, bringing their glass eyes alive. For Ellen Saint Peter's gaze was particularly creepy, seeming to lock on and follow her every move.

She dare not show up early. The monsignor had to be in place, perched under the Evangelists, straight-spined and chanting in the front pew. Ellen's role was strictly defined: to kneel silently and at attention in the pew behind. His meditation complete, Brahaney would slide back and slouch toward her, anchor his elbow on the pew back, cock his ear without looking, and then converse in a whisper. It was like sacramental confession without the screen, which she suspected was his intent since she never told him her sins for real. The act never varied. She could have done it in the dark.

He was in his trance with chest heaving when Ellen arrived, one "Miserere Mei Deus" with each exhalation. Dressed like the janitor in a soiled work shirt and black jeans, he knelt with neck extended and elbows on the rail, fingertips splayed and to his lips. The furrowed face was three days unshaven, the eyes not quite closed. Reflections from the cupola bounced off his polished dome, resembling a convex constellation.

Orion, Ellen mused.

She blessed herself as she genuflected, rattled the kneeler to signal her presence, and then dropped to her knees. His mantra ebbed and he nestled into the seat, assuming the confessor's position. Looking to the glass saints, the priest opened as usual, with no salutation.

"Parkinson was impressed, then? I knew he would be," Brahaney whispered. "The son of a bitch is a perfect ass. He's one of Bertrand Russell's arrogant agnostics— covers all bases, but believes that if God's not there, then there's no heaven or hell—and for him, no rules. But he can spot a champ when he sees one, and he had to be pleased with you." His eyes jumped to hers, their lens-less pupils quarter-sized. "Watch your ass, Ellie. Parkinson runs with the wolves. If he's involved, it's big money or big science. I hope you're stringing him along."

"I am," she said. "And it's both—money *and* science, I mean."

"Good... Well, what is it you want to know?" he asked.

"All you're willing to tell."

He stared into the pew back, tracing its dark stripes with a thumbnail. "Yeah... Well, he's a brilliant prick, a continental scoundrel—that's all you need to know— never to be trusted. Anything the bastard's involved in, Ellie, anything, it's for him and nobody else. For him the golden rule is 'Do one to others before they do one to you.' The sad thing is, Parkinson has all you'd want in an antiquities investigator ... except for a soul."

Ellen was one of few privy to the priest's sailor-tongue, and she was happy to hear it that afternoon. Whenever he used his potty mouth, she could be sure his thoughts were from the core. But something was amiss. The monsignor was cagey, squirming to find comfort in the hardwood, and his description of Parkinson was cryptic.

"What else, Monsignor?" she asked. "What else about Paul Parkinson? How is it he knows you?"

He clown-frowned as his eyes met Saint Peter's, then answered inside a pout. "Well, we've got a history, a long one. Started out well enough, as colleagues in the seventies. He was fresh out of the British Museum, full of piss and vinegar, Columbia's next big star, and I was as impressed as anybody. He made a big find in Abyssinia and his interpretation of the Antioch presbyters was brilliant. We coauthored a few papers and were friendly rivals on the lecture circuit." The priest squinted as he conjured a long-ago scene. "Friendly rivals," he repeated, "until I saw the Dark Prince, when I learned it was all about him and his bank account. It wasn't the upper-crust London ego or the cocksure attitude that went with it..."

"What else, Monsignor?" prodded Ellen.

"Well, Parkinson was beyond ruthless, damn close to sociopathic, less interested in the research than what it brought him. Think Cromwell, Ellen, in tweed. He squashed a lot of people on the way up, some of them my friends. It didn't bother him a bit ... and the bastard's as jealous as Cleopatra in Rome. He couldn't stand it when we made the Coptic find. I'd invited him along but he backed out at the last minute—too proud to go as second in command.

"Parkinson's damn good, Ellie. So good we all knew he would've found the artifacts before we did, and to this day that's galled him. After that, he abandoned me for Morton Smith[4]. It's been a Celtic feud ever since. But then..."

"Then, what?" asked Ellen.

"Well, I shouldn't judge. There may be cause for his wandering soul and reason for his condition."

"Reason for what 'condition'?"

He said nothing.

"Monsignor!"

"Well, there've been rumors—that he was buggered as an altar boy—by his vicar." He giggled. "Thank heaven the priest was Anglican."

The monsignor shifted his gaze to Saint Paul and his face congealed. She knew that expression. It was time to change gears.

"Should I take the job?" she asked.

His head whipped back. "Ellen Shea. I'm disappointed. You've already decided that, haven't you?"

Should've known better than to patronize the Old Man, she thought.

"Sorry, Monsignor. Yes, I'm taking it, even after what you told me. It's the chance of a lifetime."

"Really? I've never known you to exaggerate. What can you tell me?"

"Not a thing," she answered. "Sorry."

He looked toward the altar to hide his disappointment. "Not a hint? Okay, but like I said, cover your ass, Ellie, and always be ready to jump ship."

Touched by the priest's pout, Ellen reconsidered. "Well, I guess a hint wouldn't hurt." She put her hand on his forearm. "But you mustn't say a word."

He nodded.

"The Professor has two parchments," she said, "one in Koine and another in Aramaic, second century—he's sure there're more and wants me to look—said they were from something he called 'the Quelle.' It was embarrassing. I had to pretend I knew what he was talking about."

6

THE QUELLE

Saturday, 9 May, 5:05 P.M.
Fordham University Church
Rose Hill Campus
Bronx, New York City
USA

The monsignor jumped to his feet. She'd seen the priest off balance a time or two, but this was a first.

"The *Quelle*? Did he use that word?" he asked, almost shouting.

"Yes," Ellen answered from the kneeler, "but after what you just told me, about how good Professor Parkinson is, I doubt I'll do any good. He and his buddy searched all winter and still couldn't find it."

Monsignor stood mute, eyes wide with hands to his mouth.

"So what about this 'Quelle' thing? What's the big deal, Monsignor?"

He recovered quickly and answered prickly. "You took my Doctrinal History course, didn't you? Did you sleep through that lecture?"

Ellen smirked. "I must've been bored. It happened a lot in that class."

Monsignor made a sourpuss as he took his seat. "Well, you couldn't have been paying attention, that's for sure. We go over it every time. 'Quelle' is German for 'source', as in the source of Christian scripture. It's hypothetical, postulated two hundred years ago. Until the Nag Hammadi discovery in 1945, only a few scholars believed that Quelle documents existed, much less survived."

Ellen interrupted. "The professor said that if we found the Quelle, it would be as big as the Dead Sea Scrolls. I told him he was exaggerating."

"No. He wasn't exaggerating," said Monsignor. "It'd be bigger, Ellie, much bigger. If someone found 'the source,' what Parkinson called 'the Quelle,' it would tell the truth about the New Testament and revolutionize Christianity. Tell me, Ellie, have you ever wondered why Catholics go so light on the Bible?"

"Sure," she said. "I remember asking my granddad about it when I was little, about why Catholics studied Catechism instead of Bible, like the Protestants. He made one of his 'Bibledygook' jokes and said they were 'trying to hide something.' But what's that got to do with the Quelle?"

"Your grandfather wasn't joking, Ellie. The Church has known for centuries that what's come down to us in the New Testament is only part of what the first Christians recorded, and that what we do have, the modern Bible, has been doctored. Of course, there was the mysterious Papias. Do you remember that part of the lecture, Ellie, about the martyr, Papias?"

She mimed an "Oops!"

"Saint Papias spent his life documenting firsthand accounts of Jesus, from John the apostle and every other eyewitness he could find. He lived in Ignatius'[5] time, at the turn of the first century. Papias carried his collection around and preached from it—he called it 'The Logia'—first-hand accounts of Jesus and his teachings, in essence, what's now called 'The Quelle.' It would have been bulky, maybe hundreds of pieces, but no one thinks Papias' documents survived. Like most of the Quelle, it was left out of the Bible on purpose, especially the parts that said a church wasn't needed.

"What was on Parkinson's parchments, Ellie? Were there sayings? Parables?"

"I can't say any more, Monsignor. I promised the professor, and I know you wouldn't want me to commit a sin."

"Oh, no-o-o-o!" he mocked. "But to answer your question? 'How big a deal?' To my mind, after Saint Paul and besides Luther and the Protestants, only a few things have changed Christianity. Constantine's[6] edict was one, Galileo's solar system another, and for sure Gutenberg's press and Darwin's book. But if someone found the Quelle, *the source*, it would do more. The churches would be forced to 'fess up, explain their cover-up, and prove their worth in the face of scripture that says they have none."

Ellen gawked. "What? Are you serious? How can you be so cynical? You're ordained, a priest, a defender of the faith."

"Of course I am—a defender of the faith, I mean—but count me out as a defender of the Church. Like every scriptural scholar, I know how the Bible was made and how the Church was born. It wasn't pretty, and it wasn't clean. Like John Adams said: 'Facts are stubborn things.' My faith is in a different compartment, Ellie, on a different floor. I believe in Jesus of Nazareth, in who He was and in what He taught, in His example and sacrifice, in His ministry and mystery. I believe in the Kingdom of God, not of man. The rest is—well, it's *the rest*, and sad to say, it's all we've got—manmade and corrupt as hell... Think of the Crusades, Ellie, or the centuries of priestly abuse, or maybe the bottomless greed of those damned TV preachers. Anyway, I don't buy a lot of the New Testament because I know where it came from, but I do believe, with all my heart, in Jesus of Nazareth."

There was an awkward pause, reason for Ellen to pivot. "I may need you after it starts, Monsignor. That's why I'm here."

He slouched as before, this time leaning in with the grin she'd hoped for. "You got it," he whispered. "Vicar makes us carry cellphones now. Try that first, but you can call chambers again if you have to. Just don't tell anyone I said so. I've got a reputation to keep, and it'll confuse those assholes if they think I'm soft on you."

"Thank you, Monsignor. You're always on my side."

"So Ellie, where is it that Parkinson has you looking?" he asked.

She hesitated. "Spain. Andalusia... Granada."

"O-o-oh shit!" he exclaimed. "Granada? That's why Parkinson perked up when I told him about you. It makes sense. So many treasures ended up there. But take care, my child. You know what happens when you go to that place. Promise me you'll guard your heart this time. Walk away from temptation if you can, and run if you must."

"Yes, Monsignor. I promise."

He stood to embrace her, patting her back as he hugged. "Let Him be your guide," he said, and then retreated to his pew.

Ellen peeked back as she eased the chapel door closed. He was kneeling again, ramrod straight and chanting with Saint Peter staring down. Hurrying home across Martyr's Lawn, she thought about times to come. *If I find this 'Quelle', I'll present it to Monsignor Brahaney as a gift, just like he did to his teacher. Besides, the department will need a new chair when he goes, and if I succeed in this project...*

7

MISTER SMITH

Sunday, 10 May, 12:55 P.M.
Astor Faculty Lounge
New York Public Library, Manhattan Branch
42nd Street and Fifth Avenue, New York City
USA

It was her usual end-of-semester rush. Ellen was ready for final exams but there were bunches of loose ends to tie, and now she had to pack for a summer in Spain. She carved out two hours for her appointment and was careful to show up early at the library. The man Parkinson called Mateo was waiting outside the faculty entrance, again at attention in his lint free three-piece and shiny shades.

Without words she was escorted to the threshold of a small oblong room where she recognized the Englishman in the near corner, slouched in a high-backed chair with legs crossed and nose in a journal. Facing him was a matching chair with a tensor lamp burning on the table in between. In the opposite corner she could see another man sitting, his broad form visible in the diffuse light but with face cloaked in shadow. The little lamp's sharp reflection bounced off the man's open eyes, and she could tell he was looking straight at her. There was a second table in the other dim corner, with dual urns glowing alongside fixings for coffee and tea.

Ellen cleared her throat, waiting in vain to be recognized as Mateo stood motionless at her side. Finally, she spoke.

"Professor Parkinson?"

The professor's turtle neck stretched over the journal. He set it aside and stood as Mateo stepped into the hallway and closed the louvered doors behind.

Parkinson's manner had changed. "Welcome, young lady. How good of you to come, and so promptly this time."

"My pleasure, Professor." She looked to the corner anticipating an introduction, but the silhouette didn't move.

"Yes, and this is our patron, Mister Smith," said Parkinson. "Forgive him for not rising."

The elliptical reflections from the shadowed man's pupils shimmered like tiny mirrors as he spoke. "Pleased to meet you, Miss Shea. Thank you for coming."

She smiled back, but had to wonder. The slow voice rumbling across the room was warm and welcoming, but the staging seemed corny and over the top.

"Coffee or black tea, perhaps?" asked Parkinson. "We have every variety."

"No thank you."

Parkinson showed her to the chairs and then gently placed a sealed document and magnifying glass on the table. She took the glass in hand, bending forward to focus without touching. Both men were silent as she perused the specimen. After most of five minutes, she looked to Parkinson.

"It's remarkable. Simple, yet elegant," she said.

The professor smiled. "Did you have any trouble with syntax, Miss Shea?"

"No. I've translated whole lots like this for the monsignor," she said. "It's first century vernacular, second at the latest, and from the Eastern side, for sure. The Greek might as well be punctuated."

"Exactly," said the professor.

"And this unknown prophet—The Hierophant? Amazing." "Ellen added.

"Quite," he responded before handing her a second unprotected piece, a facsimile of the Johns Hopkins' document.

She took only seconds to examine that one. "I don't know what to say. I would've known it was Aramaic, and it looks like the other, but as I told you, I can't read a word and forgot all I knew about material analysis. You'll have to teach me."

The professor gave a crash course. Her queries betrayed sophistication. Then he fetched a small testing kit housed in a Maybelline compact: two miniature glass vials, one eyedropper, and a scalpel blade. A tiny parchment sample was wedged inside the lid.

He demonstrated on the sample. "Two drops from the black-capped vial for one of the white. It must be soaked, Miss Shea. Wait at least one minute for the green color to appear... There! Do you see the fine lines, crisscrossing like a spider's web? Both color and pattern must match."

Ellen peeked toward the corner. The little mirrors jiggled, but the boss stayed still.

Parkinson handed Ellen the compact. "Shall we review the terms of your employment?"

"Sure," Ellen replied.

The mystery man's baritone broke in. "Before that, I'm curious as to how you might approach the task. Have you given it any thought, Miss Shea?"

Her answer was quick. "Yes sir, I have, quite a bit, but I have to ask. Are you sure that the scrolls came from the bazaar?"

The professor answered. "The bazaar makes most sense. Old Granada was the last seat of the Caliphs, where all their treasures migrated, and nowadays there's more, should we say, *informal* antiquity trading in the bazaar than anywhere in Europe."

His eyes pinched. "Besides, Mateo is convinced that the scrolls are there, and he's the best—the man has uncanny sense, a remarkable ability to read people and roust a lead—he's yet to be wrong. Don't be fooled, Miss Shea. Mateo may look like a gorilla in an uptown suit, but he's as bright as they come. Mister Trump was furious when Mister Smith convinced Mateo to join us."

At last she detected a nod from the shaded figure. Parkinson was yammering now, his nose shuddering off and on. "And again, we have no reason to doubt our original contacts, both of whom describe the same shop and its owner, though their memories of the location have failed. Of course, that should surprise no one. The bloody place is a maze." He winced. "We count more than nine hundred businesses there, and as I told you, my own survey was fruitless. Most of the dealers are Moroccan, charming and cunning at the same time, and you're right, they prefer French or Arabic."

"How did you go about it?" Ellen asked.

"I asked the buggers directly. There was no reason to be timid with their kind."

"Forgive me, Professor," she said, "but there was *every* reason to be modest. The Andalusians have a special style, one they value as much as the deal. There's an odd ritual to it, and a proper sequence. They've been doing the same dance since the days of the Caliphs and feel cheated without a performance."

Parkinson's scruffy eyebrows arched.

"I'll play a struggling student, inquiring about my thesis," Ellen said. "As I'm sure you noticed, most shops sell a hodgepodge of items and there's no telling where more scrolls might be. I'll have to look through every pile and cabinet. It'll be dog work, and unless I'm lucky it'll take the whole summer."

Her hints were a few grams heavy.

"Yes, well, it appears a good plan," said the professor as he looked to the dark corner. "We require that you communicate frequently, Miss Shea. We'll continue our efforts on this side and should we discover anything germane, shall inform you. As you're aware, you'll find ample resources upon your arrival. Should you require more, simply ask."

"And my compensation, Professor?"

Again the Englishman looked to the corner, and this time the hearty voice responded. "Five hundred Euros a day, plus expenses. You're to work whenever the shops are open, all day. No days off. Ten thousand dollars per intact scroll as you requested, but I must approve them myself. Is that acceptable, Miss Shea?"

Ellen masked her glee. "Yes, sir."

"Best of luck, young lady, and please, take great care. I'm afraid the competition doesn't play by the rules," said the mystery man.

"Thanks. I'll be careful."

She and Parkinson stood. "We must guard against aiding our rivals," the professor said. "You may tell no one of your mission: not relatives nor boyfriends, and especially not that fossilized priest. Only Mateo and I may be informed. Use your eyes first, speak in generalities, and by no means say the word 'scroll.'"

"I get the idea," she responded.

He called through the louvers for Mateo.

"Bon voyage and good hunting," said Parkinson.

As Ellen exited, the patron rose to stand between Parkinson and the quiet man, six silent shoulders crowding the doorway as they watched her shrinking figure disappear. At last, the boss spoke over the dimming echoes of her clicking heels.

"Well done, Paul. I'm happy with this one. She has the spunk and savoir-faire we need, candid and more resourceful than either of the others. See that she lacks nothing."

"Yes, Stephen," said Parkinson.

Then the boss turned with a deep frown to the younger man. "Let's hope you can keep this one alive," he said.

Mateo's lips stiffened as he nodded.

"Stay on her this time," Smith commanded.

Again came a grim nod.

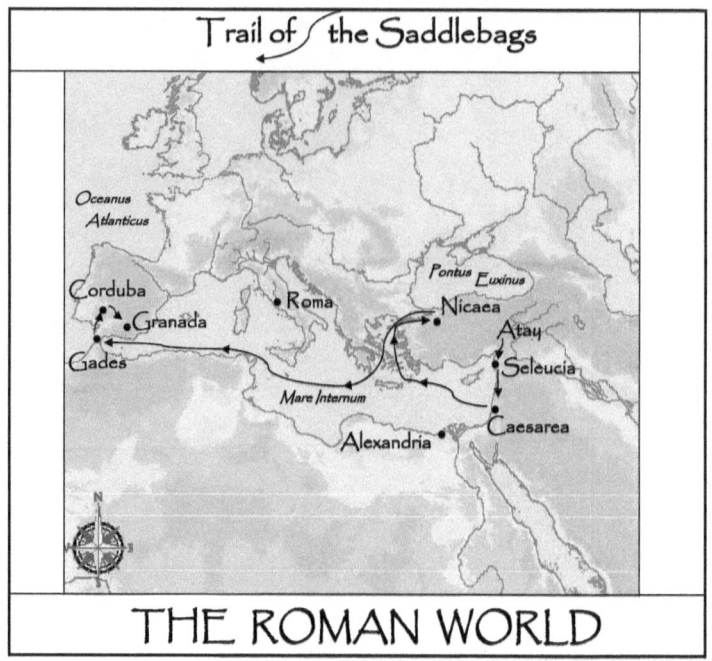

Trail of the Saddlebags

Oceanus
Atlanticus

Corduba
Granada
Gades

Roma

Pontus Euxinus

Nicaea
Atay
Seleucia
Caesarea

Mare Internum

Alexandria

THE ROMAN WORLD

BOOK TWO
THE SADDLEBAGS

alpha

PAPIAS OF HIERAPOLIS

A.D. 112
Atay, Vallis Lycus
Cilicia, Asia Minor
Imperium Romanum

Three men advanced with stealth, concealed in the cover of the wooded ravine that led to the rim of the gorge—a wiry old man astride an ass laden with bulging saddlebags flanked by two much larger men crouching low and close on each side. They slowed and moved left toward the edge of the wood, still hidden among the cedar saplings, stretching their necks to see the canyon from between the crowded branches. The younger brute separated the limbs with one hand as he cupped the other to his ear. Sensing no threat, he dropped to the ground and crawled on his belly into the bare sun, creeping by inches toward the rim. With trembling fingers he gripped the edge, peeked over, and then bounced to his feet, turning back to throw a broad grin and come-quickly waves.

The old man whipped the donkey's rump. They exploded from the thicket in a cloud of needles and fractured branches, the beast squealing louder with each lash and the third man fast behind. As they neared the rim the donkey's legs locked stiff, throwing its rider headfirst toward the chasm, but the tiny man seized its mane and regained his balance, leaning forward and tall for a clear view. Energized by the sight of the crowd spread across the near slope, he dismounted, eyes to the path and ignoring the outstretched hands. His companions followed with chins to chests and the beast in tow.

Once at the bottom, the old one cleaved the mass with a backhand wave. Without delay the big men boosted their master onto an oxcart, purposefully positioned to project his passion up the sandstone walls. Concentric waves of silence spread from the cart when the multitude saw him, and all went still.

Papias' voice was as grand as he was small, a resonant and forceful cry propelling his zeal past the last ear and over the ridge beyond. His recital had long ago become a performance and was introduced as always, with proof of his source. "I am Papias of Hierapolis, hearer of John and companion of Polycarp[7], keeper of Jesus' sayings and sayer of His teachings, come to you from Colassae to give the words. They are today exactly as He spoke them, told by those who stood by His side. The last witness is gone now, martyred in the Romans' dungeon, but no matter." He shook his head. "No longer need they be amongst us, for we hear their voices still. Our Master stands bedside us because the words He gave were set safe on the parchments we carry."

Papias motioned to his escorts. They stepped forward in unison and onto their toes, each holding a donkey bag high.

"This is the Logia!" he bellowed, gesturing with open palms toward the saddlebags. "The testament of those who were there. These parchments come to us as from the font, from His mouth to your ears, uncorrupted and with no change or amendment. Let no man doubt the source." He called the men back. "Jebidiah, Joel."

The tall one jumped onto the cart and eclipsed his master, a saddlebag draped over each shoulder, their oiled leathers aglow in the blonde light of the canyon floor. An acrostic fish was branded on each flap, enhanced with indigo and clearly visible to the throng. Expressionless, the man raised his bare arms, each muscle taut and defined in sweat. Then, with a shrug, he dislodged the bags and relaxed his arms, allowing them to glide by inches to his wrists. At that moment and again by degrees, he raised them level and stood balanced, like a set of human scales. That was Papias' cue to tuck each flap behind and extract one scroll.

With baby steps the tall man rotated, arms quaking from the load but fully extended so that all could see the protruding parchments. Each gaze was fixed and every mind in awe. Then he handed the bags down and jumped from the cart as the silent faces returned to the old man, greedy as eaglets for the mother's beak.

Papias unrolled the scroll and began to read. "And Jesus said to John, 'I am in you and in all that surrounds you. You need only my words to find the way.'"

beta

ORIGEN OF ALEXANDRIA[8]

A.D. 248
Amphitheatrum, Caesarea Maritima
Palestina Prima
Imperium Romanum

The Roman road ran true and smooth along Judea's Coast, as fine as when Herod's slaves set its stones three hundred years before. The man from Phrygia crouched forward on the buckboard of his covered wagon as it rattled down that plumb-straight highway, squinting westward at the city silhouetted on the pink horizon. As dark collapsed he was heartened by the shine of harbor lights bouncing off the bay, no more than a league ahead. It had been a whole moon's journey from his home in Seleucia. He was cold and spent, but Origen's promise of silver drove the Phrygian on and he lashed his ox through the damp night, impatient to make the trade of a lifetime. He would send word of his arrival and arrange to meet the teacher in the marketplace of Caesarea's amphitheater.

The Phrygian's Christian friends in Antioch told of Origen and his adopted city, Caesarea. It was there, they said, that Simon Peter planted the Christian seeds, there that Paul of Tarsus[9] established his first community, and there that the Jewish secession began, ignited by a deceitful Roman massacre in that same amphitheater. For those traditions it became the site of a Christian school founded by the man he was seeking, the renowned and freethinking Origen. According to the Antioch churchgoers, Origen was the greatest Christian scholar. He'd fled Alexandria for Palestine, content to live out his days as an ascetic, teaching the catechism and collecting a library of the fledgling faith. The Phrygian used the sailor's post to inform Origen of the scrolls he found, and the scavenger anticipated great profit.

Marching abreast and in double-time through Caesarea's crowded streets came Origen and his acolyte, Theodore[10]. There was purpose in Origen's eyes. His student had rarely seen the scholar so eager and wanted to know why.

"Pray tell, Master," said Theodore. "What is it about the Phrygian's scrolls that makes you so keen?"

"Well my boy, in the early years, as we compared each document in our collection, we came to realize that it is only the oldest writings that can be trusted—the newer the transcription, the more likely there are to be mistakes and alterations. Indeed, with each reproduction the manuscripts change, through the negligence of some and audacity of others. They either err in transcription or, in the process, make additions or deletions as they please. Whole passages are lost and new ones created."

"Scribes *change* the holy words?" asked Theodore.

"Yes, scribes and their masters. They change words, omit them, and add new ones. It's why we're so strict in our school. If the Nazarene's message is to survive, the writings must be strictly copied upon the most durable material, unambiguous to every eye, and exactly as first written. It is our righteous charge."

Origen continued. "If the Phrygian's tale is true, the scrolls he poached are those of Papias, the oldest record and hence closest to Our Lord. I have devoted my life to finding the earliest accounts of Jesus, and pray that on this day that the angels bring more."

Theodore could only nod and wonder.

Teacher and disciple arrived to meet the trader as agreed, with the sun on high. They identified him easily by his floppy Asian cap, standing on the freeboard of his rattletrap and looking about. Theodore approached alone as Origen dropped off and pretended to shop—their Christian sect was tolerated in the city, but not openly, and they feared a Roman trap. The Legionnaires billeted in Caesarea were Mythrians, hostile to the rival Christian ethos and as likely to arrest professors of the upstart religion as to look the other way. With local judges just as fickle, both men knew they must be wary.

Sensing no treachery, Theodore signaled Origen. The Phrygian from Seleucia was surprised when the old fellow approached—he'd expected more. To him the burly gray-hair seemed a commoner, clad in plain robes and workman's sandals, distinguished only by a thin velvet sash, tailored beard, and refined manner. There were no preliminaries.

"How did you come by these scrolls of which the Antioch bishop wrote?" asked Origen. "I'm told you're a forager."

The Phrygian rushed his reply. "They come from the Greek quarter of the new port, sir, saved by my son and me from the smoldering cinders of a wine merchant's villa on the night of the great summer fire. There they lay hidden, covered with seed inside two amphorae, in the depths of a grain larder. We worked hard to free them in the black night, with soldiers prowling about. And know you that my journey was of great length and hazard." He stepped toward his wagon, pointing at the undercarriage with his whip. "Look here. My ox has gone lame and one axle is askew. It will be two days with the wagon smith... Know also that I am no fool! My uncle tells that the writings are of the forbidden god. I carried them through great danger, down the pirate road and beneath the legionnaires' noses. They delayed me thrice and would have strangled me on the spot had they known of my cargo."

Origen grinned at Theodore. "Oh, my. Such a brave man. What an *odyssey* he's had." With rising eyebrows he turned to the trader. "Is your name Ulysses?"

The Phrygian sneered and spat. Wordless, he mounted the backboard of the tilting carriage, parted its ratty curtains, and disappeared inside. The menagerie of tins and tools tinkled as the wagon rocked and muffled curses leaked out. Finally he emerged with two branded saddlebags, grunting as he handed them to Theodore.

"The skins are soft and of the finest vellum," he boasted. "They'll do well in your collection."

"Pray let us examine them," said the stone-faced Origen.

They moved to the cover of a vacant stall where Theodore removed the scrolls and arranged them across the top of a broad, chest-high table. Origen's twisted fingers unrolled a scroll and anchored its corners with stacks of polished coins. The Phrygian focused.

Like the bags, the parchment was unspoiled— flexible and discolored only at the margins. Origen's pupils swelled when he recognized Papias' calligraphy, but otherwise he masked all emotion. It was his biggest find, the oldest documents he'd ever seen, with hundreds of new sayings and tales from the man-god's years in Nazareth. The inspection took most of four hours. All the while the Phrygian fidgeted with his whip as he paced in wide circles around the stall, spitting once at the men's feet with each revolution.

None in our collection are as diverse, Origen thought, *nor as pure.* Then, as he perused a Greek scroll, Origen gasped. He called Theodore to him and pointed at the parchment. "Look, here."

The youth found the tip of Origen's finger and read in a whisper. "At first light the women of Magdala gathered at the well. Jesus greeted each by name and then spoke to all. 'As the last days approach, I will send to you the Hierophant. Pray with him and heed his guidance. Unto those times, search for the light within.'"

Theodore turned wide-eyed to his teacher.

"There it is again," said Origen.

His chore finished, Origen nested the last scroll himself, turning as he did to the scrounger. "These are of some value," he said. "What sum do you ask?"

"As I told you, sir, I have traveled far and made great effort on your behalf, each day placing my life in peril. My uncle says seventy-five of the old coin for each lot. I will take no less than sixty!"

Again the silver eyebrows vaulted and Origen tossed a tiny, fleeting smile. "Your uncle is no doubt wise, dear sir, but ignorant as to price. They are of much less worth to me. We possess many of the same in papyrus, and require these only in reserve. Perhaps the Romans would care to bid. Shall we call them over?" Origen feigned a wave toward a pair of passing soldiers patrolling in tandem two stalls away.

The Phrygian blanched.

"I shall offer fifty for both, and no more," said Origen.

"Sixty!" was the Phrygian's loud retort.

"Fifty-five, the pair," countered the glaring Origen. "One axle from the blacksmith, salve for your beast, and your wagon filled with fodder. No more."

The Phrygian tried to match Origen's menacing stare but saw only his own fear, reflected in the old man's eyes. The trader spit once, and then again. At last, he mumbled. "Agreed."

gamma

EUSEBIUS OF CAESAREA

A.D. 325, Vernum Aequinoctium
Scriptorium Scola Christianus
Caesarea Maritima, Palestina
Imperium Romanum

Clop... Clup... Clop... Clup...
Eusebius paced in swaying steps down the aisle between his students' desks, the echoes of his wooden sandals puncturing the hollow silence of the scriptorium like a slowly dripping spout. With matching cadence he tapped an ivory staff against his palm as he surveyed each boy's work, bending low from time to time to dissect their penmanship. All at once, his lips pursed tight and the tiny nostrils flared—he'd caught the scent of error. Looming over his unlucky apprentice, Eusebius began a strident censure.

"Acacius! For the love of God, my boy! You're supposed to be the smart one... What *are* you doing here?" He pointed with his middle finger as the other scribes looked on, thumping it like a mallet on the errant letters.

Acacius jerked back, pop-eyed and quaking. Eusebius took a breath to complete the scolding but before he could release it his ears were turned by the rumble of approaching chariots. The elfish man shuddered, neck twisting and eyes snapping toward the sound. Acacius stared at his teacher's forearm, its hair erect and the finger coarsely trembling.

It's the same sound as in Diocletian's time, Eusebius remembered, *the one that carried so many off to torture and death in the Roman jails.* But then reason reminded him that for more than a decade it was Christianity at the side of the Roman state instead of on the tip of its sword, and he exhaled. Hurrying outside to the landing atop the library's staircase, he watched the crimson colors of a military cohort approach as his students swarmed around, chirping like a flock of hungry sparrows.

The leading horsemen halted at the foot of the stair while soldiers rushed forward to steady their teams. Of the modest contingent, only the centurion and his junior officer stepped down. Straight-spined and in step they climbed slowly, their scarlet capes lifting in the ocean air. The senior man was courteous though patronizing, formally delivering a scroll holder after removing his helmet and slapping a salute. The loud smack of his muscled forearm against the leather breastplate caused the youngsters to go quiet and their teacher to shiver once more.

Eusebius extracted the scroll. The Chi-Rho imprint on its rose wax seal signaled the source—it was Imperial—from Constantine himself. With all eyes to him, he broke the wax and unrolled the papyrus, adjusting his arms to focus. From habit, he read aloud. The book-boys huddled closer and the soldiers cocked their ears.

"Know ye, Eusebius, Bishop of Caesarea and master of the library at Palestine. You are summoned by your emperor to court at Nicaea, Bythnia, upon the ides of May next coming. It is a gathering of bishops which you shall attend, its purpose to confirm the righteous and purge the profane. Attention shall there be given to the Arian question, holy dates specified, and practices scrutinized so that all of Rome's Christians may worship in harmony."

Then Eusebius read the post scriptum, silently but with lips in motion. "Soon will come a second summons requiring that you carry to Nicaea one copy of each sacred scripture for the purpose of crafting a collection for my churches. There can be no omissions. Prepare you now for this. Safe passage of the documents is charged solely to your person. Deviance will result in execution."

Assured that the summons had been duly served, the soldiers slapped chests and bade farewell in Constantine's name, descending as deliberately as they'd climbed. Leaning on his baton amidst the gaping students, Eusebius watched the chariots lurch forward, and as the cohort's clatter faded dust settled from its hooves, shrouding the little crowd in a dry brown fog. His mind was entranced but racing as he watched the cherry lines break into a canter, then shrink to red ribbons as they reached the water's edge.

It was astounding yet welcome news, news Eusebius struggled to comprehend, a cacophony of thoughts colliding in his mind. *Alexander[11] and the Patriarchs will be there, and I pray that Osius[12] attend, the man I have longed to meet... At last comes our chance to confront the Arians, set firm the order of feasts, and advance Iraneus'[13] wish for one canon.* With eyes focused on the fading crimson strings, Eusebius reflected. *We have but two moons. I must order a manifest...*

His trance dissolved. "To your tables!" he shouted. "We shall work without supper to recover time lost!"

The boys answered with a collective groan but he herded them inside and made fast for his desk, anxious to put plans in ink.

delta

ACACIUS OF CAESAREA

A.D. 325
Navis Longa Agrippa
Mare Internum
Imperium Romanum

The day of departure arrived at last. It was Eusebius' first time at sea, and the book-bishop acted like the landlubber he was. Standing alone on the foredeck with manifest in hand, he marveled at the barefoot Roman sailors when they cast lines and weighed anchor, then gawked as they scampered along the side rail and fast up the mast. The bireme made way gracefully, shoved from the dock with staves and propelled into the glass-flat channel by a single pair of oars.

Eusebius' eyes shifted to the horizon. *We've gathered the documents as Constantine commanded, including the damnable Gnostic and Essene scrolls. Even the scribblings of the hermits are there... These writings are our greatest treasure, the sparks igniting the Christian inferno, and I am the fire keeper.*

He moved to the gunnel as the *Agrippa* made way, fascinated by the crew deploying the foresail. Then the mainsail fell, unfurling with a thunderclap as it caught the fresh wind. Eusebius turned to the saltwater fan arching beside him and moved to the sideboard for a closer look. He stepped over, latching onto a lanyard and leaning out to touch the bow-spray. A pod of white porpoise appeared and the scrawny man stretched further, almost to the horizontal. Playing like a child, he dangled gate-like above the dolphins, straining to touch a fin. But then Eusebius felt a sharp tug on his robes. A strong hand gripped his waist and pulled him upright. It was Acacius, his one-eyed acolyte, holding tight and stuttering in staccato.

"T-Take care, B-Bishop. You-You'll fall oh-oh-oh-verboard."

"Nonsense. Let go!" Eusebius screamed.

"But M-M-M-aster. Y-y-you'll be lost."

Acacius refused to release Eusebius until he stepped to the safety of the deck.

"Such insolence!" Eusebius shouted. "Take your hands from me, you wretched boy. I was quite safe, and relaxing for a change. Now go. Be quick to your duties. I shall ponder your penance, and believe you me, it *will* be brisk."

The boy didn't move.

"What else?" asked Eusebius.

Acacius stared down, straining to spit out his question.

Eusebius glared. "What is it, boy? For heaven's sake, what is it?"

"I c-came to ask about the r-r-recognized list of scriptures, sir. We-we all wa-wa-want to know wh-wh-why you've ch-chosen so few and ex-cluded so many."

Eusebius flared. "I can't believe, Acacius, that you, of all my students, could fail to understand our mission. You were chosen as my sole acolyte, the most gifted in our school. Despite your lonesome eye and troubled tongue, many believe you will succeed me some day. Ergo, you must learn to appreciate..." His voice softened. "Come, let us find a place in which to discuss these matters."

Eusebius led Acacius by the arm to the Captain's bench, amidships, to do what he'd always done best: explain the holy words. They sat close, centered on the cedar plank like a pair of dueling mimics with shoulders square, forearms brushing, and palms precisely pat. Together their eyes tracked the rising sea.

Eusebius began. "You've heard all of this before, my son, but seem unable to grasp the whole. Pay attention, for one day, with God's grace, *you* shall be giving this lesson. By the will of Constantine we Christians are ascendant, but err not. We could easily fall from the Romans' favor, back to the days of terror, unless ..."

The youth looked to Eusebius as his teacher stared forward, distracted by rising whitecaps on the open sea.

"Our religion stands apart, Acacius, but not by chance. First, unlike the heathen, we believe in a single God of salvation and in his soon-to-come Kingdom here on earth. In that way we give hope to those who have none. Second, our roots reach through Moses to Abraham, succoring in soil that tells of our Messiah. And like the Romans, we welcome converts and their traditions. Many bishops object, but no matter. If a practice be popular, we may adopt it. Because we are *flexible*, Acacius, more souls are brought to the fold."

The boy was flattered by his private lecture. It was true—he'd heard it all before, but never so ordered or intense. His eyes asked for more, so Eusebius obliged.

"Our faith prospers because it is *infectious*, Acacius, and our sole purpose here on earth, mine and now yours, is to nurture the agents of infection, God's written words. The documents we bring to Nicaea are our most potent weapon, unmatched by the Mythrians, Zoroastrians, or any shallow creed."

Eusebius' eyes fixed on the deepening swells. Sure that he was passing the spark, he continued.

"From the beginning, stories on papyrus and parchment passed from one Christian hand to the next, winning converts with every exchange. The first writings were eyewitness accounts. After that came

Paul's letters and then scores of gospels. Over time, some came to be regarded as essential. It's true that at first only Jesus' words were holy, but then those of others were included. When giants like Ignatius or Iraneus favored a script, it was hallowed. Soon the record was in excess."

"But-But what of Pa-Pa-pi-as?" Acacius stammered.

"Allow me to finish!" the teacher admonished. "The writings are our keystone, my boy, but only a fraction may become canon—their sheer number dictates that—and that fraction must be scrupulously chosen. There are many errors and much duplication. Take the gospels about end-times, for instance, those called 'Revelations.' There are dozens, each from a different seer, and none speak the same. We must cull the list and choose but one. And as with our feasts, in Theodore's example, we must be flexible. Those texts which bring converts should be given special consideration."

The sea was full angry and the pair held tight to the bench, lurching from side to side like camel drivers on a grade. Their eyes were drawn to the rigging by the shouts of sailors lashing canvas to yard. That task accomplished, the seamen scrambled down and dove through the foredeck like rabbits to their hole.

As the last sailor disappeared, Eusebius looked to his pupil, shouting above the howl. "Now, Acacius. Your question?"

"Yes, B-B-Bishop, it is of the very f-f-first writings, those scribed by Pa-Pa-pi-as, of which we wah-wah-wonder. Why have they not been included on the r-r-recognized list? They-They are our favorites, by far. And did-did not Origen regard them highly? Why-Why-Why have they been d-d-designated as s-purious'?"

Eusebius sighed. "Yes, Acacius, Origen did deem Papias' scrolls righteous. I will not deny it. But Origen? He was wise and saintly as God knows, but deeply tainted by his Greek experience. You must realize—much of Papias' collection is confusing—and dangerous."

"D-D-Dangerous?"

Eusebius bellowed over the wind. "Yes, dangerous! It contains only quotations and witnesses' memories, with sparse mention of miracles, none of resurrection, and with excess reference to the mystery prophet—the herald of end-times, the one He called the Hierophant... True, the Logia's verses are as poetry, and I can see why your young minds are taken, but they are simplistic and prone to misinterpretation. Many advocate knowing God not by instruction, but by looking within... And in Papias' script, the words of the Magdalene are elevated to an unnatural level, nearly equal to that of men. Preposterous. Many passages stress the need for only the teachings of Jesus, his divinity is but implied, and there are repeated cautions against the creation of structures that might dilute His words. That notion is particularly offensive to me as a churchman, as it should be to you. How can our faith grow and defend itself without organization, discipline, and a hierarchy of champions?"

Acacius' shoulders slumped as Eusebius ended the lesson.

"So, my young colleague, despite Origen's high regard for the oldest writings, we must be wary. But fear you not: they lie alongside those on the 'recognized' list and will be considered for Constantine's collection, as will every scrap we carry."

A fierce squall was on them, firing volleys of horizontal rain through their robes. The deck went awash, drenching their lower parts, but Eusebius would prove his point. He opened the manifest with one hand while holding fast with the other. Thumbing to his reference, he leaned into the young man and thrust the flapping pages in his face. "Here!" screamed Eusebius. "You'll find the old scrolls inside their saddlebags, in the crate marked 'IV'. Unlike us, they're quite safe."

Eusebius shrieked as a gust ripped the list from his hand. It cartwheeled to the side rail and teetered on the gunnel, but Acacius crab-walked through the slosh to make a saving grab. At that moment the deck officer appeared and yanked him to his feet by the scruff of his robe, soggy manifest in hand.

"Foolish Christians! Get below!" he shouted.

So the *Agrippa* sailed the shores of Asia Minor, stopping en route to collect other holy men and their cargoes. The captain caught spring westerlies and passed early into the Propontus, one day's sail from Constantine's convocation.

epsilon

CONSTANTINUS AUGUSTUS

A.D. 325, Adventum Solsticium Aestatis
Cius, Portus Nicaea
Bythnia, Asia Minor
Imperium Romanum

Eusebius was in a sorry state when the *Agrippa* docked in the early morning light. His first voyage had been a nightmare—constantly seasick with that first storm, he endured dry-heaves until the final day. For his weakness, Acacius and a Syrian acolyte carried him dockside on a litter. Eusebius insisted that he lay atop his crates until he could stand, and in the late afternoon, when at last the bookman felt able, he supervised their transfer to the Roman armory. Wobble-legged, with teeth clenched and shedding sweat all the way, he straddled the boxes in the wagon bed with one dainty hand on each tie. Invoking Constantine's name, he demanded round-the-clock surveillance for his cargo before seeking refuge in Hagia Eirene's priory.

It was Bishop Osius of Corduba, the man Eusebius yearned to meet, who'd urged the emperor to call a council of every Christian bishop, but of the nearly two thousand invited only three hundred made the journey. Because of the meeting's location most attendees were from the East, with Patriarch Alexander senior in rank. There were representatives from Persia, Georgia, and other states outside the empire, but western confessors were few. Eusebius' perusal of the roster revealed the most conspicuous absentee: Pope Sylvester of Rome.

Early that evening Bishop Alexander's chamber slave delivered a scroll to Eusebius' door. Acacius carried it to the bedside where the quaking little bishop was slurping salted broth.

"M-M-Master! A m-message! It bears the mark of his ho-ho-liness, Pay-Pay-Patriarch Alexander."

"Very well, you may read it, Acacius."

The boy severed the seal. "Your s-s-singular p-presence is re-required at the R-R-Red Gate upon the next sun," he read. "C-C-Carry this missive for p-passage and inform none of your duty."

Eusebius slept fitfully for the first hour but then dozed deep until Acacius shook him awake at dawn. Arriving early at Constantine's palace, he was escorted by a pair of legionnaires down an echo-filled passageway into a circular antechamber just off the throne room. Minutes later, as he paced the frescoed perimeter, he heard voices approaching. It was Alexander and his young secretary Athanasius[14] who emerged, and to the delight of Eusebius, Osius of Corduba was with them.

As they exchanged pleasantries, all were commanded within to find Constantine waiting at the foot of his throne. Dressed simply in thin robes, without scepter and wearing a plain pewter crown, he addressed each man by name, sprinkling his greetings with focused flattery. His physical presence was unimposing but from the first moment his voice and affect were commanding and as brisk as the morning chill. He chatted with each churchman in turn, face-to-face and holding their hands as the others milled alongside, averting their eyes and pretending not to listen. There followed a few minutes of communal conversation, but all smiles straightened when Constantine declared that it was time to compose the agenda. As the ruler ascended his throne, attendants darted out to spread lambskin chairs in a tight arc facing the Emperor. All settled comfortably, but the mood was strained as each holy man waited for another to open.

At last young Athanasius spoke, his delivery nearly equal to that of the regent's. "By my count, we shall outnumber the Arians six to one, but with arguments contentious, especially when the rogue Arius takes the front. His tongue commands the thunder, and Bishop Alexander must mute it. I propose that the question be presented immediately. There should be no wine until the vote is cast."

All shook heads in agreement.

"The Sabbath matter should be less controversial," said Alexander. "Perhaps we can link it to the Passover discussion."

Again came accord and they continued, enumerating each issue and a strategy to suit it. It grew tedious, and all sensed the Emperor's impatience. When the discussion finally ended, he demanded their attention.

Constantine wagged his finger at each man as he spoke, his tone an octave shy of reprimand. "Arius came as a serpent from the shadows, and we shall put fire to his den. As for the scriptural squabbles I have no concern, but require one act—whichever writings you deem proper must be defined without ambiguity—all others deserve a natural death, never to be copied and at the mercy of time." Constantine's finger lingered on Eusebius. "I commission you, Eusebius of Caesarea, to choose from your documents a collection of those sacred scriptures you know to be necessary. Hence it should be copied, bound, and delivered to me in a lot of fifty."

The librarian dry-gulped as Constantine looked to the vaulted ceiling. They thought he'd issued his last dictum, but quickly the cold eyes returned. "I repeat, gentle men—once the texts are chosen, all others must be sequestered—they cannot lie about, liable to fall into the hands of another asp who would spew new poison. Know that your compliance is required and that disobedience will bring a full measure of wrath." He ended with a silent stare, stabbing each man's center as it moved left to right. Again Eusebius was last to feel the sting.

Athanasius answered for all. "We are whole in our accord, my lord. Be assured. There shall be a single, universal creed."

Constantine descended, driving chins to chests and knees to the floor... "I leave you to your task. May the gods be with you!" he shouted as he walked away.

The prelates held their bows until he disappeared, and then returned to the calfskins. Queasy glances prevailed before Alexander spoke. "How fortunate we are to have this great man as champion. We must retain his favor at all costs."

Athanasius seconded. "Indeed. We can allow no excuse for the emperor to falter. Were it not for his mother... Constantine is a gift from above, and compliance with his requests essential. He views a common creed as the sinew that will bind our church and hence his empire."

zeta

ALEXANDER OF ALEXANDRIA

A.D. 325
Cathedrali Sanctus Eirenea
Nicaea, Bythnia
Imperium Romanum

Emperor Constantine's convocation began with a grand spectacle. In a rare gesture of humility the emperor led the opening procession barefoot, preceded by a picket of crucifixes and trailed by a crimson column of clergy. Bathed in the pink blush of the Asian dawn, the scarlet line descended the flower-strewn causeway, snaking beneath the marble arch and into the great hall. A thick crowd of dutiful citizens lined every stone of the half-league long route, each falling to his knees at the sight of his regent.

As the march ended, Acacius boosted the giddy Eusebius onto his shoulders to better witness Constantine's entrance. "Look there, my boy, it's *our* Emperor," shouted Eusebius, "with Alexander and Osius at his side!"

"A-A-Alleluia!" cried Acacius.

Eusebius scrambled down and melted into the merging mass, hollering back as he entered. "We shall meet here at day's end, Acacius! Bring a beast to ride!"

Resplendent in plush purples, bejeweled with the rarest stones, and smothered in clouds of incense,

Constantine surveyed his assembly. Following the eunuchs' hymn, he launched the proceedings with a wink. The Council was patterned on the Roman senate with the much esteemed Osius presiding. Constantine chose to sit among the holy men and not at their front and he declined to debate or vote, though his presence was intimidating. Many of the bishops were simple men, illiterate and with church duties secondary to their vocations: Spyridion of Trimythous was a shepherd, and several like Nicolas of Nisibus were hermits. As lettered men like Osius led, they would follow.

All were aware that Constantine's mother was a back-room player. A pious Christian proselytizer, the unseen Helena was rumored to consult with her son every night. Her influence was much welcomed by the bishops since the depth of the emperor's own faith was obscure. Most realized that the legend of his Chi-Ro vision was embellished and that despite their pleas, he remained unbaptized. They were jealous of his parallel contacts with other faiths, knowing that he took part in their rituals, wore a pagan talisman, and sought their alliance in much the same way as he did the Christians'.

The proceedings at Nicaea were uneven from the start but the cunning Constantine cajoled the conferees, resulting in the declarations he desired. The Arians were rejected by an overwhelming majority and the Easter calendar agreed. When the unifying creed was read aloud, he honored Eusebius with a place between him and Alexander.

Eusebius exited the conclave to find Acacius tending an ass at the edge of the mumbling crowd. "At last, my boy, it's done." he said. "From this day forward, Arius is excommunicated, the holy days are fixed, and the path to one word is chosen."

"A-Amen." said Acacius.

Though no canon was produced at Nicaea, its cause was advanced. Years later Eusebius delivered Constantine's bibles, an orthodox selection that mirrored the consensus. Added later by Athanasius was the gruesome gospel of John of Patmos, a hermit whose chilling apocalyptic visions made hell and its devils conspicuous, neatly matching the pagan myths.

The contents of Papias' saddlebags and hundreds of other documents deemed unworthy were, by Constantine's will, refuse. The emperor hosted a feast on the eve of the first bishop's departure, concluding with Athanasius' soaring bonfire in the priory courtyard. Led by Alexander's rubied crucifix, the bishops chanted the beatitudes acapella as they circled the pyre, ignorant of the holy nature of its kindling.

eta

OSIUS OF CORDUBA

A.D. 325
Portus Gades
Hispaniarum
Imperium Romanum

The warship furled its sails and sprouted oars as it plowed toward the Gades naval dock, shields shining on the side rails and Imperial banners boasting from atop its masts. All but the oar hands were on deck, weary from their voyage and keen to reach the last anchorage, having hopscotched the length of the Mediterranean as they delivered each bishop to his native shore. The sailors awaited their first night's liberty in the Atlantic harbor, known for its sweet wine and subsidized bordellos. More than anyone on board, the Roman captain was relieved as he bade Bishop Osius farewell, content on completion of his mission with safe transfer of the last bishop to his homeland.

"Fare thee well, holy traveler," said the Captain to Osius. "You have been my longest and most gracious charge. May the gods protect your last way home."

"Thank you, brave Captain. I pray He do the same for you and your men," Osius answered. "One could not have had better companions."

Osius was fatigued but at peace, and joyful for his return to Spanish soil. Wobbling down the plank, he climbed on a crate to address the clergy who'd come to greet him. "Praise be. We are delivered from the present peril. Arius' teachings are forbidden, feast days established, and there is a common creed. Deviant documents shall be sequestered, post haste. Already the libraries in Caesarea, Alexandria, and Granada have been quarantined, and censors comb the provinces as I speak."

But under the censor's nose and aboard Constantine's own vessel, Osius had smuggled an ironic contraband. Amidst his mule train on the overland leg to Corduba rode souvenirs of his trip: chalices from Antioch, silk vestments from Persia, a jeweled crucifix from the Emperor—and in the same container, a special present from his admirer, Eusebius—the saddlebags of Papias. Osius and the Caesarean made quick friends in Nicaea, sharing metaphysics and Asian wine under the Bithynian moon. Osius had expressed his fascination with Jesus' Galilean tongue, and to his surprise, Eusebius presented him with a farewell gift on the day of departure—the saddlebags. Cloaked in sheepskin in the hold of the ship and transferred to the Corduba caravan, they were Osius' special reward.

The good bishop supervised the storage of his treasures upon his arrival in Corduba, ordering them sealed in a sarcophagus and placed in the basement of St. Acisilo's church, his intent to enjoy as time allowed. But it was not to be—the holy man would never see the ossuary again—a few years later, emboldened by Alexander's demise and led by the dead emperor's son, the Arians challenged the outcome of the council and its conclusions about the trinity. Osius fought on, but was exiled to Pannonia until his hundredth year. His treasures from Nicaea became a forgotten dream, Papias' saddlebags among them, untouched inside the stone box in St. Acisilo's cellar.

theta

MUGIT-AL-RUMI[15]

A.D. 711
Portum Pons
Corduba
Regnum Gothi

At the trot and beneath a rippling white flag, the Berber horseman approached the Visigoth ramparts. With saber dangling and sweat dripping from all points, he dismounted with flag in hand and marched across no-man's land. In stride he climbed the pine stairs to face the Christian soldiers hunkering across and above on Corduba's outer wall. It was quiet all around, so quiet that the hollow echoes of his boots and tinkling of his chain mail lofted up to the cowering defenders. As the Christian bowmen drew their strings, they saw tenacity on his face and aggression in his stance.

With legs wide, knees locked, and fists anchored on his hips, Mugit al-Rumi yelled in Vulgar Latin toward the Visigoth banner. "Hear ye, hear ye! To all noble men of Corduba and to ye, honorable governor, for your king! The servants of Allah stand at your gate with respectful notice from Caliph al-Waleed!"

The unstoppable Islamic tsunami that breached the straits of Gibraltar and was drowning the Iberian Peninsula had reached Corduba, and Mugit al-Rumi was the crest of the wave. In less than a hundred years, the prophet's messengers grew from a handful of

Arabian zealots into a host of inspired armies sweeping in every direction and consuming dozens of cultures along the way. The sea protected Europe and Visigoth Spain for only a few seasons. After capturing Toletum, Tariq-ibn-Ziyad dispatched al-Rumi and a thousand battle-wise soldiers to the gates of Corduba with orders to negotiate its surrender. Generous terms were to be offered and resistance seemed unlikely.

"Hear ye, honorable governor, hear ye!" al-Rumi repeatedly bellowed, until at last an obese man in ill-fitting iron appeared on the parapet, his sheepish subordinates filing behind. The governor shed his helmet to better display conceit and then gave a lazy "let's-hear-it" wave.

Seeing that, al-Rumi shouted across. "Fine sir! By the will of Allah and his humble servants, Musa-bin-Nusair and Tariq-ibn-Ziyad, and through me, Mugit al-Rumi, their respectful vassal—know that your city is besieged!" Three times he slammed his wrist against the steel breastplate before bowing in the elegant Amazigh fashion. Quickly erect, he delivered the decree. "This city and its dominions are today subject to the rightful jurisdiction of his highness, Musa-ibn-Nusair, Emir of Tingi and liege of al-Waleed. You will now hear the terms of surrender."

The smug Visigoth interrupted before al-Rumi could begin, his flapping jowls spewing a train of insults. "Spare thy foul breath, pagan!" he screamed. "Your African carcass shall never cross these battlements. They have denied their attackers since the days of Caesar and shall repel your vermin in kind. Back to hell with you! Be gone!"

The governor thrust both middle fingers forward, whirled around to bare his cheeks, and then disappeared. Unaffected, the Muslim commander recited the Caliph's offer to the empty parapet, his voice washing over the wall and into the courtyard. The terms were indulgent, including safe passage for all who requested it, a guarantee of tolerance to those who stayed, and an invitation for every citizen to join the new realm. All the while, the pudgy governor slumped in a stony nook, picking at a pomegranate and mocking the Moor to an audience of smirking subordinates.

That night Caesar's walls were breached by al-Rumi's sappers. The gatekeepers accepted silver bribes and abandoned their posts, allowing Muslim scouts to slit the sentries' throats, lower the gate, and lead the host into the city. The less numerous Visigoths were overwhelmed in their barracks, two hundred or so escaping to shelter in the Church of the Martyr. Attempts to burn them out were unsuccessful, so the attackers camped on the grounds and waited. Starving but defiant, the Christians were slaughtered to a man two months later. On the following day, the governor's much slimmer cheeks were presented to the Caliph inside a wicker basket.

It was a decade before the Emir's clerks sorted the booty from the church basement. They correctly identified the artifacts in Osius' stone box as religious, and as such they were reverently transported to the repository of the central mosque. The ossuary containing Papias' saddlebags was placed in the corner of a low level storeroom and was soon obscured by other treasures.

iota

AL-HAKKAM II[16]

A.D 969
Minaret Noreste del Gran Mesquito
Madina Qurtubah, Al Andaluz[f]
Caliphato de Qurtuba

The Caliph and his Imam relished the spring sunrise, their dark tunics billowing in the upwelling breeze as they surveyed the city from atop the Great Mosque. First prayers completed, the elders gazed silently with arms crossed, necks extended, and legs wide, enjoying the most spectacular urban panorama the world had ever seen.

By the tenth century, humble Visigoth Corduba had been transformed by its Muslim conquerors into the most sophisticated city on earth. Five-hundred thousand of the caliph's subjects bustled below in the hundred square mile metropolis, chosen by Hakkam's ancestors as capitol for climate and strategic location. The city's name morphed from Corduba to Qurtubah at the beginning of the Umayyad dynasty, and from then on was the unchallenged center of the Muslim west. Under the tolerant wings of its emirs and caliphs, science, art, and literature flourished to the benefit of all. No place rivaled Qurtubah's physical beauty: a blend of inspired architecture, vivacious landscaping, and urban engineering.

While the adjacent Christian kingdoms wallowed in superstition, poverty, and disease, al-Hakkam's dominion enjoyed a complexity not to be equaled on the continent for ten centuries. Hundreds of mosques, churches, synagogues, public baths, and hospitals were scattered through the city, and three dozen libraries served his literate populace. Free secondary schools fed budding scholars into universities supported by royal benevolence. Qurtubah's paved streets were lit through the al-Andalusian nights, and sanitary systems flowed beneath. Like Muhammad, al-Hakkam regarded Jews and Christians as fellow children of Abraham, "people of the book" as the prophet labeled them, and they functioned as integral members of Umayyad society, serving in all but the highest office.

The principled leader staring across his city, son of the first caliph, was the most learned ruler in Europe, one who preferred the solace of his library^g to the intrigue at court. Early in his reign al-Hakkam began his most ambitious project, the translation of his five-hundred thousand Greek and Latin volumes into Arabic. An army of linguists, scribes, and bookbinders toiled for their caliph, and by that blustery morning they'd been working for a decade.

Both men turned toward the echoes of quick feet ascending the minaret's stairwell. It was al-Hakkam's master librarian, Ali ibn-Nassar who emerged, panting from the climb and as excited as the ruler had ever seen.

"Sire, I beg your indulgence. God is the greatest!" the puffing librarian exclaimed. "We've made a marvelous discovery among the Visigoth artifacts. It is a wonder."

Al-Hakkam responded. "Take your breath, my good man. What put you in this state? Do you require my presence?"

The wheezing bookman spoke with hands on knees. "Yes, Sire. You will delight in the treasure. Pray accompany me to the copying hall."

Hakkam bade the Imam good day. The pair descended and fast-stepped through the courtyard's jasmine trellis, past the gushing fountains and into the tiled passageway. All the while Nassar teased his sovereign, parsing only hints until they entered the replication suite. The librarian led between rows of copying easels to one on which two yellowed scrolls were stretched, with fresh paper receiving the Arabic translation in between. The scribes jumped to their feet and bowed away.

Hakkam needed no direction. After fondling each scroll, he focused on the Greek one, fingering its margins as he read aloud. "'It is through your heart that our Father guides you. Look there first for His wisdom and not to those who pretend to know.'" He read on silently, and then again, aloud. "'It is he who loves himself that can love all things, he who knows himself who can know God.'"

He turned to Nassar. "Amazing, Ali. So profound, yet simple, without doubt from the mind of a prophet. Is it the one they called the Baptist?"

Nassar answered. "We think not, highness. It is the wandering preacher of the Qur'an and Christian book, disciple of the Baptist, son of Mary, and he who both faiths call Messiah—the Jew who foretold the coming of Muhammad and the Hierophant—Jesus of Nazareth."

The caliph fired questions. "Where were they found, dear man, and how many there be? Any scripted in Latin? Are there stories of his mother?"

"Yes, much about Mary and the brother James," responded Nassar, "but none in Latin, Sire—and not at all like the Vulgate[h]—all quotations and proverbs. Look here."

Nassar moved to the workbench and hoisted one of Papias' saddlebags. "There were two of these to be found. Their scrolls have lain in our storehouse since the liberation, buried under things of lesser note, cool and dry within these fleece-lined leathers, inside a Roman bone box. The first emir's log tells of their rescue from the Visigoth church in the old city, the same as besieged by Mugit al-Rumi. There are ninety-seven in each bag, all intact, and they're odd for their time, of parchment, not papyrus. The Greek is in one hand, from the time of Vespasian, we guess. Just look at their condition. There is no god but God!"

"And the other script, Ali? It resembles that of the Jews," said the caliph.

"Aramaic, your highness, Jesus' language, a sister to Hebrew. By the look of the vellum, from the same lot. Alas, we have no translator for that dialect here in Qurtubah. We think the Aramaic scrolls copies of the Greek, or perhaps the reverse, but will know soon enough. I've asked to borrow a Hebrew master from the Syrian library. He arrives in the planting moon."

Hakkam responded. "Praise God! Wait until Damascus learns of this. The Grand Caliph will be sick with envy." He stroked his beard. "Translate the Greek at once, and on the finest fiber. Use Ibex paste, cat's black, and golden linseed. Be sure the senior staff does the work. I would have the copy when finished."

The ruler moved to examine a saddlebag, focusing on its branded flap. "What of this fish design, Ali, and the letters inside? 'I-X-Θ-Y-Σ'? Is it of the same age as the scrolls?"

"I cannot say, your majesty. Perhaps, but of course the fish symbol is much older, one the Christians stole from the Greeks, and they from the Persians. We think 'ICHTHYUS' an acronym, but can only guess what the letters stand for."

"Very well, Ali. Inform Damascus and stake our claim with the law keepers. I do not wish these gems usurped. When finished, fortify the leathers with angel's oil, return the scrolls to them, and again to the box. Its humors may account for their fine condition. If Allah wills it, they shall remain that way."

"Yes, sire," answered Nassar.

"God is the greatest!" shouted the Caliph as he strolled away.

kappa

FERNANDO OF CASTILE[17]

A.D. 1236
Muralla Ajarquia
Qurtuba
Al-Andaluz

Even the riders at the front of the galloping column were covered in mud, with only the whites of their eyes reflecting the sputtering torchlight.

"Adelante, Caballeros! Forward!" shouted the young king as he set the pace, one length ahead but otherwise indistinguishable from his men-at-arms. The freezing drizzle soaked to their skin and made a chore of staying in the saddles. All were numb with fatigue but they rode determined into the darkness, hell-bent to reach Qurtubah before dawn. To horse since nightfall, the Castilians were eager—their mercenaries had breached the Ajarquian wall and requested reinforcements for a final assault.

Sunrise confirmed that the outer wall was theirs, but the Moors had retreated in good order and full force to the Madina, and that bastion would prove an expensive prize. One year before the same enemy had meekly capitulated at Úbeda, but it would take five months and scores of his soldiers' lives before Fernando would have the keys to old Corduba.

In that same moonless night on the opposite side of the city, a Muslim captain rode to and fro along an organizing wagon train with clumps of muck shedding from his horse's hooves, splattering nobles and commoners alike. Swearing and shouting, he commanded his men. "Be quick! The infidels have breached the Ajarquian wall and shall next assault the citadel," he cried. "Castilian horse approach from the west and will soon be upon us. Form your lines! Order the wagons!"

It was bedlam, Nasrid style.

His patience depleted, the captain approached the vanguard and bellowed. "Open the gates! All mount and take to the road! Do it now!"

Whips cracked and drivers cursed at their teams. Like an earthworm, the wriggling column crept through the eastern gate and down the stone highway. Carriages were first in line, followed by wagons, carts, and a long pack train. Animals stalled in the downpour, with the quickest exile delayed by the slowest. Hundreds trudged alongside and a thousand straggled in the rear as the pathetic conglomerate trekked toward Granada. Terrified and shivering, the once proud people wore the empty eyes and rounded shoulders of the vanquished. They knew that the Christians would offer no quarter and that their only future was fifty leagues distant, behind the high walls of the Alhambra.

It had been decades since Qurtubah's lamps lit the night. By the twelfth century, the caliphate had fragmented into a Babel of quarreling city-states, torn by jealousy and weakened by royal deceit. Then, beginning in Galicia beneath the banner of Saint James the Apostle who'd supposedly erupted from his grave for the purpose, the Christian Reconquista[i] began. Its momentum grew with every liberated city until the outcome was inevitable—expulsion of the Muslims from all of Spain.

As Fernando approached Qurtubah's western gate, the custodians of the Great Mosque acted. Successive caravans were dispatched to the east while the opposite border resisted. Papias' saddlebags, plucked from the sarcophagus and tossed into a royal wagon, were in that first contingent. Along with the exhausted refugees, they found haven in Granada eleven days later where they were stashed in the Alhambra's old livery, their Christian acrostics obscured by a heap of Qur'ans.

lamda

MUHAMMAD XII – BOABDIL[18]

A.D.1492
Orilla del Río Genil
Granada
España Reconquistada

It was the most elaborate surrender Europe had ever witnessed, staged with the air of a festival. Scarlet banners flew from the Alhambra's battlements a half-league distant and from every lance flanking the royal procession at the riverside. King Ferdinand[19] and Queen Isabella[20] settled in their saddles at the front of the host, resplendent in the shadow of a towering gold crucifix held aloft by three Benedictines. The regents were about to receive the keys to Granada from Muhammad XII, its last Muslim ruler. The captivating refrain of *Te Deum Laudamus* wafted over the crowd, chanted incessantly by scores of clergy. Captain Christopher Columbus, who would soon plead for the royals' favor in his adventure on the Western Sea, was among thousands in the audience. Every Spaniard dressed in his finest on that second January day, anxious and giddy to know that they were about to witness the final act of the five-hundred yearlong Reconquista. Seers predicted that Saint James would sprout from the foot of the gold cross, and for that the royal guards kept their pikes low. Men cried openly, women swooned, and pickpockets had their best day since the caliph's induction. Souvenirs, prayer beads, and freshly crafted relics commanded premium prices.

By this painful act, Abu 'ab-Allah Muhammad XII, the man the Spaniards called Boabdil, would allow himself to become the last Nasrid ruler. He approached on the riverbank at a canter, leading a column of ninety-nine unarmed men in tight military formation. With backbones erect but heads bowed, they rode up to the cross. Boabdil dismounted and paced forward to kiss the hands of the regents. He was received by the Catholic monarchs with much courtesy, for he'd been a friend and ally before becoming their vanquished adversary.

"My old friend," said Ferdinand as Boabdil took a knee. "You are now the most noble of my subjects."

"And you, lord king, are my liege," answered Boabdil.

The king ordered the release of Boabdil's hostaged son and as they embraced, Ferdinand waved to his signalmen. In seconds all eyes were drawn to the massive cross of Christ as it unfurled from the distant parapets of the Alhambra. Cries of "Alleluia" merged into a boisterous roar as frenzied bodies crushed forward to kiss the crucifix.

A few days later and without notice, Boabdil and his family rode south into exile. Ferdinand and Isabella had gifted him an estate in the Alpujarras, a rugged mountain land on the southern slope of the Sierra Nevada. From there, on a clear day, Boabdil could glimpse the Rif mountain peaks of his ancestor's homeland. As the entourage made the ascent from Granada and reached the crest of the pass, they paused at a small meadow below a rocky promontory, the last vantage from which the city could be seen. Boabdil cinched the reins and turned for a last look, but the memories were too much and he lost control.

His mother scolded when she saw his tears. "You do well to weep like a woman for what you could not defend as a man."

The monarchs allowed Boabdil to carry whatever he wished to the Alpujarras, so there were scores of pack animals in his train. Falling behind on a lame mule at the end of the line rode Papias' saddlebags, tossed over its flanks by a clerk who, not knowing their value to his lord, feared reprimand should he omit them.

mu

FATHER ESTEBAN GOMEZ

A.D. 1658, Nochebuena
Capilla de la Virgen
Barón, Alpujarras
España

Counting five babes-in-arms, sixty-nine parishioners sought shelter inside the whitewashed chapel at the center of the pueblo, certain that the crowd gathering outside would respect its holy sanctuary. Father Esteban Gomez wasn't so sure. Peeking through the slats, he saw a mob—fifty men pumping shears and torches into the air, shouting "Allahu Akbar" without pause. These were the same men who'd greeted him all week long as he prepared his little church for Christmas. The simple priest knew only a few Arabic phrases, but he realized that the men huddled at the front of the crowd were debating the fate of his congregation.

"What do they mean to do, Padre?" asked a mother from across the pews.

"Settle a score," Gomez answered.

The woman looked to her husband for comfort, but none was there.

It was happening all over the high country—the Morisco Revolt[j]. Planned for sundown on Christmas Eve, the descendants of the Moors would rise up and expel their Christian neighbors as a first act of independence from King Philip of Spain. Aben Humeya, previously

Fernando of Válor[21], patterned his insurrection on the successful French purge carried out on Saint Bartholomew's day seventy-five years before. On that night, French Catholics massacred thousands of their Huguenot neighbors in their beds and declared their nation Catholic. Humeya would do the same, and this time the new state would be ruled by the righteous descendants of the Moors, the Moriscos.

Boisterous newcomers muscled to the front of the swarm and the shouts changed from "God is the greatest!" to "Death to the infidels!" The predictable happened about nine o'clock. Two men dragged an oxcart through the crowd and wedged its yolk against the chapel's oak doors. Others jammed the window latches with scythes. At last, an anonymous torch was tossed onto the tinder-thatch roof. Another followed, and soon every one was there. For a few seconds the children's cries quieted the rioters and a few regretful faces stepped toward their screams, but the leaders bellowed louder, their shouts and the blasting fire masking the last tiny squeal. In ten minutes it was over and in less time the mob dispersed, eyes to the ground. Only smoking rubble remained at first light.

It was the third near-immolation and the latest close call for Papias' saddlebags. The bags, with Hakkam's book tucked inside, had been jammed into the stone tabernacle by the priest, and it acted as a firebox. Along with the consecrated hosts, they were all that survived the inferno. Gifted to the founders of the church when Boabdil quit his estate six generations before, they'd been the sole relics of the parish, their nature unappreciated by a string of peasant priests. Father Gomez was their final protector.

Soon the bags and Hakkam's book became booty in the short-lived rebellion, scavenged that morning from the embers by an itinerant Morisco named Zegrí in an act eerily similar to the Phrygian's. Zegrí was no rebel, just a lucky looter, and he had the double good fortune to remain in the pueblo after King Philip crushed the revolt. The king allowed one Morisco family to stay in each village to teach the tricky mountainside farming techniques to Spaniards imported from the North. In that way, Zegrí and Papias' saddlebags were spared from exile.

nu

CAPITÁN ZEGRÍ[22]

A.D. 1936
Plaza Central
Bubión, Alpujarras
Segunda República Espanola

There were no uniforms to issue the recruits, only Republican berets and a few tricolored armbands. Most carried their own pitiful weapons: shotguns they called "spitters," single-shell hunting rifles, and one boy his father's Mauser from the Spanish-American War, its barrel gunked in Cosmoline. Of the fifty or so men in the village, barely a quarter showed up, mostly teens with their mothers in tow and begging them not to go. There was no gaiety or strident crowds as in the cities–only weepy faces wishing anxious good-byes.

The men filing into the open bed of the Ford AA were the last of the White Village volunteers, and Bubión was the bottom of the barrel. The recruiting sergeant was unimpressed with his skinny charges but pleased to see their bodies—war fever had long ago subsided and replacements were hard to come by since the Nationalists seized Granada—they would make fine fodder in the ever more brutal Spanish Civil War[k].

Seated stone-faced among the naive youths was one very different volunteer, Rodrigo Morales de Zegrí, a strapping twenty-seven year old deserter from the Spanish Foreign Legion. Only his striped trousers betrayed his past, but the sergeant noticed them at once and invited the man into the cab. Zegrí's sole weapon protruded above his belt: an eight-inch Jambiya dagger, Mecca style, its bronze hilt a cross of Agadez inlaid with Rif rubies, the engraved blade sharp as a barber's razor. The knife was both souvenir and practical possession, retrieved from the body of a Tuareg he killed in the first night at Aladir.

"How long with the Legion?" asked the sergeant.

"Eight years, plus," responded Zegrí.

"Why with us, now?"

"I hate them. Always have," said the recruit. "Want to kill as many as I can."

"Good reason," said the soldier. "You'll get your chance."

Zegrí's Legion comrades were fighting alongside General Franco[23] and his Nationalists on the outskirts of Madrid, but Zegrí slipped away from his regiment when they disembarked in Cadíz, ashamed of killing Africans in the name of the Spanish King and repulsed by the Royalist cause. He loathed the monarchy and its lapdog church as much as he did the provincials, who for centuries had oppressed his Morisco ancestors. For those reasons and more, the Republic was exactly what Zegrí wanted, and he was willing to die for it.

Before he could do so, Zegrí advanced to Captain and was the last surviving officer in the Republican battalion defending the Guadalajara salient, cut off from his comrades and besieged by an Italian brigade. Neither side considered surrender—all knew that no quarter would be given—this was the Spanish Civil War, a cockfight that would leave only one rooster standing. The courageous Zegrí fell in a bold breakout attempt as he urged his men forward, the first machine gun bullet entering his braincase through the mouth, rendering the next two post-mortem.

His flag-shrouded body was returned to Bubión that same week, thanks to the Republicans' counterattack and their control of the railroad. Zegrí's mother placed the corpse upright in the family mausoleum, a limestone shrine ringed in wrought iron and Jerusalem roses at the apex of the meadow where he'd played as a child. To make room for his body, one chamber had to be emptied. A repository for eight Morisco generations, it was stuffed with heirlooms: framed portraits, family records, and in the far reaches, keepsakes from the time of the Christmas revolt. In the very back against the cold stone squatted two leather pieces wrapped in muslin and again in deer hide—the saddlebags of Papias. Zegrí's grieving father tossed the whole lot into a hay wagon and then dumped it in a birthing pen at the rear of the shearing barn, covering it with a tattered ship's canvass.

omicron

FRANCISCO FRANCO

A.D. 1965
66 Camino San Giorgio
Bubión, Alpujarras
España

It was a peaceful time, but the price of peace was freedom. The dictator Franco's civil code was known as "La Ley de Vagos y Maleantes," roughly translated, "The Law for Bums and Hooligans." A hooligan was anyone who didn't follow the state's rigid edicts or the strict moral constructs of Franco's chief vassal, the Spanish Catholic Church. A bum was anyone his personal police force, the tricornered Guardia Civil, decided was not toeing the line. In Franco's Spain there were fewer bums and hooligans as the years progressed, thanks to jail time for meager offenses like mocking Franco or cursing in public. A perfect order was the tyrant's goal, intimidation and imprisonment his tools, and that goal was nearly achieved.

In the beginning, summary execution was commonplace, but by the 1960s Franco's tactics had grown subtle if not less pervasive. One of many forbidden practices was the use of languages other than Spanish. Greek and Latin were permitted in the schools and some academies taught French or English, but only the Castilian dialect was sanctioned. Basque and Catalan tongues were the primary targets of Spanish-only laws, but others like Arabic were likewise stifled.

Thanks to the purge that followed the Morisco revolt, few remnants of the Moors' language survived in Andalusia, but there was at least one Arabic refuge—a prayer-room shrine hidden in a farmhouse on the road to Bubión, in the home of the hero Zegrí's only son. There, in a windowless cubby off the shepherd's kitchen, the keepsakes of Rodrigo Zegrí's short life were arranged around his wedding portrait on the west wall. The opposing bare wall facing Mecca was painted sky blue and the room's entrance was disguised with a beaded curtain since Muslim worship was forbidden in Franco's Spain.

Republican banners draped along that west wall, and on shelves beside the photo Capitán Zegrí's medals from the Legion and Republic were displayed. Prayer rugs waited in the corners, and on the lower shelves sat objects retrieved from the birthing pen: a Berber scimitar, antique Qur'ans, al-Hakkam's book of sayings, and on each end, a bulging saddlebag of Papias. Zegrí's Jambiya dagger hung above the shelves, its ornate scabbard polished and edge sharply honed. The objects were the only connection the son had to his never-seen father, and as such were his most cherished possessions.

Each night in that prayer room Zegrí's son told of his father's exploits to his own boy, Chori, teaching the child to speak the grandfather's forbidden language by immersion in those Arabic texts. The tales Chori heard about grandfather Zegrí were enthralling if inflated, and like his father, he developed a cult-like devotion to the man neither knew. Every session ended with the same ritual: little Chori climbed the shelves, unsheathed the dagger, and then read from the engraving on its blade.

"To Allah we belong and to Him we return."

pi

CHORI ZEGRÍ RODRIGUEZ

A.D. 1994
Barrio Central
Granada
España

Franco's restrictions eased as Zegrí's grandson grew to man, and when the dictator died, the year Chori turned seventeen, they were all but extinct. Franco willed his absolute power to the young king, Juan Carlos de Bourbon[24], reasoning that his repressive regime would be perpetuated by the monarch, but in one of the wisest political acts of the twentieth century, the king gave his authority to the fledgling Spanish democracy. In the decades that followed, the ancient nation was transformed from an irrelevant backwater into a respected force in the European Union.

Young Chori reveled in the new freedom by discovering girls, spending his sheep-shearing money on African kitsch, and praying without fear. He was a skipped-generation copy of his heroic grandfather: intrepid, charismatic, and always the risk taker—a success looking for a place to happen—and that place was Granada. On his eighteenth birthday, he set out from Bubión for the ancient city, branded with his Morisco mores and eager to exploit any opportunity. Capitán Zegrí would have been proud.

It was his bicultural skills that allowed Chori to prosper, his two-tongued charm combining with ambition to guarantee a career. After acquiring a skillset from his first boss, Zegrí's grandson opened his own business, with time a profitable cog in Granada's urban machine.

Chori fell in love with another newcomer and they wed in Granada's Capilla on her feast day, followed by a fairytale reception in Alhambra's gardens. His family came down from the Alpujarras to witness their union, and for one afternoon the scene was as before—Muslims and Christians sheltered in the shadow of the majestic palace as they engaged in an act of respect. His bride was a convenient Catholic, and for love he accepted her faith. She returned his kindness by allowing their children to steep in his creed.

With his father's death came the contents of the prayer room, moved from Bubión to their second story flat and arranged identically inside a larger chamber. Chori chose that condo with the prayer room in mind— one of its balconies faced the Alpujarras, and Mecca beyond. He carved oak shelves to hold Zegrí's heirlooms and hung the Jambiya dagger above. True to Muslim custom and as in Bubión, the prayer room door was cloaked with a beaded curtain to shield it from female eyes. Papias' saddlebags rested as before, bookends for the growing collection of prayer books and Qur'ans, with Hakkam's book in the center.

rho

FAMILIA SALAZAR

A.D. 1999
Hospital de Niños
Plaza de Medicina
Granada
España

He was the handsomest preemie in the nursery, blessed with his mother's sculpted features and Chori's endearing eyes. His brother was seven years older, and though his parents had hoped for balance with a baby girl, they decided this second child would be their last.

The mother was first to notice that something was wrong when he was in the crib. His cocoa eyes tracked the mobiles hanging above, and at night the car lights as they ricocheted across the ceiling, but they never captured her eyes like his brother's had. The infant was slow to crawl and then to walk. He ignored his family from the beginning, preferring to rock on his haunches in the far corner of the living room, muttering odd intonations and ignoring all else. He connected only with the cat.

Instead of baby talk there was a noisy babble, with clicks, pops and whistles erupting from the toddler's mouth in unpredictable spurts. He mimicked sounds exactly, like an Amazon parrot, but less often words. The little boy never used language, at least nothing his parents could decipher, and not a peep was directed to them. Playdates were impossible and the neighbor kids shunned him, mocking his vocalizations and teasing without mercy.

Chori and his wife ignored the obvious until the boy they'd nicknamed "Paco" turned three, when they decided to seek help at Granada's Children's Hospital. After weeks of testing, they were summoned to the chairman's office. Chori was surprised to see a crowd of medics there, standing behind their boss and whispering like children in church. The parents took seats in front of Doctor DeLaPeña's metal desk with the child oscillating on his father's lap.

A stern glance from DeLaPeña made the white coats go quiet.

"Señor, we must be frank and tell you that your son will be very different from his brother," DeLaPeña said.

The frightened parents looked to each other.

"Paco is severely autistic," he continued. "His ability to process information is compromised, and his reactions to stimuli inappropriate."

"What do you mean, Doctor?" Chori asked.

The M.D. answered. "Your son's personality is isolated. Secluded. He processes sounds and sights in a different manner than other children. His mind is poles apart from ours, and the way he perceives the world is ... special. The child's social development will be slow, but please, don't be too concerned. The condition is well known. We have many children with this diagnosis." The doctor leaned back and extended both arms. "These are my colleagues who will be working with your son."

All exchanged polite smiles as Chori's mind raced. *If my boy's problem is so common, why are all these people here? There has to be more.* He reached for his wife's hand as DeLaPeña droned on.

"There's something else about the boy you must know—something that fascinates us and that we've read about, but never seen—our tests show that your son has a co-morbid condition, a concomitant trait known as 'savant syndrome.'"

The terrified mother interrupted, trying to repeat the terms. "What is it you said, Doctor? I don't understand. Please speak Spanish!"

A young physician on DeLaPeña's left stepped forward.

"Señora, if I may? It means that in some ways Paco is a *genius*, an au-tis-tic sa-vant. It's unclear why this happens, but it regularly occurs in autistic children, in some fashion nearly five per cent of the time, and most often in preemies like your son. Usually they excel in mathematics or music. Most have prodigious memories. They can do things that the brightest normal, err ... *regular* kids can't do."

Chori held the little fellow close as if to protect him from the news. "But Doctor, all he does is babble, with words we don't understand."

The same doctor answered. "Yes sir, and that's what's unique about this patient—it's not babble. The boy's pathology involves the *left* side of his brain. Almost all savants have changes affecting the right hemisphere, the side that deals with math and music. But our studies show your son's condition to be on the opposite side, in the language part of the cerebrum, and his fMRI demonstrates high activity there, the highest ever recorded. We propose to call him a linguistic savant. There is only one other case in the literature, a Hungarian female, now thirty years old."

One by one each professional stepped forward to explain his or her role before leaving the room, until only Doctor DeLaPeña remained. He asked permission to study Paco and publish their findings. When the papers were signed, he wrenched the child from Chori's arms and carried him screaming from the office as the terrified Señora covered her ears. The door slammed shut, leaving the parents alone and staring into the silence. At once they embraced, in tears.

sigma

THE FORTUNE TELLER

A.D. 2002
Plaza Central
Bubión, Alpujarras
España

At first Chori and his wife rejected Paco's diagnosis, but with time they realized that the doctors' labels were just that. Besides the hospital's regimen and drugs, there was no therapy they wouldn't try, but they found only frustration until their trip to Bubión.

Chori loved going home to the White Villages, a string of pueblos clinging to the southern flank of the Alpujarras. Those hamlets have changed since Boabdil's time but the mountain folks' spirit has not. He delighted in visiting his birthplace where his kin lived like their Morisco ancestors, scratching a living from their terraced gardens and Merino sheep.

Good-weather Saturdays fill Bubión's steep streets with gay colors and happy faces. Chori's brood waltzed toward Plaza Central with the sun on their shoulders, browsing leisurely among the vendors but with no plans to buy. They reached the corner of the tiny town plaza and came upon a thin woman squatting at the base of Saint Teresa's fountain. She stared down at a stack of Dali Tarot cards inside an empty pie pan marked DRABARNI. In traditional gypsy dress, with tangerine scarf and a long patterned skirt, the woman sang a mountain Caló, her falsetto the only sound there. Paco trailed a few meters behind, gibbering as he tapped a stick on the stones.

All at once the little boy froze and his eyes went to the woman. The stick rattled as it fell. His brother turned to the sound and tugged on his mother's skirt.

"Mama, look!"

As the family watched, the woman's gaze turned to Paco and she rose, still warbling. She stepped directly toward the child, toe-to-heel with head cocked left. The brother moved in between to halfheartedly challenge but she looked through him and he stood aside. Then she went quiet, touching Paco's face with her fingertips as if reading Braille. Her expression changed to his and she led him by the hand to the fountain. Retrieving a book from her bag on the rail, the Gypsy leaned against it and began to read. Paco inched closer, almost nose to nose. Balanced and lilting, her words were sung more than spoken. She smiled when she finished the verse and then leafed forward to another, a call to the Almighty for insight and favor. All the while the little boy stood still, content for the very first time.

Then, as she began a third reading, he tried to repeat her words. She waited as he struggled, but then continued. This went on for ten or twelve minutes, with the boy occasionally parroting a phrase. Closing the book when she reached the last page, the lady kissed Paco's forehead, turned to the rail, and replaced the book. She returned to her spot and descended yoga-like to crouch on the stones, staring into the pan and chanting as before.

Chori dropped to his knees in front of her with the tearing brother on his shoulder. She acknowledged each question with a faint nod but never looked up or stopped singing. With a litany of pleas, they threw every Euro they had into the pan. At last she quieted, shuffled the Tarot cards and blindly drew one, displaying its face to them without looking—The Hierophant.

Stone-faced and with eyes fixed on the back of the card, she spoke. "Know that the boy has the rarest of gifts, Señores, the same as the first Romani. He can see heaven. Read to him of godly things, of things that never die, and he will come to you..." She peered over the card. "... and then to the world."

Amazed and shaken, and only when they could provoke no more from the woman, Chori and Raphael stood to join the others. Paco retrieved his stick and the family moved on. They drove down the mountain that night without speaking and as Chori's eyes tracked the string of tail lights snaking through the cascading turns, he resolved to take the Gypsy's advice.

tau

PACO RODRIGUEZ SALAZAR

A.D. 2002
Apartamento 203B, 44 Calle Colón
Granada
España

He may not have had the pediatricians' diagnostic skills, but Chori was just as keen an observer, and thanks to their encounter in Bubión he was certain that Paco was more than a medical freak. He believed the gypsy, that reading to his son would make him whole, so he tried every presentation. Quotations gave a first success and the lyrics of certain songs seemed to calm the boy, but Chori found that more complex constructs, especially poetry and hymns, tranquilized like no others. Paco focused when his brother read from the Qur'an or Bible and was quieted by Neruda's verse, but nothing pleased him like his father's metered voice as he read from al-Hakkam's book of sayings. More and more, the child brought that battered old book to Chori.

One evening as dinner ended, Paco ran to the prayer room and fetched Hakkam's book from between the saddlebags, but instead of handing it to his father he spread it on the table, turned to a chosen page, took a huge breath, and began to read.

"And Jesus said to the Zealot, 'Heed my words. They shall guide you on your journey, along every path and in all directions. It matters not who leads or which pilgrimage you make, only that you tread in my footsteps.'"

His family gaped as Paco leafed forward to read a second passage.

"Listen to your soul and not to false prophets, for they will descend as locusts, in all seasons and in every guise and garb. Many will claim my robes, but only the Hierophant will speak for me."

They were awestruck. Soon the boy abandoned the corner as well as the cat and was reading every book they owned. Then, when he learned that asking his father to recite from Hakkam's text brought quicker results than throwing a tantrum, he struggled to speak. At first chaotic, his words became ordered and articulate, in two languages.

On Paco's birthday he received an unexpected gift from his sitter: a pocket radio. Twirling it's dial, he sampled FM in the daylight and shortwave after dark. The radio's molded earphones became a body part, removed only when he slept or listened to his father as he read from "Paco's book," the name he'd given to Hakkam's translation of Papias' scrolls. At breakfast he'd prattle about last night's BBC or Al Jazeera programs, reciting verbatim in the language broadcast.

There was one unnerving episode. On a late summer night, Chori eavesdropped on Paco from the prayer room balcony as the boy listened to a Civil War documentary in the living room. He got chills as his son aped the speeches of Lorca and Franco. Then Chori closed his eyes and was afraid—the boy's voice and delivery wasn't just similar to the dead dictator's—it was identical.

The doctors didn't buy it. They were sure they'd turned the tide with their rigid remedies, but Chori and his wife knew better, and they said so. They withdrew Paco from the school and flushed his pills. The boy thrived, roaming the condominium with earphones dangling. He still had to endure the playground bullies and there was no spontaneous socialization, but Paco gained a measure of control and on the surface resembled any boy his age. He was most content when his father read from Hakkam's book, occasionally singing the phrases that pleased him in the exact pitch of the Gypsy's falsetto.

Chori and his son established their own nightly ritual and it bonded the pair as hot rivets do steel. After dinner, Paco would run to his father with Hakkam's book in hand yelling "Read, Papi! Read Paco's book!" When he had his fill, the boy ended their session by shelving the book and fetching the dagger, reciting its inscription just as Chori had.

"To Allah we belong and to Him we return."

upsilon

SERHANE FAHKET[25]

A.D. 2004
Tren 21431
Alcalá de Henares, Madrid
España

"After you, Señora, please," said the handsome
young man through an African accent before
helping the fragile lady to her seat.

Commuters streamed into the car as they did
each morning, squeezing close as the last passengers
boarded. Most were bound for Atocha station in the
heart of the great city—families, couples, teens, and
little children—business folk, teachers, clerks, and
students, all anticipating their new day. They chatted
and daydreamed, people-watched and flirted, reading
newspapers and schoolbooks as the train pulled away.
Sales meetings, shopping trips, final exams, and lover's
trysts were on their minds, but for an unlucky many, it
was the Thursday that never came. They clutched their
briefcases, purses, and backpacks in the last moments
of life, not noticing that the polite foreigner who exited
one stop before Atocha left his backpack neatly tucked
under the old woman's seat. It was 7:36 A.M...

The Madrid Metro is among the world's most efficient,
moving millions under the city in clean comfort and
fair cost. Three days before the Spanish election, a
handful of Al Qaeda fanatics armed their explosive

devices, slipped their passes through the turnstiles, and then boarded the strategically targeted trains. The cowards stuffed their bombs under the benches of the densely crowded cars and stepped off as they neared the city. Detonating the plastic explosives with cell phone triggers, they killed one hundred ninety-one Madrileños and injured two thousand more. Atocha was rocked with the first blast at 07:37. Others followed in less than a minute. The mangled corpses and screaming wounded lay amidst the smoke and twisted metal as panicked survivors stepped over them to escape the terror, the stench of charred flesh staining it all. Mercy missed the train that day.

The bombing[1] occurred exactly two and one-half years after New York's 9-11. It was the first deep trauma for the young democracy, and the nation convulsed from the blow. The culprits were North Africans, including the mastermind, Sherhane Fahket. Most were captured within a month and Fahket blew himself up when cornered, but his goal was achieved—the Spanish government, a partner with America in the war against Al Qaeda, was thrown from office and replaced by a left-leaning regime.

All of Spain was on edge in the days after Atocha. Four hundred kilometers south of Madrid, in Old Granada, the specter of African aggression was reborn. Muslims like Chori were numb and in families like his there was fear and confusion.

On the following Saturday, election eve, bands of thugs roamed the bazaar, fueled by alcohol and incited by constant images of the carnage. Intent on revenge against anything Muslim, they wandered the streets shouting slogans and throwing rocks at targets of opportunity. About midnight a cluster of fools gathered below Chori's living room balcony, alerted to the presence of Moroccans by its Amazigh tiles. They hurled epithets and stones at the veranda, and when a lucky throw shattered a pot, the family came running. Taking advantage of the commotion out front, someone climbed a trellis onto their eastern balcony and looted the prayer room. Gone were the scimitar and Foreign Legion banners, every antique Qur'an, Hakkam's book of sayings, and both saddlebags. Only the Jambiya dagger remained on the wall, its scabbard tangled on the ornate hook.

Chori discovered the theft minutes later. Falling to his knees in front of the looted shrine, he sobbed as his boys watched through the parted curtain.

Paco rushed up to his father and screamed. "Papi! Papi! Paco's book! Paco's book!"

The loss of their heirlooms was a trauma for all, but for Paco it was a calamity—his heart wailed when his father couldn't produce Hakkam's book. Chori could recite the passages from memory and occasionally it calmed the child, but just as often Paco was enraged, reminded of his loss when there was nothing to carry to bed. Soon he shed the radio and retreated to his corner, scooping the confused cat into his lap. The theft scrambled the boy's nucleus and he slowly regressed, sinking by degrees into his old self—insular, morose and babbling.

phi

MIGUEL VALENZUELA

A.D 2005
Barrio Terraza del Rey
Granada
España

Some parts of Granada's royalist quarter are shabby, but on the whole the architecture and atmosphere of its glory days remain, especially in the neighborhood called Terraza del Rey, near the crown of the hill overlooking the old city. Scattered among the winding streets just below the hilltop are strings of colorful shops, their ornate facades removed from the touristy bazaar and free from its trappings. Serving locals and the few visitors fit to scale the steep stairs, they offer bargains along their angled streets and dead-end nooks. Each shop deals in one commodity or service: dresses, haircuts, candy, etc., and in the big corner store at Marquez and La Posada, in *Libreria Valenzuela*, books, more used than new.

Señor Miguel Hernan Valenzuela founded his business in 1958, financed with his teen bride's dowry. In the first years Valenzuela sold only new books, and thanks to his rank in Franco's auxiliary he secured the Catholic textbook franchise. He lost that privilege when the despot died and his place gradually became a secondhand warehouse. The once, often, and never-read titles supplanted new ones bit by bit until the only shiny covers were romances displayed in the rotating racks up front. By the nineties, his store was known to bibliophiles as the best place outside Madrid to find out-of-print works, neatly stacked on every surface of the single level, wall-to-wall and floor-to-high-ceiling, creating a grid of dark aisles wide enough for one person to pass, and only sideways in some places.

For decades Valenzuela was renowned for his ability to locate a book among the thousands of volumes. With time his trick became a performance, an excuse for buyers to climb the steep grade, and the reason the business flourished. His act never varied. Dressed in a cardigan with ascot and gray slacks, the bald bookseller would shuffle up to the customer, snap to attention and cheerfully ask "May I show you a title?" When they named it, he'd beam and shout "Follow me!" Then the gangly man led through his maze, straight to the book with the customer in tow, jimmying it free and dusting it with the velvet cloth that lived on his shoulder. Finally, after a gentlemanly bow, he'd present the prize along with his punch line: "I believe this is what you requested." Many asked for a random book just for the show, and all felt obliged to buy.

Through his early and middle years, the bookman was an affable contributor to his Royalist neighborhood. It was in the late '90's, after he was widowed, when his granddaughter and only assistant, Maria Luisa, noticed the onset of disease. He began to leave lights on, repeat done tasks, and speak of conversations with people long gone. Annoying to customers was his habit of mumbling. The decline was relentless if slow, one IQ at a time, and by the millennium his genial mind had gone hollow, distilled to the routines of his young-man days.

In the first week of the new year, a youth whom Valenzuela befriended as a boy entered the shop. The sticklike twenty-something was a physical waste—

powder white, stooped, and with hands coarsely trembling—a junkie nearing his end.

The wretched man greeted Valenzuela across the dusting bench as he spilled the contents of his backpack on it. "Señor Valenzuela, good day, sir. It is your friend, Reynaldo! I have brought you things of great value."

By habit, Valenzuela aligned the items as the man talked—a half-dozen texts and two bulging saddlebags.

The sick man pointed. "Look at these ancient books, no doubt very rare. And these leather satchels. Have you ever seen their like? Filled with priceless writings, from the tent of a sultan, I bet."

The granddaughter interrupted. "How did you come by these things?"

"I acquired them last year, during Atocha, from the estate of a rich Muslim," Reynaldo answered. "I offer them to you at a good price: five hundred Euros."

As had been his lifelong custom, the old man answered the friend he did not know. "I will pay exactly half that," he deadpanned.

In seconds, they agreed on three hundred, and just as quickly Reynaldo fled.

Then Valenzuela repeated another routine. He and his granddaughter gathered the goods and snaked through the aisles, placing them on the top shelf of an open bookcase in the rear. It was Maria Louisa's idea to remove a scroll from each bag for display out front.

Their task accomplished, she closed the store for siesta and led her grandfather by the arm to their flat across the street. Valenzuela tapped the pavement with his cane and saluted everyone he passed with someone's name, all the while mumbling about Franco's coming visit to the Alhambra.

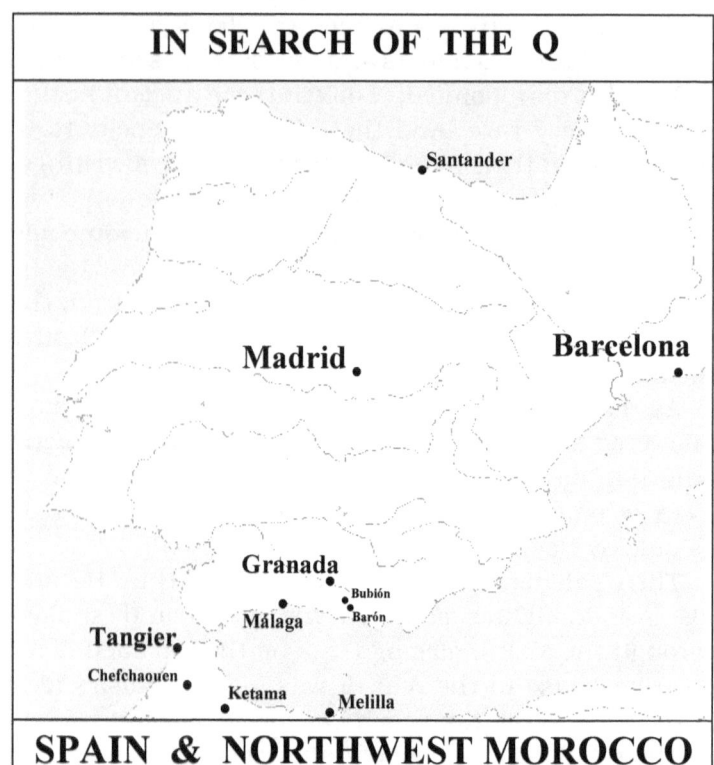

IN SEARCH OF THE Q

Santander

Madrid

Barcelona

Granada
Bubión
Málaga
Barón
Tangier
Chefchaouen
Ketama
Melilla

SPAIN & NORTHWEST MOROCCO

BOOK THREE
THE SCROLLS

8

MATEO BAREFOOT

Wednesday, 13 May, 2:12 P.M.
Federico Garcia Lorca Airport
Granada
Spain

Ellen Shea was exhausted after her last all-nighter, and she fell fast to sleep in the airliner's recliner with thoughts of the Quelle scrolls on her mind. First-class was a new experience for the frugal student, as was arriving in Madrid rested and ready for the day. Waiting in the boarding queue for her connecting flight to Granada, she watched a young father tending his toddler and was reminded of her affection for all things Spanish. To her these were a dignified and sweet people—quite proper and often stiff, but genuine—something she imagined the Americans had been before their age of excess. Her sparkling persona and near-native fluency flattered the Spaniards and explained the courtesy they extended. She carried her grandmother's Mexican accent, to the provincial Spaniards an annoying trait, but her refined bearing blunted their bias, and she thrived among them.

Ellen was at ease in her favorite Spanish city, Granada: a handsome, happy, and magical metropolis filled with students, tourists, and business folk from all points on the planet. The sun-soaked city of fountains and antique squares was the original European melting pot, the last seat of the caliphs, and as such a living remnant of the ancient world. Home to the magnificent Alhambra palace and a prestigious university, it's a young and energetic place, a place where Ellen could belong. The medieval palace is the country's premier tourist attraction, with its formal gardens and stunning Moorish architecture setting a noble yet gay mood for the city that fills the plain below. She delighted in the exotic atmosphere of the neighborhoods gathered around the Alhambra, as much North African as Spanish, and she knew those teeming streets were safe, places where a woman could walk day or night.

Mateo stood above the crowd to greet her at the customs gate, or at least to nod and grunt, perfectly pressed and robotic as usual. Her swollen suitcase had a frozen wheel, so he toted it out front, plowing their way through the crowd. As they reached the curb Ellen realized that he might be mute, but Mateo answered her first query with a soft reply, and when she asked him to shed his sunglasses there was a pleasant surprise—he was Native-American, all right—with high, sharp cheekbones and warm, dark eyes, his coal-black hair and slashing eyebrows giving contrast to the clear complexion and perfect teeth. Ellen thought she could tell men by their eyes, and these intrigued her. The margins of his chocolate irises were ambiguous, indistinct from the pupils, creating the illusion of dark suns on a cotton-white sky.

"Seen enough?" he asked, holding the sunglasses aside.

"Yes, thanks," she replied.

Back they went.

She tried chatting with her new partner as they drove into the city, but he didn't make it easy, answering with grunts and one-breath phrases. He wasn't rude, just efficient, and as she increasingly appreciated, shy. When Mateo did say something, he spoke haltingly, enunciating his proper nouns like a child in front of the class.

"And your ancestry, Mateo? I hope you don't mind my asking."

"Mes-ca-ler-o, A-pach-e," he replied. "And on my mother's side, Co-man-che."

"Where'd you grow up?" she asked.

"New Mexico, Rui-do-so. Spent my summers in Old Mexico."

"Your Spanish is native," she said. "Chihuahua or Sonora?"

"Chi-hua-hua, Pa-lo-mas, both grandmothers," he said.

"Really? My grandma's from Cuauhtémoc... Do you enjoy what you do, Mateo?"

"Not lately."

The dead spaces in their conversation evaporated as the Mercedes wallowed in traffic and soon he answered briskly, in whole sentences, and with wit. All formality dissolved when they took turns making fun of Parkinson. Mateo told one anecdote after another about the geeky Englishman, and she laughed out loud.

"Parkinson tries to stump me with trivia and silly riddles," he said, "but I'm pretty good at it—the Apache teach with riddles."

"Can I hear one?" asked Ellen.

"Okay. I'll make it easy. What's better than God, worse than the devil, something poor people have that rich people want, and if you eat it, you die?"

Ellen eyes pinched. "Easy, you said?"

"No hints... Gotcha stumped?"

After a long pause, she nodded. "Yes."

"Nothing," he said with a grin.

She pretended a pout and said "My turn."

"Okay. Shoot," answered the beaming Indian.

"This one's the Monsignor's: What do Christmas trees and Jesuits have in common?"

"Good one," he said, and then deadpanned. "Their balls are for decoration."

It went on and on. Oblique and straight-faced, Mateo's set-ups were clever and his punch lines seamless. *He could do stand-up in the Village*, Ellen thought.

His last quip was a caution. "One thing about Parkinson, Miss Shea—never say 'Thank God' in front of him!"

"Why?" asked Ellen. "Would it offend him? I thought he was agnostic."

"No," he chuckled. "Because he'll say 'You're welcome.'"

Then Mateo sobered. "I've worked with some real personalities since the Corps, Miss Shea, but Parkinson takes the prize. He's too smooth for his own good. Always tries to stay *two* moves ahead, and he really believes he's the world's smartest human. The guy has no patience with anyone unless they have something he wants, and then he wants it all, yesterday."

Mateo quieted as he threaded the car through a whirling roundabout, but continued as they spilled onto Calle Neptuno. "He's not all that bad. He'll work just as hard as you, and he'll say when you've done a good job. You should've seen him in the bazaar last winter—a bulldog, twelve hours a day, with no breaks outside of siesta. My bet is he finds the scrolls. He knew he'd need big money and influence, so he hooked up with the boss right away. That's when I met him. I've been reporting to the professor since Christmas, and now, well, it's got to where it doesn't bother me."

"What's going on between Parkinson and Monsignor Brahaney?" Ellen asked.

"The old priest? Ha!" Mateo threw his head back. "Parkinson hates his guts, and 'hates' is the right word. Whatever happened with those two must've drawn blood. The professor gets red in the face just hearing the guy's name. I bet your teacher beat him at something.

Parkinson can't stand to lose, doesn't matter at what. He blows up, like the time last winter when the boss had to bail him out after he totaled a guy's Porsche in the library lot. The jerk stole Parkinson's spot, so he rammed him with his Land Rover, over and over, until the police came. They used those pneumatic jaws to get the guy out. The boss had to call the mayor and dish a wad of cash to make it go away."

Mateo told more as they inched through the snarl. He worked for the fat paycheck, to support his family on the reservation, he said. She joked at that comment, thinking it was more humor, but Mateo's pained expression said not, so she changed subjects to blunt her error.

"What's with the fancy suits, Mateo?"

His frown inverted and there was a light shrug. "Yeah, well, I couldn't afford real clothes until I worked for Trump, and he picked on every mistake, really teased me, so I made it my business to learn what to wear, and when. Pretty soon The Donald was calling me 'Fashion Master.' Now I enjoy duding up. Sorry if you don't like the look, Miss Shea."

"Oh, no. You look great, just not what I'd expect from a guy in your line of work."

The commute was a gentle surprise. They chatted long after he parked, across and down the street from Casa del Moro, the residence hotel he'd chosen. She learned about tribal schools, New Mexico State ROTC, and his tour of hell in Fallujah. He went for the big money after the DEA, working for Trump until 'Smith' made the offer.

"So what's up with your 'Mister Smith'? He could've dreamed up a better name."

"You're right about that," Mateo replied, "Parkinson picked it... Well, I like him, a lot. He's a Hollywood kingpin, a behind-the-scenes mogul. Tries to keep a low profile, but he's bigger than any of 'em, and twice as rich. He's a little intense, and he expects you to do things right, but the boss is flesh and blood. If he asks how you're doing, he wants to know. We hit it off right away—spent a lot of time together before he sent me to Spain, in his Jetstream and the chopper. He likes to talk, and once he gets it going, it doesn't stop. He calls out of the blue sometimes, wanting to 'kibitz,' that's what he calls it, to talk about nothing. You'd never know he had billions, and believe me, Miss Shea, he's into this 'Quelle' thing as much as Parkinson."

"What's with the cloak-and-dagger?" Ellen asked. "It's lame. Why was he hiding in the dark? I felt like I was in a Hitchcock movie."

"I can't say any more," said Mateo.

"What about—"

"That's it, Miss Shea. I've said too much already. You can ask him yourself if you get the chance."

"Okay," she replied.

"It's your turn again," said Mateo.

"My turn? Another riddle?"

"No. I just told you my whole life story. How 'bout yours?"

She stared down the street. "I don't think you'd be interested. Not very exotic, not like yours. All white bread and vanilla."

"Wonder Bread or Sunbeam?" he asked with a grin.

"Who wants to know?"

"The boss," he lied.

"Okay... I grew up in a college town. Western Pennsylvania. Both of my parents were language profs, boring but sweet. They traveled a lot, so I grew up on my Granddad's tree farm, mostly ... I'm hopelessly Irish: three grandparents, from Galway and Roscommon, and like I said, my mother's mom is Mexican. I have four older brothers and they're great, but easier to love from a distance."

"Are your parents still teaching?" he asked.

She blinked. "They're gone. A small plane, in a blizzard, two years ago. Peru."

"I'm sorry," he replied, then blurted the first thing that came to mind. "Parkinson says you're a big-time egghead. Do you like what you do?"

She laughed. "Yeah, I do. But I'm looking for more … more adventure, I guess. I want something in the field, not the classroom, but it'll be hard to find without experience. That's why I jumped at this job, that and the idea that the scrolls might exist. It seems farfetched—a pile of scriptures, older than the rest, stories from people who knew Christ? Don't tell the boss, but it sounds like a wild goose chase to me."

"I wouldn't know," he said, and then delicately, "So, is there a guy?"

"A guy, are you kidding? What guy would be interested in a 'big-time egghead' like me?"

He winced. "Parkinson wanted to know."

"Yeah? Well, you can tell Parkinson to stick that question—"

"Okay," Mateo interrupted. "What if *I* wanted to know?"

"What if *you* wanted to know?" She wiggled her mouth. "Okay, this'll sound silly, but it's true: I do fine with men, anywhere except here, in Granada… So far it's happened every time. My friend Emilio says my landlady put a spell on me when I broke her lease—something about a magic moon—a 'Gypsy moon,' he calls it. Like I said, it's silly, but it's real, and it messes me up. It won't happen this time though, because this time I've sworn off romance, completely, for as long as I'm here."

Mateo's brow crinkled. He wished her good night, declining to get the door by saying that his suits were too easily recognized. "You may not see me, but I'll be there, Miss Shea. Sixty, sixty, twenty-four, seven. I'm number one on your Europhone. Remember, no free rides and only meet people in public, in the daytime."

She pixie-smiled and gave a mock salute. "Yes, sir, Lieutenant Mateo!"

The sass brought a straight-ahead stare. She jumped out and dragged the bag onto the pavement, crossing to the hotel with its wheel chalk-screeching all the way. Ellen looked back as the doorman took her bag, but the Mercedes was gone.

Her top-floor suite was digitally robust. She found bank checks, credit cards, and a Europhone on the desktop with a note in childlike script telling of Friday maid and laundry service. Scrawled across the bottom were Mateo's signature and a smiley face. After a reunion for tapas with her old roommate, Maria, she fell to sleep at twilight, again with the Quelle scrolls on her mind.

9

EMILIO RODRIGUEZ

Thursday, 14 May, 10:02 A.M.
Café de Valor, Calle Zacatín
Granada
Spain

Ellen loved the Iberian routines. Spain's workday hasn't changed since the Middle Ages: commercial establishments open about ten in the morning, close promptly for siesta at two, and then reopen between four and six, depending on the mood of the owner. The exceptions are the ubiquitous bars and cafés. They're almost always open and are the citizens' social crossroads, each with a unique ambiance evolved to match its clientele. She appreciated Spain's Daylight Savings Time as well, two hours later than the rest of Europe, with June's twilight lapping the midnight hour in cities like Santiago and A Coruña. Andalusia's leisurely pace is opposite the New York push, and she dressed for the role.

She beelined for Café de Valor that first morning, in search of a special friend: the busy restaurant's owner, Emilio Rodriguez. He was her favorite Spaniard, one with whom she'd shared many a midnight sherry debating things that mattered. They were an odd pair of soul mates considering the wide age gap and contrasting backgrounds, but their friendship was synergistic from the start, and during the two years she spent in Granada it grew into a deep, familial bond. She'd lingered many evenings in his home, tutoring his older son at the kitchen table, baby-sitting the younger boy, and enjoying the Señora's nuanced cuisine. It was a sugar-tears good bye when Ellen returned to New York, but she and Emilio remained e-pals, regularly sharing their dreams.

Emilio was at his station that day, polishing crystal behind the café's mahogany bar and prospecting for customers through the cut-glass façade. He recognized Ellen's gait from across the street and quickly shed his apron, rushing out to greet her with a hug and pair of kisses.

"Rubia! My Rubia! God be praised!" he exclaimed.

"Uncle Emilio! Tio Emilio! How are you?"

"Well, Rubia, well."

He'd nicknamed her "Rubia," "Blondie," on the first day they met.

"We missed you very much, Rubia. Why didn't you tell us you were coming?"

She shook her finger. "Emilio! You're behind on your e-mail again, and I wrote twice. Sorry, but it was crazy and every time I thought of calling, it was the middle of the night over here."

His grin said he forgave her and they took seats at a sidewalk table. Emilio hadn't changed: fair and taller than most Spaniards, he was trim save a small paunch and was poised as always in pressed trousers and satin vest. A thin silk hid the top buttons of his ice blue shirt, secured with a crescent-and-star cravat. Graying temples and salted eyebrows gave away Emilio's age and his dignity was palpable, displayed in the expressive gaze, textbook posture, and slight but ever-present smile.

"What's new in the bazaar?" she asked.

"Very little, Rubia. More tourists come each year and more Moroccans follow, selling junk at even higher prices. The bad times hurt, for sure, but business is steady. I get home late every night and almost never go fishing. No matter. These times will pass, and soon Rafael will be running this hole-in-the-wall. I'll be sunning on the beach in Almeria, sipping sangria and ogling the girls. There's one thing that's changed, though: there're more Americans lately."

"I bet you like that," Ellen mocked.

He gave an "uh-oh" look. She knew what it meant. Easy to distinguish by their bad manners, big bellies, and bigger mouths, Americans remain the bane of Europe's tourist meccas despite their free-spending ways and odd habit of tipping. Spaniards know the roving tour groups as particularly condescending and put Texans in a class of their own. Their habit of mobbing restaurants, demanding ketchup, and making fun of the sophisticated Andalusian cuisine galls the natives, who call them "vaqueros," "cowboys." Ellen was happy to pass for Scandinavian on account of her looks or for Mexican because of her accent. Most were surprised when she said she was from the U.S.

"Tell me of your family, Emilio, what of your beautiful family?" Ellen asked.

"They're well, my dear. Graciela's still smiling, and wait 'til you see Raphael. Thanks to you his English is excellent, a good draw for students and foreigners. He watches over Francisco, and Francisco keeps amazing us all... He had a setback, but it's better now. All is as God wills. God is the greatest."

Ellen loved both boys. She used to babysit the young one, ten or eleven by then. He was everything darling, but vulnerable and housebound. His teen brother Rafael was Francisco's opposite, an extroverted young bull groomed to take over the café. His little brother's constant guardian, Rafael was even more patient with him than the mother. Ellen taught Raphael English, initially in trade for his father's help with her Arabic studies, and then just to give. They had a great time when the teenager visited New York the summer before.

"Allahu Akbar," said Ellen. "I'd be glad to sit with Francisco again."

"I was hoping you'd say that," Emilio replied. "He misses you."

They continued the gab, catching up on gossip and repeating old lies. She told of her task, omitting specifics as instructed by Parkinson. "Tio Emilio," "Uncle Emilio" as she called him, was eager to help.

He fetched a street map and spread it on the table. "Believe me, Rubia, it won't be easy. I speak from experience. To find what you're looking for, you'll need a precise system and the patience of a monk."

Fingering each neighborhood, he suggested methods to canvass the huge shopping area, "the bazaar" to foreigners. His café was central, he said, and they decided to plan her day there each morning.

Emilio marked the map with a crayon, circling bookshops and other places where artifacts might be found. "Rafael and I will ask around, and we'll get the staff to help," he promised. "The more eyes, the better. And be sure to mark precisely where you've been. If you don't, you'll go through the same shops twice." He shook his head. "The bazaar makes the Alhambra's labyrinth look like a child's puzzle."

Emilio folded the map and handed it to her. "Now tell me of your triumphs, my dear. Have you finished your schooling? Are you a professor at last? You've been in Granada for ... how many hours now? Have you fallen in love yet? How many times? Oh, Rubia! You really should settle with that Gypsy woman. It's not too late."

Ellen's nose wrinkled. "Not funny, Uncle Emilio, not funny at all, but I'll tell you this—the number of romances will be *zero* this time—I promised Monsignor Brahaney, and I'll promise you. Zero. And no, I'm not done. My course work is finished, but there's still the dissertation, and after that ... Who knows?"

Ellen excused herself and walked to the Ayuntamiento, a kind of jumbo city hall where she used the public copier to magnify Emilio's map. Dividing the jumbled web of passageways into quadrants and again into sixteenths, she penciled numbers overtop each square. At the end of siesta, she made her first stop on square number one and used that place to craft her method. Working her way down each aisle, she fingered every item before questioning the clerk. Satisfied that there were no scrolls at that shop, she crossed it out on the photocopy and moved next door. Thus came her habit, efficient and ordered, but from the outset tedious and mind-numbing. Her search for the scrolls had begun.

10

FRANCISCO RODRIGUEZ

Sunday, 18 May, 7:35 P.M.
Apt. 203B, 44 Calle Colon
Granada
Spain

Ellen wasn't keen on small children. Her girltime neighborhood swarmed with little-boy pests and girls who did things she didn't, and for as long as she could remember she preferred the company of adults. As the last of the litter she never had to be mother, and as a teen she did bookwork for her parents' colleagues instead of sitting their kids, so Ellen's nurturing skills were untried. It seemed all she got when her friends brought their little ones to visit was ringing in her ears and stains on her blouse. For those reasons and more, she kept her distance from kinder.

Emilio's little boy changed all that.

Her babysitting sessions with Francisco became a twice-weekly favor, Tuesdays and Sundays mostly. It gave Emilio and his family time for themselves and was one way to repay their kindness. Earnest as in every chore, she spent the first night on the floor, facing the boy on her knees and trying to connect. But Francisco had regressed—he was distant before, but now he was utterly withdrawn—always muttering or whistling and never responding or even acknowledging her presence. Nothing she did could provoke him. The second night Ellen faked disinterest by sprawling next to Francisco as she read her cheesy novel, and when she got bored, by doing Pilates planks and sit-ups by his side. But no matter that ploy or others, the child ignored her, hidden behind his invisible screen.

Things turned on the third night, when she brought her yoga pad. Cross-legged beside him in a Dhyana pose with eyes closed and emitting a soft Shanti mantra, Ellen realized that the boy had gone quiet. Opening her eyes, she was startled by his peeping stare, inches from her nose. She jerked back and he retreated.

Ellen found that other melodies brought him out, but they had to be delivered like her mantra, *ostinato*. With the right pitch and cadence, he'd go quiet and move close, engaging her eyes with wonder in his own. Certain chants prompted hints of emotion, and rarely he'd mimic a sound. One night she remembered Monsignor's Latin canticle, fetched her iPad, and found the Vatican's version on You-Tube.

♫ Sanctus Michael... Ora pro nobis.

Sanctus Gabriel... Ora pro nobis.

Sanctus Raphael... Ora pro nobis. ♫

It brought his first smile.

It was the only time a child had reached her, a wonderfully fresh interaction that stirred her little girl instincts and made her realize what she'd missed. Beginning that night, Francisco was the little brother she never thought she wanted, albeit without touch or speech. For an hour they'd sing the litany from their knees, she the saints' names and he the refrain, with giggles and horseplay to follow. Their time together became precious for both, a twice-weekly respite and the best reason to look forward. For Ellen it was a deepening affection, one without rules or language, something she'd never known. His parents remarked how their sessions pleased the boy, but she didn't tell why. It was their little secret, too special to share with the grown-ups.

11

RATTUS NORVEGICUS

Monday, 1 June, 11:58 P.M.
Pasillo Estrecho, Restaurant Row
Granada
Spain

By its nature the bazaar's crisscross of cobblestoned corridors, crammed with congested shops and crowded tourist traps, is suffocating. Every square meter swarms with patrons and sales folk, dodging each other and gobs of protruding merchandise. Most businesses have a single narrow entrance, one tall step up per their medieval architecture, with goods hung thick and crammed into every cabinet and rack.

As expected, Ellen found the shopkeepers too busy to be bothered by her stream of questions, with some pretending not to speak whichever language she tried. Tall piles and dangling clothes limited visibility, causing occasional collisions with oblivious shoppers. And for Ellen the work wasn't just tedious—sometimes it was terrifying—she was a congenital claustrophobe, and once in a while, especially in the airless afternoons, the panic closed in and she had to rush into the open skies of the fountain squares to get her breath. Dreadfully bored from the start, she labored without pause in the manner of a honeybee, hovering from one shop to the next. Ellen thought none about money, but much of the prize: a two-thousand year old trophy that would open her world. So on she plodded, dissecting each shop, one day as dreary as the next. Only her evenings with little Francisco gave respite.

Ellen fell into the habit of dining after the last store closed, along with most Spaniards, around nine-thirty. She wound down and recharged in that way, sampling Granada's cuisine courtesy of Mr. Smith's Amex card. Most nights the walk home took fifteen or twenty minutes, depending on where she ended up. In prior years she'd navigated Granada's dim streets without fear, but this trip was different. From the first night, Ellen felt a sinister anxiety that cooled her skin and quickened her pulse, imagining danger in every doorway and a bogey man around each corner. In the daylight she dismissed the creepy feelings as a remnant of her time in the Bronx, but each night the dread returned. Unexpected sounds were thunderclaps, alley cats jaguars, and always she felt eyes on her back. More than once she whirled around to confront a stalker who wasn't there. Altering her routes to busier streets, she took cabs when she could, each time scolding herself as she reached the shelter of her suite and vowing to be brave the next night.

To top it off, there were rats. Granada is among Spain's cleanest cities, but the hairy rodents that hitchhiked with the Visigoths fifteen centuries before have evolved into an aggressive subspecies the Grenadines call "sewer lions." Bulky, bold, and covered in shiny caramel-brown fur, it's the cats that are afraid. With the dark come teams of hungry vermin families, emerging from the sewers to forage. Hardly a night passed when Ellen didn't see at least one slimy rodent.

Then, one Monday midnight gray with fog, she challenged her fear. Exhausted from her day and blocks from home, she peeked down the alleyway behind restaurant row, an inky passage that funneled directly to her hotel. The slender lane was her favorite shortcut in daylight, but not after dark—only a few shafts of streetlight penetrate the tapering corridor and its rough stucco walls narrow to shoulder width near the end.

On impulse, she dared herself. *It's only twenty meters long,* she thought, *just what I need to beat this silly fear...* In she went.

At once Ellen heard quick footsteps closing from behind. She turned to look. The point of her shoe caught a crack. She stumbled. Careening off the stucco and scraping her bare arm, she reeled from the pain and ricocheted off the opposite surface, falling face-first into a heap of kitchen garbage. Choking in the putrid waste and in a claustrophobe's panic, she tried to dig free but only bored deeper into the slop.

The mother rat attacked first, its wet fur clinging to Ellen's exposed skin as the fore claws pierced her shoulder. Biting the nape of her neck, it burrowed into her loose bun. Brother rat latched onto the left ankle and shimmied up the calf, nipping as he went. Sinking further into the greasy refuse, she tasted his squealing litter mate as it brushed across her lips. Enraged when she reached the pavement, Ellen struggled to her knees, plucking the mama by the tail and hurling it against the wall before swiping the other from her thigh. Kneeling tilted and dripping with slime, she watched their chittering silhouettes flee along the gutter and down the grate.

To her feet, she retrieved her bag and staggered barefoot toward the light, squeezing through the gap and barely avoiding a cruising taxi as she stumbled into the street. She took that cab to the emergency room. From then on, Ellen made sure to walk home through the most crowded streets as soon as work was done, bringing take-out or dining in the hotel's restaurant.

It was terror in the alley that changed her ways, but it wasn't the rats. As she fell Ellen caught a good look at her small-man stalker and his shiny butcher's blade.

12

SISTER MARIA TERESA

Monday, 8 June, 1:19 P.M.
Humanities Library, University of Granada
Granada
Spain

Sunday mornings in Spain are for sleeping. Just
hospitals are open, with only their emergency doors
unlocked. The idea that anyone would want to work,
shop, or study during those hours is absurd to the laid-
back Spaniards, but a few of the university's foreign
students, Germans and Americans mostly, suffered
from a different ethic, and they'd gained Sunday access
to the library.

Ellen took advantage. The peace she found in the
stacks allowed a diversion from her weekday routine
and opportunity to research the Quelle. Like Professor
Parkinson, she had trouble believing that the Quelle
could be real, though the more she studied, the more she
wished it were so. The idea that the earliest accounts of
Jesus might be preserved, free from editing, omissions,
and forgeries was exhilarating.

Her investigation was comprehensive by habit, but
she struggled with the esoteric literature—the Quelle
hypothesis was an academic Pandora's Box. She was
reminded that scholars see the New Testament as
serendipitous, that much of what Jesus said and did
was lost in a sea of scribes and forgers, and that parts
of the record were purged. She read that the accepted

or "canonical" gospels, recorded in Greek between at least forty and seventy years after Jesus' crucifixion, weren't written by his illiterate Aramaic-speaking apostles, but by pseudonymous Greek-speakers with complex motives. The more Ellen researched, the more she struggled—most biblical scholars' bias seemed naked and their conclusions impossible to value. Long ago she'd decided that all historians were liars, but the religious writers seemed particularly allergic to the truth. Monsignor Brahaney touted Ehrman[26], Crossan, and Pagels[27], but Ellen was unconvinced, knowing that the careers of most religious scholars depend on pleasing their sponsors with expected results. The bottom line was that without the Quelle, the historical Jesus was whoever they said he was.

Then Ellen got creative. Scrutinizing the signature cards inside the pockets of the library books, she noticed that at one time or another every text even mentioning Quelle had been borrowed at least once by the same person, H.M.T. Frasco. She figured the guy to be a bible geek, someone who might help her through the scriptural morass, so with the aid of the librarian she arraigned to meet Frasco at the main desk on a Monday afternoon.

Ellen waited there impatiently, past the appointed one o'clock hour. Only a portly old nun in full habit and her gaggle of third-graders loitered around the desk, with no sign of the Frasco character. Thinking he was a no-show, Ellen gathered her things and was about to leave when the cherubic sister waddled up.

"Señorita Ché?" asked the nun.

"Why, yes. And you are?"

"Hermana Maria Teresa Frasco, Señorita, at your service. Señora Garza said you wished to see me. Forgive me, but I wasn't expecting ... a girl."

Ellen excused her own error and thanked the sister for coming. The Carmelite commanded her charges to mind their schoolwork at a nearby table and they obeyed with a harmonious groan.

"How can I help you, my dear?" asked the nun, peering over top her spectacles.

"Well, Sister, I'm doing a paper on the source of Christian scripture, and I noticed that you've already surveyed the literature. I was hoping you could help me understand a few things."

Sister Maria Teresa was clearly bothered. "You speak of the Quelle, don't you? Do you come from the Archbishop's office? Please, I promised silence, and you must tell them that I have kept my word."

"Oh no, Sister, I have nothing to do with the archbishop. I'm a student at a Jesuit school in New York, trying to learn about the Quelle for my paper. It would mean the world to me if you could help."

Sister hesitated. "You're not with the archdiocese?"

"No, Hermana, I'm just a student."

The nun threw a prayer at the ceiling and blessed herself before responding. "Very well then, but I must ask that all I say be entirely anonymous. I have not spoken of the Quelle for years, and my name may not cross your lips."

"Of course, Sister. On my honor," Ellen pledged, hand over her heart.

They moved to a desk beside the children's table and their chat began, with an explanation.

"I was a youngster when I started, about your age," said Frasco, "a novitiate just out of university, fascinated by the early church and its martyrs like Perpetua and Papias. Not long after, because of my degree, I became convent historian and was allowed to spend my free time here. I stumbled on the Quelle right away."

Ellen leaned in.

"From the beginning I was captivated, you might say infatuated, with the idea that there could be a trove of lost scripture, writings that would reveal more about our Lord. For years I helped scholars by searching the Alhambra archives as well as the diocesan libraries here and in Madrid. I learned much about the first Christian writings. Mother Superior encouraged me until the archbishop intervened. He was quite ... strict. So now, my dear, what questions have you?"

"To be frank, Sister, I'm confused and a little skeptical. If there really were such documents, what happened to them? Why don't we have them today?"

The nun's eyes sparkled. "How much time do you have, dear?"

"All you can spare," said Ellen.

"The first thing to know is that they did exist, and that some may still exist," the sister said, "but those first scriptures, the verses the German theologians called 'Quelle?' Some were discarded and others deliberately not copied, an effective means of extinction in those days. We don't know how much Quelle there was to start with, but we do know that what's survived has been edited by a thousand hands, for a thousand reasons. The fact is that most of the New Testament isn't close to what was first written."

"Most?" Ellen asked.

"Yes, most," said Frasco. "No doubt some of the original remains, but we can't be sure of which, or how much. There've been rumors for a thousand years. Some say that the Quelle ended up in the Vatican's secret archives... I could find no proof of that, but only heaven knows. In my opinion, all that's left in today's Bible is a hazy sketch of Our Lord, a jigsaw puzzle with half the pieces missing. There've been several attempts to pick out the genuine verses. Mister Tolstoy tried, and Mister Jefferson. To me, Jefferson made the best guesses. His work was my first inspiration."

"Jefferson?" Ellen questioned.

"Yes, your wise president, Thomas Jefferson, the man who hoodwinked Napoleon. He recognized the New Testament as holy paella, a mix of the fake and the real, and thought he could 'abstract'—that's the word he used—'abstract' the essence of Jesus from the King James' Bible. Mister Jefferson literally cut out, with a scalpel, the parts he thought true to Jesus, then rearranged and pasted them together to make his own bible. He said abstracting the 'real' from the 'rubbish'— that's what he called the rest—was like separating 'diamonds from the dunghill.' The Smithsonian in Washington just restored the original. You can find copies of the *Jefferson Bible* in any library."

The nun paused for a smug smile. "And Jefferson wrote another book about Christ, *The Philosophy of Jesus*. But like the Quelle, it's been lost.

"Remember, Señorita Ché, every scripture we have was written well after the fact. For decades the story of Jesus was only spoken." She pointed toward the children. "It's as if you told a nursery tale to that skinny boy there, the freckled one on the end, and asked him to whisper it to the next kid, and so on. It wouldn't be long before the story changed, and just as in the early church, by the time it came around to the first kid, he'd barely recognize it."

Ellen was taking notes.

"The record in those first years is murky," the sister said. "In the beginning there were many rival sects, Jews who believed that Jesus was their Messiah and that he would soon return, free them from the Romans, and found his own kingdom. They were a minority, separate from the mass of Jews who didn't accept Jesus. Each group had its own traditions and scriptures, often competing and sometimes drastically different. It got nasty, especially between the Orthodox and Gnostics— they tried to outdo each other—changed verses to fit their ideas and made up new ones, like the details of Pilate's trial: a way to gain favor with Rome by blaming Jews instead of Romans for Christ's death."

She waited for Ellen to stop scribbling.

"We know of many alterations as well as outright forgeries, and that the writings evolved, especially when they were translated into other languages. For instance, the first believers taught that Jesus was the son of God, but not always that he was equal to his father, or even divine. By the second century, when Ignatius and others began to call themselves 'Christians', beliefs were fluid. In a few generations, it was impossible to tell firsthand accounts of Jesus from the altered, mistranslated, or made up ones. Origen and a few others saw what was happening. They tried to save the oldest writings, but theirs was a losing cause."

Again the sister paused for Ellen.

"From time to time though, what people call 'lost gospels' appear, some real and some not, like the gospels of Peter, Thomas, and Mary Magdalene. My dream when I started, and one I still have, is that someday we'll find more."

Ellen questioned. "But the concept of Quelle—it's a modern invention, isn't it, Sister?"

"Modern? Yes, relatively. Nineteenth century. A string of German theologians came up with the notion of Quelle by comparing the accepted gospels and listing their common texts. They saw that many passages in Matthew and Luke match the older gospel of Mark. But they recognized other congruent parts, parables and sayings like the beatitudes which couldn't be found in Mark. Their idea was that those passages came from another, even earlier tradition. They called it 'The Source,' in German, 'The Quelle.' Quelle has come to mean every lost datum from the tumultuous first decades. Saint Papias was one of the first Quelle hoarders."

"Has any of Quelle been identified, Sister?"

"We think so, in the nineteenth century and again in 1945, at Nag Hammadi," she answered. "It was that discovery which gave new life to the Quelle."

"So why wasn't the Quelle included in the New Testament?"

"That question has many answers, Señorita, answers I've sworn not to repeat. But I will say that the omitted parts didn't fit, and I don't mean for size."

The nun finished her story. "I was active in my research until the morning Mother Superior called me in. She said I'd been credited in a journal, that the Vatican had alerted our Cardinal, and he the archbishop. I was summoned to Madrid and *educated*. It's unfortunate, Señorita Ché—Christian scholars have known the truth for centuries, but nearly all have been afraid—afraid to reveal that the modern bible isn't what their churches say it is. For me, it's the opposite. Why wouldn't we want to know more about the real Jesus, about what he said and did? He'd still be our Lord, but there'd be more lessons and stories, and they'd be true. The deceit makes no sense, and I doubt Jesus would approve, but I shall honor my vows and remain silent."

At that moment one of her pupils approached.

"Yes, Alicia," said Maria Teresa.

"Is it not time for siesta, Hermana? We are *very* tired."

With that, the sister excused herself but offered to help again.

"I'd love that," Ellen said.

From then on, Ellen and the affable nun met every Monday before siesta, more for friendship than education.

13

ONE YOUNG STUDLY

Sunday, 28 June, 12:10 P.M.
Humanities Library, University of Granada
Granada
Spain

There was sparse relief from the monotony of Ellen's daily grind. She enjoyed her morning meetings with Emilio and dined every Sunday in his home, savoring Graciela's scrumptious meals and time with the family, especially her babysitting sessions with Francisco. One week's wages were wired into Ellen's account every Friday. Each deposit netted more than she'd made in a summer's hosting in the Village, and she had money to burn though little time to burn it. She supped in restaurants she couldn't afford during her student days and shopped in Granada's trendy boutiques, but amusement was limited. No matter. As a rule she was spent at day's end from the tedium of the bazaar, seven days a week as she'd promised the boss. On Saturdays she and Maria hiked up to Sacromonte for wee-hour Flamenco, and once they taxied to Granada Diez where she danced close with a guy who made her flush, but she honored her promises to Monsignor and Emilio, fleeing before the music stopped.

But there was one young studly who made her tingle: a really handsome Nordic type who'd been making eye contact from across the library on those Sunday mornings. She'd peek back when he wasn't looking, enjoying his great looks and lithe body, but she was coy, parrying the smiles he tossed her way. There seemed no harm in looking.

He made his move when Ellen was waiting in the always long line at the library's photocopier, at first queuing behind her and then, when she didn't look around, by showing interest in the books she was holding.

It came in a sugary drawl. "I declare! *Misquoting Jesus* and *The Golden Bough*." he said. "Are you a divinity student, ma'am?"

By habit, Ellen didn't turn around. She'd adopted the New York girls' practice of ignoring anonymous flirts and feigned deafness while staring at the ceiling. She was curious about the silky accent, though, one she thought she recognized—melodious and molasses slow. *From Old Virginia*, she guessed. Glancing over her shoulder, Ellen was surprised to see that the flirt was the attractive blonde.

"Oh, yes, err, I mean no, *not* a divinity student," she said.

"What a shame," he quipped. "Then a student angel, perhaps?"

Both giggled at his corn. She thought of walking away, but didn't want to lose her place in the queue. His invitation came as he helped her make copies. "How 'bout a gelato? Have you tried that shop across the street? They have five kinds of mint."

Ellen knew she had to escape, but she dallied in his eyes as she groped for a turn-down phrase, triggering the neurochemicals that denied her the words. Like hummingbird to orchid, she flew.

His name was Hendershot, "Howard Harold Hendershot," he proclaimed, and sure enough, he was from Virginia. As they leaned in to share their two-straw shake, Ellen struggled to focus on what the tall boy was saying. His gallant diction was too distracting, the lean physique too well cut, and the exotic eyes captivating—icy and translucent like an albino's, but blue. He seemed the complete package: a serious grad student with suave manner and subtle humor wrapped in the body of an underwear model, his outfit and hip hairdo flattering the confident posture and easy smile.

"I'm working on a school project like you, Ellen, and I'll be here all summer," Howard said. "Only two years to go, and I'm hoping this trip will move me to the head of the class."

She could only grin.

"I guess I shouldn't assume that everyone who reads Ehrman or Frazer is a bible student, should I?" asked Howard.

He had to wait.

"No, you shouldn't," she answered.

"So why're you readin' 'em, if you're not studyin' religion, I mean?"

Ellen's answer was rehearsed. "It's for my thesis, about how ancient texts change as they're copied. I'm researching al-Hakkam, the librarian-caliph. I was expecting his scribes to be as naughty as the Christians, like Ehrman showed, but so far it doesn't look that way... Sorry if I'm boring you."

"No, ma'am. The opposite. Whatever you say sounds interestin'."

Sobered by that schmaltz, Ellen thought of leaving but was paralyzed. She was "just bitten, soon smitten," to use her grandfather's Irish cliché, and she knew it. Foreheads touched as they neared the bottom of the mint chocolate, but just then the brash notes of *Beethoven's Fifth* rang out.

"Excuse me," Ellen said as she reared up and retrieved her cellphone. Stepping to face the tile wall, she shielded it with her hands.

"Hello."

"Miss Shea? Paul Parkinson here. Mister Smith is on speaker. We've heard nil for so long. May we have a progress report?"

"It's been two days, Professor, but yes, just a moment." Ellen covered the phone, turning to thank Hendershot and excusing herself as she pushed through the door, leaving the boy dog-faced and slumping on the table.

"Yes, Professor. Sorry." said Ellen. "I was taking a break and it was hard to hear... I've been through six grids of sixteen, but found nothing. I stumbled on a cool Nasrid text and picked up a Spanish first edition of *The Old Man and the Sea*, but the few scrolls I've come across are facsimiles. I've got every friend looking, but nothing's come up."

The boss broke in. "You should take care, Miss Shea. That's why we called. We've just confirmed that an Eastern syndicate has joined the hunt—they're more than thugs—aggressive and plainly dangerous. Please be discreet and don't hesitate to call Mr. Barefoot."

"Mister who?" she asked.

"Barefoot, Mateo Barefoot," said Smith.

"Oh, Mateo." Ellen answered. "I'll do that, sir. Thank you. Goodbye."

14

HOWARD HENDERSHOT

Wednesday, 1 July, 11:35 A.M.
Al Kaftan Bookstore, Calle Catedral
Granada
Spain

Good timing, Ellen thought as she hurried away from the ice cream shop. *If Parkinson hadn't called, I'd be loopy again. The next time I see that guy, I'll be on guard...*

The following Wednesday she spotted Howard in the bazaar, from across the lane and between the dangling scarves of a Tuareg store. She congratulated herself for having dodged his arrow and then deliberately looked away, but soon she was peeping. Howard's back was to her as he arched over a deep glass case, long arms wide and fingertips splayed. Like a GQ model, his tight end stretched the slacks just right, the triangular torso broadcasting raw strength. She rubbernecked until he moved out of sight, resisting the urge to cross—but she'd watched a moment too long—that night, as she burrowed into the bedcovers, images of the blonde boy intruded. Drifting toward sleep, Ellen could see him spread across the glass, bottom taut and shoulders strong. Tingling as warm waves washed through her, she touched her breasts and then, below. Soon they were sharing ecstasies, one after another, ending in a shuddering cascade.

Two mornings later she was working a string of shops near the cathedral, inquiring of an Algerian owner about "antique papers" she might have in her bookstore.

The woman looked puzzled. "Do you speak of 'rollos', Señorita?"

Ellen's heart skipped. The Spanish word for scrolls is "rollos," the only term used, and the one Parkinson forbade.

"Why, yes, rollos would do," Ellen responded.

"No, I have no such things, but wish I did. You're the second one to ask this morning, and the man said he'd pay well if I could produce them. Is he your brother?"

"My brother?"

"Yes, a tall young man, handsome for an American, with hair and eyes like yours," said the woman. "My English was better than his Spanish, but I understood that he was searching for scrolls, for his teacher's collection, he said. I sent him to the intercambio in Virgin Square. Sometimes those kinds of things can be found there."

Ellen asked for a description and it matched her suspicions: Howard Hendershot. She finished the cathedral shops and as siesta approached, remembered the woman's tip. *If there're scrolls at that market, I don't want to miss them. It's been two hours since I talked with that shopkeeper, so Howard should be gone.*

Intercambios are Andalusian flea markets, with goods traded and sold in the open air. Cash only, no refunds, and no tax if you're discreet. Hurrying to make it before the midday break, Ellen turned the corner onto Virgin Square and froze. There he was, his towhead poking above the crowd as he fussed with a vendor. She took a step back, but Howard must have felt her eyes on him because he looked up at once and hurried to her.

"Hey, Ellen!" Hendershot gleefully greeted. "Takin' a break from the books?"

"Sort of. I heard there're some good deals here."

"What'cha lookin' for?" he asked.

"Some tops for this hot weather, maybe. And you?"

"Just browsin'," Howard said, "but there're no clothes at this one, only junk."

"I hear you're looking for scrolls," said Ellen.

"Scrolls? Oh, you mean for my project? Not scrolls in particular. Anything about *Revelations* will do. How'd you know I was lookin'?"

She ignored his question. "For your dissertation?"

"Not 'til next summer," he said, "but my major requires a field project, and I'm searchin' for apocalyptic writings, any kind." His smile stretched. "It's almost siesta. How 'bout lunch, my treat? I know a bodega up the street. There's a gui-tar man, and it's cheap."

She looked away knowing she must resist, but the chemicals catalyzed the second time, and again she flew. "Okay," Ellen blurted, "but only for siesta. I have a lot to do."

"Yeah, me too. Hope you don't run off this time."

"Sorry about that," Ellen said as she silenced her cellphone and took the arm he offered.

The cantina on Calle Elvira was delightful. They lounged at a tiled table on its sun freckled patio, sampling trio tapas and La Rioja rosé with a Segovia imitator strumming out front. Their seats were framed in San Diego Bougainvillea, the intense red blossoms quivering in the breeze. Howard's slow-mo speech was charming, complimenting his Old South etiquette and wit. *Everything but his name is right*, she thought, *'Howard' just doesn't fit.*

"I'm two years shy of my D.D. at Oral Roberts," he said, "and I'm lucky. My research is sponsored. I even get a stipend. We're lookin' for old writings about judgment day, and if we find 'em it'll put our program on the map."

"Who's we?" Ellen asked.

"My classmates," he said, "the Whitcolmb boys. They've been here since winter term. They're Oakies, whip-smart. Hope you get to meet 'em."

He was no church school geek. Candid and clever without being slick, Howard showed a dry humor and didn't boast. There were a few churchy clichés, but he seemed the exception, a Southern Baptist who drank like a Catholic and spoke like a sage. *One notch too pious*, she thought, *but he contains it well and doesn't preach...*

As she dawdled in his eyes Howard's phone gonged. He read the text and jumped to his feet. "I forgot about my meetin' with the Whitcolmbs. Sorry!" Tossing a twenty Euro note on the tile, he kissed her hand and shouted "See ya!" as he jogged away.

Ellen lingered in the spotty sunshine, tipsy but quite pleased and with only a smidgen of guilt. Her mind churned as she strolled away. *This curse thing is silly. Granada's no different than New York. The same thing would've happened there... He's not really that cute... It's because I haven't had sex in so long. Nothing's happened yet. I just need to go slow ... and stay in control.*

15

AHMAD AL KHOURY

Thursday, 2 July, 9:55 A.M.
Café de Valor, Calle Zacatín
Granada
Spain

For once, Ellen awoke thinking of something besides her tedious task. It was the blonde boy on her mind that morning, with snapshots of his crystal eyes and snug hind intruding. She giggled at the happy face primping in the mirror and caught herself skipping on the way to the café. Emilio was alone at the counter that morning, frantic to serve the rush of Alhambra workers and early-bird tourists. When Ellen reached the front of the line, he presented her usual coffee with churro and then asked her to stay, saying he had some news. Moving to the end of the bar, she leafed through *El Mundo* with daydreams of the Virginian rising from each page. As the last customer cleared the counter, Emilio waved her to him.

"Rubia, I'm sorry to delay you, but..." He jerked back, wrinkling his brow.

Ellen reacted. "What is it, Emilio? What's wrong?"

"It's happened again, hasn't it, Rubia? You seemed so determined this time—and you promised me, and your priest. Really... You should go back and pay that Gypsy!"

"Never mind, Emilio," she scolded, "Never mind. What's up?"

"Some news, from Oscar. Have you met Oscar, our new kitchen boy from Mali? He's been keeping an eye out as I asked and says he saw something, in a pipe shop. It's next to a Kebab King, against the massif. *Para Fumar* I think he said. Anyway, he saw a very old book there, but the shopkeeper wouldn't show it to him. Said it wasn't for sale. I have trouble understanding Oscar's Spanish. You'll get more with French. He's working the side sink in the dish room."

"Thanks, Emilio."

She made her way through the steamy kitchen and found the young immigrant slopping plates. It sounded promising until he described a small leather book with Arabic numerals on its cover. It wasn't large enough to be a folio of pressed scrolls and she couldn't imagine that binding, but she'd follow the lead as soon as she finished the cathedral grid.

It was after siesta when she entered the smoke shop. *Para Fumar* was isolated, near the dead end of a pasillo in a niche where the bazaar abuts the Alhambra's northern cliff. The place was weekday empty with one clerk at the counter, a nice-looking young man in plain jellaba robe. A North African shop, they sold "antique" Berber pieces made in Vietnam, overpriced jewelry from the Atlas, and the main items, Fez-style water pipes, replete as any store in Tangier.

She spotted the book Oscar described when she entered, right where he said it would be, lying flat on the top shelf of an illuminated glass case. It was clearly not a collection of scrolls, but at once she recognized that it could be of great value. In the library the Sunday before, she'd seen a photo of a surviving al-Hakkam translation—this book looked just like it, washed-out numerals and all. That day she read about what happened to Hakkam's library. After the caliph's death a fanatical invasion swept through al-Andaluz, led by literary assassins averse to any writing that wasn't the Qur'an. They sacked Qurtubah and burned every book they could find, including Hakkam's collection. She knew that any surviving volume was worth big money.

Afraid to alert the clerk, a pleasant fellow who introduced himself as Ahmad, Ellen turned away and pretended to browse. She anticipated a haggle but was seasoned from her summers in Tangier and had a ruse ready. Returning his flirtations, she pretended curiosity as she approached the cabinet.

"Hmm... What about this beat-up old book, Ahmad? The faded red one in the middle."

He moved behind the case. "Oh, yes. Malmut brought that in last winter," he said. "It's a collection of proverbs, handwritten in the old style. Very quaint, at least a hundred years old, but it's not for sale. The owner saves all the Arabic stuff for his Saudi buyers. They come every fall and buy all we've got, for near the asking price. But I don't think it would hurt if I let you see it."

She shrugged. "Okay."

He fished it out, dusting the cover before handing it across. The undersized book creaked as it opened, revealing a six character code atop the first page, the same as on the cover. Below was the caliph's imprimatur, confirming her hunch: it was an intact al-Hakkam translation, at least a four figure find. Ellen turned the page and gasped—the frontispiece described it as a translation of the scrolls she was after.

With goose bumps rising, she turned to the text. In crisp indigo, it screamed. "And Jesus said to John, I am in you and in all that surrounds you." Her pulse galloped. With open mouth, pink cheeks, and swollen pupils, she looked to Ahmad, realizing she was about to blow it.

"You like it?" he asked with a happy face.

"Have you read this little nasty?" she countered with a devilish grin.

"Well, not yet. It's a busy shop, as you can see. What do you mean, 'little nasty'?"

"You don't know why I'm blushing?" Ellen asked.

"No, Mademoiselle. What are you saying?"

She paged ahead and fingered a line, offering the book across as if to have him read, but before he could focus on more than a few words, she pulled it back.

"I'm glad to hear that, Ahmad. I *thought* you were a gentleman. I would've been insulted, and you? Well, you wouldn't have had a chance with me. Not all western women are whores."

"What? Mademoiselle, please. Of what do you speak?"

She explained. "Proverbs, you said? This Malmut guy must've been kidding you. It's pornographic—from some sheik's concubine chamber—an Arabic 'Fifty Shades.' But you're right, it's from the French time. I saw one of these in Mendoza's shop last week, way overpriced—the old man was asking two hundred—for the risk, I guess."

"Risk? What risk?" asked the bewildered Ahmad.

"Didn't you know? They're illegal to possess. The Spaniards put them on their heritage list last fall. I bet the Guardia keep the confiscated ones by the crapper at the police station."

"That wouldn't surprise me at all," said Ahmad.

"You should get rid of it," she advised. "It's worth a hundred at most. You might get some American to pay more, but I wouldn't leave it out. Those macacas might let Mendoza get away with it, but not a young Muslim like you. They'll bust your African ass, just for spite. Tell you what: I'll take it off your hands for fifty Euros."

His face went blank. "No. I'd get in trouble. Like I said, the royals buy them all."

"Seventy-five!" she shouted.

He hesitated. "No, Mademoiselle, I'm sorry."

"All right," she said, "One hundred Euros *and* my phone number."

He went for it. She slapped the cash on the counter and scribbled some numbers on one of the notes.

"So, Ahmad, who's this 'Malmut' guy, the one you said found the book?"

Ahmad laughed. "Malmut? 'The Rascal'? I hear he's gone home to Morocco. The cops came for him last winter, here in the shop. They frisked him and found two phony passports, but he got away. You should've seen it. He snatched the passports, ducked between them, crawled through that window there, and then climbed the big vines up the cliff and into the Alhambra. Amazing. The police could only shout into their radios. Anyway, Malmut isn't a businessman like me, but he's a great hustler. The Spaniards smile while he screws them."

"Did he say where he got the book?" Ellen asked from the doorway.

"Probably, but I wasn't listening. The kid's a big talker."

"Is he coming back?" she asked.

"Who knows? It's getting harder to cross all the time, but if anyone can make it, Malmut can. I bet we see him before long. I sure hope so."

Pressing the book against her chest, Ellen bid "adios" and made fast for home. Every few strides she glanced behind and then, three blocks from her hotel, the spooky feeling returned. It was stronger than on rat-night, with chill bumps erupting despite the warm sun. She was scolding herself for the fear when she saw him over her shoulder—the little stalker—elbowing his way down the crowded sidewalk with one hand to his belt. He was gaining on her.

16

ELLEN IN WONDERLAND

Thursday, 2 July, 7:20 P.M.
Suite 304, Hotel del Moro
Calle de Beso
Granada
Spain

Thank God I wore flats, Ellen thought as she fled from the little man. Wedging her way to the curb, she stepped into the bike lane and sprinted. Ignoring the cursing cyclists and honking horns, she jaywalked to the hotel's entrance and dared to look back. The man wasn't there. Two-stepping the stairs with keys in hand, Ellen dead-bolted her door, checked the window locks, snapped the street shutters closed, and plopped down at her desk, gasping.

Minutes later she took a cleansing breath and then stood to face the hallway mirror. "This is your time, what you've trained for, all these years," she said, and then louder, "Be smart. Be objective. Do what Monsignor would do." She sighed before whispering. "This is for you, Mom and Dad."

Ellen changed into pajamas and an NYU hoodie before selecting her gear from the desk: an Arabic dictionary, padded tweezers, and magnifier. Her laptop was linked and the voice-activated recorder on green. She wiped the kitchenette's table and arranged her tools on its deep-blue surface, encircling the little tome. A bottle of sherry and its sniffer were placed on an adjacent shelf, to be sure a spill would fall nowhere near. After donning cotton gloves she began her dissection, pausing first to describe the exterior.

Ellen dictated. "Cover heavily oxidized, red to pink, straight-grain Moroccan goatskin; central iron brand, 7-3-0-8-2..." It was the caliph's version of the Dewey decimal system. "Edges fissured. Spine warped with fungal blots. Binding glue fractured and flaking." Ellen trembled, thrilled for a moment that the great caliph once held the same book in his hands.

The hide creaked as it opened, breaking the room's silence. She fondled the royal seal and referenced the net, finding that the numbers designated the book as prophetic, from the age of Rome, one that would have been shelved among the Islamic texts, far from the Christian section. *It figures*, she mused, *Muslims have always claimed Jesus as their prophet, after Abraham and Moses.* On the second page were Nassar's annotations.

> *7097 VA. 21 Safar. AH344.*
> *Herein is converted from Common Greek*
> *By the grace of Allah*
> *And the will of our Caliph, al Hakkam the Great*
> *Collected tales and sayings of Allah's prophet*
> *Jesus son of Mary*
> *Province of Judea, Empire of Rome, circa Caesar Augustus*
> *From parchments liberated in Visigoth Corduba, AH87*

> *Royal Library, Qurtubah*   *Ali ibn Nassar, Master*

On the reverse was an affectionate note from Nassar to his Caliph. Again she trembled. Ellen tried to corral her bias but concluded that the scrolls she was seeking must be the same parchments Nasser described. Her method was routine, identical to so many times in the Fordham lab. She took a sip of courage, remembering her girly days when she'd dressed as Alice, an oval-eyed golden-hair exploring the underworld in a powder blue dress and crisp white pinafore. Many times she'd been down the hole, but this was for real.

The fading font was in one hand, strict and diminutive. There were a few familiar passages, but most was apart from scripture she knew—quotations and sayings, their poetic themes pointing inward. Occasionally she encountered something peculiar and translated out loud.

"At night a wealthy Jew clothed in white linen came to Jesus asking of the path to salvation. Jesus said to him, 'Open your mind to the light within and to the sound of silence. Only then will you hear His voice and pass beyond, to the Essence. Now go. Do good deeds in my name and prepare you for the final days, when the Hierophant will show the way.'"

Ellen worked without pause until the new sun forced its way through the blinds, painting orange stripes across her work and the wall behind. Sore-eyed and spent, she corked the sherry and made for bed, tucking her prize beneath the covers. The hypnogogic Harold appeared as her head found the pillow, but she rolled on her side and dismissed him. Eros himself couldn't have kept her from sleep.

17

SPIRITS

Friday, 3 July, 2:04 P.M.
Suite 304, Hotel del Moro
Calle de Beso
Granada
Spain

Ellen awoke feeling like a Spaniard: to bed at daybreak and up after noon. At once she reached under the covers to make sure that Hakkam's book was still there. The long night's study invaded her dreams and stained her first conscious thoughts as she stretched the sleep away. Her first impulse was to share the news with Monsignor, so she phoned him with legs dangling from the bed. She had to leave voicemail.

"Monsignor. It's Ellie. Hope all's well in New York. I'm really excited. You won't believe what I found. Please call."

She approached Café de Valor craving caffeine. Emilio was polishing the front window as he whistled a Morisco tune. On seeing her reflection he pocketed his cloth and turned to greet her.

"Buenas tardes, Rubia! How are you this beautiful afternoon?"

"I'm well, I think, but I was up all night and need a café solo to be sure."

Emilio snickered. "If it was a man, I hope he was worth it!"

She thought for a moment. "He was."

"What a lucky fellow! Oh, Rubia, did you find the smoke shop yesterday?"

"Yes, but it wasn't what I expected. Thanks for the tip, and thank Oscar for me."

"You can thank him yourself. He's learning the grill on Fridays."

Ellen did so, slipping Oscar fifty Euros after swearing him to secrecy. She returned to perch at a sidewalk table, relishing her coffee as parables sloshed through her mind. Emilio hurried through his chore to join her, and they chatted until he was called to the phone. As always, he had to pull himself away. It was hard to believe that Ellen was "giri," Spanish slang for foreigner, but she was his favorite by far, poles apart from all others, and dear in every way. *So wise for her tender age*, he thought, *so bright and so very kind. If I could wish myself a daughter, she would be the lovely Rubia.*

Standing to take the call, the Spaniard questioned. "Will you be with this man again tonight?"

She grinned. "Not with that man, Emilio."

He faked a frown and raised his finger. "It's that Gypsy moon again. I warned you. Too many stallions can spoil the mare."

Ellen was chronically poised, but not that day. It wasn't her deceit in the pipe shop that was vexing. She'd played by the same rules as the shopkeeper and knew he'd have done the same. Her quandary was more complex.

I was hired to find calfskin scrolls in ancient Greek and Aramaic, not a bound paper codex in Medieval Arabic, she thought. *Like that Hemmingway first-edition, Hakkam's book was related to the job, but I've been working eleven and twelve hour days, so who's to say it happened on the boss' time? I took a chance and paid with my money.* She lounged back and fingered the lump in her bag. *What's the right thing to do? The book's worth a lot, and it'll send me to academic heaven, but what about Mr. Smith? I wish Monsignor would call.* Then she thought of her primary task. *If the scrolls and book were together, then the scrounger the shopkeeper called 'Malmut' must know where they are. If we can find the guy, we'll find the scrolls...*

She quick dialed Mateo Barefoot and invited him to join her. He arrived almost at once and stood where Emilio had been, in a loud Hawaiian shirt with cargo pants, his braid strung through a Dallas Cowboys' baseball cap.

Ellen chuckled. "The Texans' bus just left, sir. I'm afraid you missed it!"

Mateo's shoulders slumped. "This outfit's too much, huh?"

"It is, Mateo. You were in the DEA too long. But I'm glad to see you. How've you been?

"I'm good, Miss Shea, thank you."

"Please, my name's Ellen. *Ellie* if you want. Have a seat."

The handsome strongman was his shy self again. He sat erect with hands flat as Ellen updated him on her search, telling that she'd discovered something in a pipe shop the day before. She told of its location, describing the clerk and naming his absent employee, Malmut. She asked if Mateo could find him in Morocco.

His eyes darted about under the shades. "If the pipe shop guy is like you say, it should be easy to get a lead on this 'Malmut.' I'll tell him I have some kind of prize for his buddy: an inheritance, maybe. Then I'll drop a few Euros and promise more. That usually works. But I won't get far in Morocco. My third language is Chiricahua, not French or Arabic, and I've never been to Tangier. We should go together."

"Maybe," she replied. "Let me know what you find out from Ahmad, that's the shopkeeper's name, and don't say a word about me." She leaned forward. "I'm busy tonight, so let's meet here tomorrow, around noon, and I'll tell you what I found."

He agreed and stood to excuse himself, but she asked him to stay. Just as in the car, his bashful mode evaporated and they lolled through lunch. Demanding that he stow the glasses, she teased and he laughed; a wholesome, honest laugh. Whimsical and at ease in his company but with her mind still churning with the little book's sayings, Ellen led him to things philosophical.

"Are you religious, Mateo, or are you a 'nonester'?"

"What's a 'none-ster'?" he asked.

"Nonesters are people who check the 'none' box for religion," she said. "They don't have one, on purpose. They're not atheists or agnostics, necessarily—most're younger than us, and they're lots of them—the fastest-growing segment if you believe the demographers. Nonesters think of themselves as spiritual, but feel like they don't fit into their parents' or anybody else's religion. Kind of like independent voters."

"In that case, I'm neither." Mateo answered.

"Do you believe in God?"

She had to wait. "Yeah, I guess so," he said, and then, emphatically, "Yes, I do. Do you?"

"Sure," she said with a childish smile. "I'm Catholic, *American* Catholic. Granddad calls it 'The Church of Good Choice'—you pick what you like and ignore the rest. I prefer my dogma that way, a la carte. Like he says, 'there's no thinking required!'"

Mateo passed a crooked grin.

"Granddad Shea's got another reason for being Catholic," Ellen continued. "He says we should plant his casket head-up like the Moors did, since he's going straight to heaven. According to him, it's guaranteed because he made a 'plenary indulgence' as a boy, meaning he took Holy Communion thirteen first Fridays in a row. Like Constantine's baptism, only it took longer."

"You're kidding," said Mateo.

"No," she replied. "He even had the cojones to write his bishop. It took a year, but he sent Granddad a letter confirming his perpetual state of grace. He's got it in a fancy frame on his woodshop wall—says he was the happiest thirteen year old in Galway after that, and that he's been a champion sinner ever since." She threw her head back and cackled.

Mateo grinned back. "My grandmothers are Catholic, sort of," he said. "They meet at my aunt's house every Sunday and walk to mass at Nuestra Señora, the mission church in Palomas."

"What do you mean, 'sort of' Catholic?"

"Well, they grew up on the Mexican side, off-reservation, hanging around Mescalero diyans and getting a full dose of 'Bikagoihidan.'"

Ellen pretended shock and tried to repeat the mouthful. He smiled when she asked what a diyan was, and what the long word meant. "Diyans are like shamans, Ellie. Apache wise men. It's pronounced 'Beek-ah-goy-hee-dahn', a religion I suppose, but the Apache wouldn't call it that. There's no word for 'religion' in Chiricahua, and none for 'time,' but their beliefs are as deep as the white man's, only different—no gods, no heaven or hell—just a code, about good and evil, about spirits and powers. They think everything has a spirit inside and that some spirits make magic—people, animals, trees, mountains, the wind, a thunderstorm— everything is home to a spirit. The Mescaleros meditate more than pray, and they have special ceremonies and dances, some with peyote. They can go on for days. The diyans teach that the way you live is a prayer. Every minute of every day you have a chance to gain power from the spirits, 'with each act and every breath,' they say. And the Apache don't expect anyone to be watching. The act, by itself, is what matters."

Ellen leaned toward him, astonished at such eloquence from the former mute.

"Anyway, my grandmothers got both barrels from the diyans," he said. "They believe in the Earth Mother more than the Virgin Mother. Me, too. It's corny, but I try to live the code... If you really want to know."

She did want to know. The more time Ellen spent with this man, the more she wished for. He was pleasingly odd, perhaps even unique—a genuine First American—gorgeous, sweet, and built like a power lifter. Ellen compared him to her Manhattan lovers as he spoke, daydreaming in the brown suns and half listening. *It's been a string of dandies*, she remembered, *Village bardogs, Wall Street hypes, and insipid academics. None were as real as Mateo, or as sexy.* Along with her dreamy thoughts came the warm waves and another neurochemical storm, even stronger than the last. Her mind stumbled to bedroom scenes, this time as she gazed at her imaginary lover.

Then, mistaking her blank look for boredom, Mateo ended his soliloquy. "So that's my philosophy, Ellie. What about yours?" He had to break her erotic fantasy by waving a hand in her face. "Ellie? Are you there?"

Her stare fractured and she squeezed a long blink. "I'm sorry, Mateo. I'm a zombie today. What about my what?"

He stiffened. "Nothing important, Ellie. I was only asking about your take on life, about our place in the universe. Was I boring you?"

Speared by his barb, Ellen fiddled with her spoon. "Sorry, Mateo. I was somewhere else. If you'd've asked me the god question yesterday, I'd've dished out my usual B.S., covered with one of my Granddad's jokes. I'm so full of shit sometimes... But today? Today, I don't *have* an answer. I've been thinking about what old man Brahaney says. Those damned Jesuits—they talk like Hindus—about a path to awareness, helping souls, imitating Jesus, and all that." She sighed. "It's always seemed so trite, but right now I don't know what to think. Today is different."

Clueless, he honey-smiled and reached across to place his hand on hers. The voltage jumped.

Just then the whistling Emilio emerged with their marisco paella, short-circuiting the enchantment. They talked on, of themselves and their gods, of their fears and dreams, lapsing into Spanglish at the end. He taught her some Chiricahua phrases and she a few French to him. It was sublime. Emilio smiled through the window, assuming that Mateo was the reason she'd slept late.

No telling how long it would have gone on or what might have happened that night, but when the Alhambra's broad shadow reached their table she remembered her date with the other boy. Wishing it were some other night, she excused herself abruptly, leaving the strongman to wonder why.

Ellen was striding toward Hotel del Moro when the Fordham fight song sounded. With the phone to her ear, she ducked into an alcove.

"Hello, Monsignor! Thanks for calling back. I hope I didn't disturb you."

"Never, my child. How goes your quest?"

"I'm excited. I stumbled on something special," she said.

"That's what you said in the voicemail. What can you tell me?"

"It's a Nasrid artifact, an al-Hakkam text, prophetic translations from Koine the legend says, intact and in fair condition."

"Wow! Congratulations! Where did you find it? Anything new?"

"I bought it in a pipe shop for a few Euros. It's a virgin."

"No shit! Which prophet?" he asked.

She didn't answer.

"You gotta be kidding! Ellie! ... Ellie!"

18

KING JAMES

Friday, 3 July, 10:05 P.M.
Fountain of the Giants
Plaza Bibarrambla
Granada
Spain

She looked hot for her date with the Virginian. Ellen's Celtic beauty could overwhelm when she gilded, and that night she was dazzling in crimson silk and black lace. With eyes framed in cobalt, her mane fell past strapless shoulders and the clinging dress teased. She took more time to preen that night but decided against stockings or heels. *Don't need them to be sexy*, she thought, *I'll be Marilyn tonight, in Spanish lace.*

They'd arranged to meet at Bibarrambla fountain. Ellen advanced unseen and paused in a shadow to peep at Howard. He was a genuine good-looker, near perfect in his corduroy blazer, dark slacks, and half-buttoned shirt. Circling the spouting Giants in a wide arc, he paused with each rotation to search for her and prune his wildflower bouquet. *Too pretty for some women*, Ellen mused, *but not for me.* Eyes sated, she emerged. When Howard saw her he made a sweeping bow, held it until she came close, and then with heels together, kissed her hand. His Gatsby imitation was hokey, but it charmed. The flaxen couple turned heads as they climbed the Albaicín's bending stairs, playful all the way but in a hurry to reach San Nicolas lookout in time to see the sunset. They just made it. The panorama was dreamy as they knew it would be, the orange rays setting the Alhambra's walls aglow and glancing down to bathe the valley in a soft amber neon. They strolled away as dark descended, holding hands off and on. Neither noticed the faint stains at their feet.

He announced it would be his treat at a seafood restaurant in the heart of the Arab quarter, and they got lucky: a patio table facing the castle, its walls painted with rainbow kliegs, and below, the bazaar lights spreading like a carpet of fireflies. The young man seemed a knowledgeable diner but knew nothing of wine. Just as in the bodega, he downed one glass after another as if they were little Cherry Cokes. The conversation was empty at first, but their converging postures said more. Howard was inquisitive, almost nosy about her work, she not at all about his.

"Tell me about your paper, Ellen. Just what are you looking for? Moorish mistakes, you said?"

"Yeah, but I've got less to go on than you Bible boys," she answered. "The Caliph was super-strict with his scribes. More than one lost his thumb for a sloppy translation. I should've picked an easier topic. It was one of those things that seemed like a good idea at the time. I do that a lot, but hey, I'm tired of even thinking about school. I'd rather talk about you."

He obliged with a sappy synopsis: boyhood in a Blue Ridge hamlet with four years to Eagle Scout, Messiah College on a congregational scholarship, two years at Moody Bible Institute, and now nearing his doctorate at Oral Roberts. His dream was to teach at the new Pentecostal college near his home. Howard talked on, admitting to a boring life with few outside interests save one: a Korean martial art with a name she'd never heard.

"It's cool, Ellen, ancient and forgotten—your skull is the weapon. I practice every day."

There was no need to inquire after the boy's philosophy. Howard was a no-questions-asked, rock-ribbed believer. Ellen dodged a few holy jabs before he landed a proof of salvation, sourcing Aquinas and Paul. She responded from time to time with connected comments, but her mind was on passion's path and only pips of his piety punctured her erogenous visions. What she did hear was expected: traditional and gently intolerant, but when he quoted from Job it disturbed her fantasy and she interrupted with a good natured challenge.

"So tell me, Howard, do you disagree with Ehrman? Do you think every word in the New Testament was precisely placed by the Creator—that once written, nothing was added or altered—that they got it right on the very first try?"

Instantly he answered. "Every word."

"And the Englishmen's permutation, the King James', should it be the only one?"

"Yes, ma'am," he replied.

"What about the moral inconsistencies?" she asked. "There're a dozen verses that condone slavery, and a few that praise it. Is that what God meant to say?"

His answer wasn't as quick. "That depends, Ellen, on how you interpret the words. What's come down to us is inspired, like 2 Timothy says: 'Scripture is *inspired* by God.' There can be nothin' false in the Bible, not one word or comma. It's what my professors call 'biblical inerrancy.' But they teach that it's not always easy, that it's how you look at the words that matters. I'm no theologian, Ellen, just a missionary. Wiser men will have to answer your question."

She avoided asking who the wise men were and if there were any wise women, and then returned to her racy daydream, listening intermittently and hoping for more than the missionary. When he made his n^{th} biblical reference, she had to respond.

"Tell me, Howard, what about the contradictions from one gospel to the next? They're bunches of them, like the accounts of Jesus' birth and death. They're not even close."

"They're *all* right, in their own way," he said, grinning.

"And the stuff that was added later?" Ellen asked. "There's a lot in King James' that was invented, y'know, like the last verses of Mark, or the parable about the Pharisees trying to trick Jesus. I can't cite it like you, but Ehrman does. Turns out, it was tacked on in the third or fourth century. It can't be found in the earlier copies. There's a mountain of research that says today's scripture is a long way from where it started."

It was if she'd doused him with ice water. Howard's eyes flared as he sat upright. With arms crossed he looked skyward, searching the constellations for a reply.

"You mean the passage from *John*, don't you, Ellen?"

Realizing she'd stepped on his holy toes, she tried for a joke. "Probably, but I'm Catholic, so you can't expect me to know much about the Bible."

He didn't laugh.

"You know the one I mean," she went on. "When Jesus says 'let the ones who aren't sinners throw the stones.'"

He corrected in a monotone. "Close. You're talkin' 'bout *John, 7:53*: 'He that is without sin among you, let him first cast a stone.' It's one of my favorites, but I never heard what you're sayin'. Like I said, I'm a soldier." He leaned forward with eyelids pinched. "Ehrman's a turncoat, y'know, a blasphemer. People say he's thrown in with the devil, like Carlton Pearson[27] and that Pagels woman. But where it came from doesn't matter, or when. Like I said, if it ended up in *King James*', it was inspired, and no way can it be wrong."

She conceded with a silly face and no-big-deal shrug. "And evolution, Howard? What about evolution?"

"Hogwash!" he said, smiling.

"The rapture?" she asked, with a bigger grin.

"I'll drink to that!" he exclaimed, giggling as he raised his glass.

She laughed along as their glasses met, and then posed a last question. "What if there were more, Howard?"

"More?" he asked.

"Yeah," she said. "More scripture, lost scripture, maybe—first-hand accounts of Jesus. You must've studied how crazy the early church was. There could be hundreds of lost parables, just like the one you just quoted, but *real*."

He blinked and made his own joke. "It'd be too late, Ellen. It's past press time!"

The dialog was as spicy as the pulpo picante they were eating, and Ellen feared spoiling the magic, so she horse-laughed and talked trivial. They took half an hour to share a chocolate flambé, speaking Romance as they waited for the tab.

19

SERNETA

Saturday, 4 July, 12:02 A.M.
Encima del Sacromonte
Granada
Spain

When the check finally came Ellen suggested something fun, and as they exited arm in arm, she quizzed.

"Do you know Flamenco, Howard?"

"Y'mean the pink bird?"

"C'mon, Howard! Haven't you been to Sacromonte?"

"No ma'am. It's off limits. Am I missin' somethin'?"

"You sure are," Ellen said. "Something the Gypsies have been doing up there for three hundred years. That's when they carved out those caves. Can you see them?" She pointed toward the sparsely lit hill crest. "Up there. See that line of dark circles above the Camino? It's the best place in Spain for Flamenco. Wanna go?"

He smiled "yes", so they strolled toward the ridge with cheeks rosy and hearts light. Ellen led to the entrance of her favorite haunt, *El Soltero*. To Howard it seemed no more than a dingy café wedged into a cave with a pock-marked dance floor in back. A calico cat curled behind the bar under a faded oil portrait, a life-sized depiction of the seductive Serneta, the grand diva of old time Flamenco. She was performing, her spine gracefully bowed with bosom thrust forward, her angled limbs and outturned foot accepting the bold embrace of a faceless partner. Carved benches outnumbered chairs at *Soltero*, strewn about and facing the hardwood. A mutt tried to sneak in with the couple but in seconds it was airborne and squealing, propelled into the street on the point of a boot. Eyes flexed at the blondes until a guitarist embraced Ellen and introduced her to his mates.

Taking a bench beside the stage, they waited for the show to break out. She hooked his hands and drew him near. "Granada's got two kinds of Flamenco, Howard, the predigested kind down on the Camino, and the genuine article, up here in these caves. You can tell the phony joints by the glass buses out front. They herd girls into numbered seats for shows on the hour and give what they expect, toned down for their cheesy tastes."

Howard's eyes were drawn to the arriving dancers.

"Am I boring you, Mr. Hendershot?" asked Ellen.

"No, this is terrific. Go on."

"Then there's Encima," she said. "Up here they dance both ways—Añejo and Zambra—sassy and sexy, like it used to be. These caves are for locals, amateurs, and it's what they live for. You never know who'll show up, but most nights it's hot, especially on the weekends. The dancers don't perform—they emote—like lovers on the verge."

The first heel slammed the parquet. Howard was enthralled and Ellen in flames as she clapped and hooted between sips of sangria. She joined the dancers, at first coaxed onstage by the guitar player and then a few sets later, in a falda and shoes the dueña provided, she stomped en sola through a five minute canté. Her gestures toward Howard during that second dance meant only one thing, something everyone in the place understood except him. The crowd stood as her routine ended, whistling and clapping as she whirled to the finish. Then all broke for smokes. Ellen strutted across the stage, seized Howard's hand and led him into the street, her borrowed dress rising in the small hour breeze. With quick strides but no words they marched toward his apartment.

The passion was phosphorous quick and just as hot. Orgasms had never been her problem, and she made up for the long winter's drought. They came in a train, like a string of cherry bombs, but arrived none too soon for the boy. At once he lay spent and was to sleep in seconds, still panting.

She woke at first light, disoriented and disturbed. Lying supine alongside the naked Adonis, Ellen stared into the tin ceiling with a bad case of lover's remorse and the first of a nasty hangover. She rationalized, at first blaming the pent-up abstinence, then all the wine, and finally, that Gypsy moon. Melting onto the floor to stand at the bedside, she admired the nude and debated. *As pretty as he is, there'll have to be more. He's smooth and witty, and I love the eyes and accent, but his mind is too easy and light-years from mine. Some things don't fit: an Eagle Scout, and we had to use my condom? And have the Baptists changed their attitude about booze and sex? As for the sex, thank God for the relief, but he was a missionary, all right, beyond clunky and way too quick. I must've blinked and missed the foreplay.*

For all or none of those reasons, Ellen tiptoed away. Collecting her clothes like a cat-burglar, she could find only one shoe and as she rummaged in the gray light she collided with a small table, catching it by the stem as it toppled. Its lone drawer slid open, dumping a three-hole punch onto the hardwood with a loud bang. She looked through the bedroom door to see Howard's bare bottom stirring, but in seconds he resumed the snore. As she replaced the punch, a binder at the bottom of the drawer caught her eye. One word was Magic-Marked on its cover—QUELLE. She gulped.

Sneaking into the kitchen, still naked and with folder in hand, she moved to the open window and balanced it on the sill, tilting the pages into the streetlight. The binder revealed Howard's deceit in chronological order. The first page was a letter from "The Committee of Research Evangelists for Preservation of the Truth," referenced throughout as "CREPT." Embossed with a Greek cross and seeing-eye logo, ten directors were listed in a tight column on the left, Th.D.'s and D.D.s trailing most. She recognized two names from Sunday cable. The correspondence outlined Hendershot's assignment—deviant writings survived in Granada, documents that would threaten the righteous, and they must not fall into secular hands. He was to join the team already there and bring them home or "destroy them in place if they can't be had." One instruction was repeated—there were no boundaries on his behavior— he was anointed, on a heavenly mission, and his "special skills" were to be employed as needed.

Ellen perused the folder as her lover slept but found nothing to help her own search. There was one tidbit, a memo cautioning Howard to "beware of the Turks: armed and dangerous." The last page surprised her: a hand written fax from the first man on the list ordering Howard to "get as much information as you can from the Catholic girl. Sacrifice your innocence if God wills it!"

She stretched forward for another look at Hendershot's iron buttocks. *That fax explains a lot. Looks like he was a teetotaler, and a virgin...*

20

TURKS AND CRUSADERS

Saturday, 4 July, 2:07 P.M.
Café de Valor
Granada
Spain

Ellen trudged towards Emilio's café with head shrouded in a scarf and wearing wraparound sunglasses, two hours late for her meeting with Mateo. With cotton mouth, jelly knees, and pulsing temples, she peeked through the glass to see Mateo and Emilio conversing across the bar, braced on their forearms with eyes linked and noses near. She wasn't surprised. Camaraderie among Spanish men is reflected in many ways, but none so intimate as being in each other's space.

Emilio looked up as she entered and came around the bar to take her hands. "Rubia? Is it you under there? You don't look well. Another late night? Remember what I said about the stallions. And you've kept our friend waiting."

Mateo joined them.

"Sorry, Mateo."

"No problem. It gave me a chance to connect with Emilio."

The men swapped uneasy glances as Mateo offered his arm. She chose a table in the dimmest corner and asked for an Ibérico tortilla with her coffee, intending to tell Mateo about Hendershot as soon as she got enough caffeine to her brain. But she noticed a change—for the first time Mateo was casual, almost snarky—unexpected behavior from the modest man. Puzzled but still not straight-thinking, she said nothing. The dark coffee did its duty and as the pounding ebbed, Ellen was ready to tell. She daubed her lips and sat back.

"I ran into the competition last night, Mateo."

"I know." he replied, slouching back with a crooked grin.

"You know? What do you mean, you know?"

"Yeah, the Hendershot flake," he said. "'El Guapo' is what I've been calling him. Quite a night for you two. How come you snuck out like that, in the dancer's dress and with only one shoe?"

She was lobster-pink. "You've been following me?"

"Everywhere," he said. "All day and every night, whenever you leave your hotel. It's what I'm paid for, Ellie. Parkinson said I'd be close by, and I told you the same thing the day you got here. I thought you'd've caught on by now. I guess my disguises weren't all that bad." He leaned forward and lowered his voice. "I was doing my job, Ellie. Believe me, you need protection. How do you think you made it out of that garbage pile? And on the sidewalk the other day? The boss gave orders to stay on your tail, and that's what I've been doing. It's nothing personal."

Ellen jumped to her feet, chucking her napkin to the floor. With a Jack O'Lantern frown, she railed. "It's *very* personal, you son of a bitch! What right do you have to spy on my private life?"

He was calm. "Your private life? I guess Parkinson didn't tell you about the bad guys, or about what happened to his last *two* treasure hunters. He has a knack for leaving out details."

"What're you talking about?"

He stood and extended his hand. "Please, Ellie, sit down. I know it isn't fair, but this isn't grad school. It's dangerous as hell around here, and it's time you knew about it. I wanted to tell, but Parkinson thought you'd work better if you didn't worry about, well, about what happened to the others."

She took his hand and eased into her seat. Mateo drew his chair near, keeping his gentle grip. "Believe me, Ellie, I don't like being a peeping Tom, and I really didn't like what I saw last night, but ... Why do you think you're making this kind of money? Hendershot's a holy hit man, and he's not the only one who's got you in his sights."

Mateo has more secrets than I do, she thought.

His voice descended. "This is the situation—there're two other teams working the bazaar—your pretty boy and his buddies are one, and he's the muscle. His partners are geeks, brothers named Whitcolmb. They've been here since the first of the year." His lips tightened. "Jasper Whitcolmb's a loudmouth. Acts like a tent preacher: he can cry on cue and'll preach to anyone who'll listen. He means to get a name and the money that goes with it—wants to be a televangelist—bigger than Joel Osteen and richer than Joyce Meyer, he says. Jasper's beanpole skinny, a fancy dresser, and a born salesman."

Ellen gaped.

"The younger brother's named Leon," said Mateo. "The slob could write a guide to Granada's kebab joints. Leon's odd: a bookworm and farm boy. Likes to be around animals. Volunteers at the zoo. As detectives, the brothers are bumblers. They'd have trouble finding their Johnsons in a pinch—and when Hendershot showed up, it got worse—Oklahoma's version of the Three Stooges. None of them speaks Arabic or French, and Hendershot's Spanish only gets him in trouble. There's no chance they'll find the scrolls. I don't trust 'em, though, especially not 'El Guapo.' There's an animal behind that movie star face. That's why they sent him, and not another brain.

"Then there's the Turkish gang," he said. "They've got nothing to do with the church boys, but they're twice as scary, meaner than Pecos rattlesnakes. A Moroccan kid scammed 'em early on. They found his body at the dump, gutted and sliced into quarters.

"The big Turk's in charge over here. He's built like a bowling pin. Calls himself 'Doctor Adivar.' Crows about his Oxford schooling and tries to come off like a British gentleman, accent and all. You've seen the look—seersucker suit, white-faced shoes, silk tie, and straw hat—even has a pocket watch on a fob. Packs a Beretta, quick-draw, on the left."

Ellen could only stare.

"Adivar calls his sidekick 'Kundak,'" Mateo said. "The little twerp doesn't talk much. He's a goat butcher by trade and a man-killer, for sure. Rotten teeth. Dresses like his boss but doesn't wash. Carries a gutting blade on his belt and a nickel-plated .32 in his right high top. Kundak's been on you like a duckling. He's the one that got away in the alley, the one behind you on the sidewalk, and the one ..." Mateo looked to the bar and then back. "There's a third guy who runs with the Turks, a Puerto Rican, but he's no heavy, just a translator and messenger boy. Sometimes he drives. He texts Adivar's boss in New York with disposable cellphones, in ciphers they change every week. The texts go to a Manhattan area code. There's no trace after that. Anyway, the Turks don't move until the Puerto Rican hears from their boss in New York."

Mateo took another sip. Ellen released his hand, closing her eyes as she leaned back. *How innocent and fun it's been,* she thought, *my excellent summer adventure, with big paydays, a shot at academic stardom, and two really cute men. I guess it had to end...*

She jerked upright. "What did you see last night, Mateo?"

"Was there anything new in the binder?" he asked. "I couldn't read it through the binoculars."

With teeth clenched she stared through him and then, after what seemed like an hour to Mateo and in a tone he'd never heard, she spoke with cold eyes from some other space. "All right. We'll go to Africa and find this 'Malmut' guy. Did you get his last name, and where he went?"

"Yeah, he's back in his hometown, outside Tangier," Mateo replied. "I can't pronounce it." He fished a scrap of paper from his shirt and handed it across.

"Malmut *Adjani*," she read. "*Chefchaouen*. Okay. I've been there. It's a little place. Shouldn't be hard to find him. When can we go?"

"We'll fly direct, from Málaga." Mateo answered. "I'll book the plane and pick you up at seven."

"Good, but I need a day. We'll go Monday," she said, her chair screeching as she stood.

Mateo tried to get up but she shoved him back and then shouted as she walked away. "Seven A.M! I'll be on the curb. Don't be late!"

21

MALMUT ADJANI

Monday, 6 July, 11:38 A.M.
Boukhalef Terminal
Ibn Batoutta Airport
Tangier
Kingdom of Morocco

It was a short and scenic flight to Tangier. From her window Ellen gazed across the yawning turquoise of Gibraltar bay, towards land's end with its great limestone thumb poking into the morning sky. Gazing down as they crossed the straights, she marveled at the string of white-ribbon wakes, in the near channel making for the open Atlantic and on the far shore for Mediterranean ports. She remembered Tangier as it appeared on the horizon. *Just ten miles across,* she thought, *to another world.*

Ellen people-watched from the airport's taxi stand while Mateo searched for a driver. She was taken by how much the locals' manner had changed since she lived there. Most telling was the women's western dress and real smiles. Compact blue cabs swarmed on the near curb but Mateo headed for the big white ones stacked across. The young chauffeur he chose introduced himself to Ellen as "Jabi," politely in French and then tourist English, but she yapped back in vulgar Arabic, ordering the man to drive south immediately, to Chefchaouen. Jabi's smile went flat.

They had no address for Malmut Adjani, only his name and that of the town, but Ahmad the pipe dealer said it was all they'd need. The antique village was an interesting Google for Ellen. Known for its cobalt-blue buildings and perfumed hashish, it was a refuge for exiled Moors in the days of the Reconquista and until recent times hostile to all things European. The first foreigners to visit, two foolhardy Englishmen, were murdered for their audacity. Only in the last decades had the locals warmed to tourists' and their cash. According to the travel sites, the hamlet was a launching point for Atlas mountain climbers and well-heeled adventurers bound for Marrakech and beyond.

The blue village and its townsfolk were charming. Literally everyone they asked knew Malmut, and all called him "The Rascal." Each had a Rascal story. Malmut was Chefchaouen's best mountain guide, they said, the most daring and the one sought by serious climbers. But his heart wasn't on the cliffs. He was a city boy by nature, preferring bistros and European girls to the snowy peaks. They described a loveable prankster with a perennial smile, a youngster who'd steal your heart and then your wallet, but when they were directed to Malmut's aunt, her news gave them pause.

They found the tiny woman gardening on the roof of her home in the heart of an alabaster conglomerate called Vieux Ancién, a fusion of sapphire three and four story stuccos melded through the centuries by dangling footbridges and roof planks. She was flexed and weeding as they topped the stairs, her billowing purple apron stark against the snowcaps. Alerted by the visitors' shadows crossing her sunflowers, she greeted them with an open smile, stepping down from the garden box to extend her hand.

"Hail in the name of the prophet!" she declared.

"Hail in his name, Madame," said Ellen. "We're in search of a young man, Malmut Adjani."

Her weathered face drooped. She looked toward the peaks, and then to the sky. "I'm afraid my dear nephew's done it this time," the woman said. "The green shirts came for him in the night, six months past. Malmut made it down the lattice, but more were waiting at the bottom. They beat his precious body with those black batons. He's never been in this kind of trouble, not with the green shirts. They wouldn't say where they were taking him." She looked to Ellen. "What am I to do, Mademoiselle? I promised my dear sister!"

"We're here to help, Madame," said Ellen. "Who would know where he is?"

The aunt answered excitedly. "The provincial police, on the square, under the red flag, over there." She pointed. "They tell me nothing, only that he won't be coming home for years. I'm sure they know where the green monkeys took him, but I doubt they'll talk to you, mon chere. It will take a man to find out where he is."

She translated the woman's comments for Mateo as they neared the station, marked by a huge red banner and concrete lions flanking the stairs.

Ellen wheeled around. "I'll do better alone. Bring the cab."

"Aye-aye." Mateo replied.

A dozen cops lolled around the perimeter of the office. Immune to their stares, Ellen stretched on her toes to ring the duty bell. A bald cop came forward.

"Sergeant Shriki, at your service, Mademoiselle! Welcome to Chefchaouen. It is a pleasure to see a lovely young lady in our humble place. I hope there is no problem."

"Oh no, Sergeant. I'm here on business. I must ascertain the location of an arrestee, Malmut Adjani."

The sergeant guffawed and then yelled over his shoulder, announcing that someone was looking for Rascal. Hoots and wisecracks bounced back. When the ruckus died down, he answered. "What makes you think I can tell you the whereabouts of this criminal, Mademoiselle? It is only the business of the police."

She smiled up. "Very well, Sergeant, but you might ring Rabat before I'm dismissed. You see, I've come on Minister Walid's account. We're ... associates, and share an interest in this man. Quite proper, I assure you. If you don't care to call, I'll report back. I hope he's not bothered. May I use your phone?" She peeped over the desk to read from his name tag. "Sergeant *Shriki*, is that correct? I wouldn't want to mispronounce your name."

Like everyone in Morocco, Shriki knew of the minister's penchant for foreign women and his reputation for hasty discipline. Either doubt would do.

Shriki went jolly. "Only joking, Mademoiselle, only joking! Do you have credentials?"

Ellen pushed her passport and Macy's card across. He accepted without touching.

"We all know Malmut," Shriki said, "and despite his mischief, we were sad to see the Federals take him. Rascal's a local boy, and we'd rather handle these things on our own." He raised his voice. "There's not much to do around here now that Malmut's in prison!" The laughter came again, but quickly his face turned cold. "He's in Shaleed Penitentiary, Mademoiselle, and there's no escape from Shaleed, no matter who you know."

Every cop had migrated to the desk, eavesdropping as Shriki explained. "You see, Rascal won the prize— three years for holding ten kilos of kif. And you needn't waste your time until Saturday. There's one visitors' day per month, and a long line to apply for a pass. It takes three weeks after that, if you're lucky."

She thanked the policeman and then told a bawdy joke about a French woman stuck in a Moroccan jail. As the laughter ebbed, she asked for their phone to call the prison. The sergeant fell over himself dialing the number. Ellen alternated languages depending on which subordinate she was bullying, at last reaching the warden to tell of her "mission." She'd be bringing another agent along to help with interrogation, she said, and asked what time the next day would be best for their visit. When the warden stopped swearing, she inserted her hoax about the minister. After a long silence, he told her to be there at nine. Every cop was gaping as she returned the phone.

"Thank you so much, Sergeant Shriki. I'll inform the minister of your cooperation."

Ellen rushed to the waiting cab and ordered Jabi to the American consulate in Tangier. She entered alone and returned minutes later with stationery and business cards, declaring they'd make perfect I.D.s. There was a last stop in the European quarter for passport photos and a push-up bra. All the while, the Apache was a silent spectator. Since their breakfast in Granada two days before, Ellen had become an aloof, alternate being, more like his old drill sergeant than the dashing young woman he'd known.

Turning with a smirk, Mateo tried to revive her old self as they approached the hotel's desk. "One room or two?"

Ellen winced. "Not funny, Tonto. Let's get to work on our papers."

"Okay," said the downcast Mateo.

22

IBRAHIM ALWAHARI

Tuesday, 6 July, 8:12 A.M.
Kilometer 2, Raisuni Highway
Valley of the Rif
Kingdom of Morocco

Jabi's taxi escaped from Tangier's central roundabout and accelerated into the new sun. It was an easy drive to Morocco's maximum-security prison, back through Chefchaouen and then east on an arrow-straight highway bisecting the Rif Valley. With steaming coffees in hand, Ellen and Mateo faced off in the rear seat of the Peugeot.

She opened. "North Africa has supplied Europe's hashish, what the locals call 'kif', since the Muslims took over. It's grown in family plots on high meadows, with plants that have longer pedigrees than Kentucky racehorses. You can tell by color." She pointed out the window. "Look, at the base of that mountain. See the patch of light green?"

"Same as in Texas," Mateo said, shaking his head.

"The word 'reefer' comes from 'Rif'," she continued, "but what they make here isn't for joints. It's hashish, made from marijuana *pollen*. Like Afgan poppies or Bolivian coca, it's the peoples' crop, Morocco's cash cow. The irony is that Ketama is the center of the trade."

Ellen explained that Sergeant Shriki thought Malmut shorted the federals' on their baksheesh, their word for bribe. "But it doesn't matter why he's there," she said. "We can't leave Ketama without getting the exact address of the bazaar shop, or short of that, without Malmut Adjani. He's the only one who can lead us to the scrolls." She leaned toward Mateo. "We'll tell the warden we're with Interpol. You be the bad cop and I'll be ... I'll be what I have to."

Jabi pointed through the windshield at the whitewashed prison as it appeared on the horizon, nestled in a wadi in front of Ketama. Ellen likened it to an ivory jewel box trimmed in rhinestones, an effect of the sun bouncing off the razor wire. They passed through the checkpoint with no delay: she was quick to inform the sentries that Warden Alwahari was waiting.

And he was. They were welcomed in the administration building foyer by the bony middle-aged man, courteous as could be in his sand-tan suit and lime green tie. With a constant smile, he led them up the stairs to his art-deco office, remarkable for its floor-to-ceiling corner windows overlooking the exercise yard. Armchairs squatted in the opposite secluded corner, with a tall water pipe in between. After declining smokes and Cokes, they presented their counterfeit credentials with the expected measure of American arrogance. Alwahari waved the papers away as he moved behind his desk, complimenting Ellen's French while perusing a Manila folder.

"Now, Miss Shea. You said that this man was involved with extremists? It's hard to believe—arrests in Chefchaouen for pickpocketing phones, a bad check charge in Tangier, one immigration detention by the Spaniards at Melilla, and finally, the drug conviction. It seems odd that this insect could be involved in anything substantial."

"I'm not so sure, Warden," she answered. "Intel says he ran with one of the 3-11 bombers. That one's dead, but we want to know about the others."

"Very well," said the warden. "We're eager to assist. We have extremists here, you know, in single confinement." He jumped to his feet and raged. "They're swine, a scourge to Morocco, and they soil the good name of Islam!" Alwahari's fit cooled as quickly as it came, but he remained standing. "I see you brought an expert to persuade the man."

"Yes," she said, "DEA."

His eyes fixed on Mateo's as he asked Ellen to translate. Mateo stared back.

"Leave him alive," Ellen interpreted for the warden. "And with no marks. It's you who'll answer to Rabat if we dispatch another of these pigs. Thanks to Adjani's insolence, he's already halfway to paradise. Avoid the head completely, and none of these 'enhanced techniques' we hear about. Do you understand?"

Mateo stood and saluted. "Yes, sir, err ... Oui, Monsieur."

After an all-points frisk they were led to a holding cell two floors below. Square, squalid, and lit by a bare bulb, it smelled strongly of urine. The pathetic prisoner looked up from his stool, sunken eyes expectant and pale skin hanging from a delicate frame. He was much younger than they expected. With cheekbones bruised and sores erupting from beneath his boy-beard, Malmut Adjani looked like he'd been in hell for six years, not six months, a long way from the lively joker his friends described. The guard straddled the doorway with one ear tilted in, so Ellen used Spanish and went straight for the kid's hope. In a wavering voice, Adjani admitted to buying Hakkam's book.

Ellen questioned. "What else did you see? Any scrolls? Maybe unrolled: yellow pages with brown edges and faded writing, with Hebrew or Greek letters?"

"Yes," Malmut said. "There were two leather bags fat with such rolls, but I didn't see the writing. The bags were dried up, with fish signs on the flaps. I remember them well. It was last year, in the crazy Spaniard's place. They were on the top shelf, inside a glass cabinet, along with the book you asked about."

Her pulse fluttered. "Where was it?"

"Against the back wall. Inside the glass, as I told you."

"No, no, I mean where in the bazaar? The street name and number."

"Oh." Malmut looked to the bulb. "It's off Calle de Beso, I think, on Calle Limón, or, maybe … I can't remember exactly, but I could find it if I was there. The shop carried the owner's name. Vasquez, or Valdez … I know it started with a V!"

Ellen spoke to Mateo in English. "He's just a kid. Do you think he's straight?"

"I think so," said Mateo. "He's been worked over good, and I doubt he wants any more. His answers were quick and the pupils stayed small, but you never know. Everyone in that little town said he was slick. There's only one way this chump can help us, though, and that's impossible."

Ellen blinked "yes". As they exited, she shouted through the door at Malmut. "Get ready! And you'd better be telling the truth, or what's happened here will seem like teatime!"

She led up the stairs and rushed down the hall, rapping sharply on the warden's door before barging in. Startled, he turned from his perch at the window. The guard hustled behind, apologizing. Alwahari dismissed him with a wrist flick.

"Back so quickly, Mademoiselle? A successful interrogation?"

"Partly, warden. Our sources were correct. We'll need traveling papers for Adjani's transfer to Rabat."

It was as if she were asking to borrow a book from the prison library. Alwahari stared down at the yard. "That's impossible, of course. It will be at least two years before the inmate is discharged, assuming he lives that long. Conduct like his can result in an unexpectedly short sentence, if you know what I mean. Understand well, Mademoiselle. We may be one Muslim country America can call friendly, but we are *not* your lackeys!"

"Yes, sir, of course. Please forgive me," Ellen replied. She turned to Mateo. "Wait outside."

Mateo watched their fuzzy silhouettes through the frosted door. The warden took to his desk and Ellen joined him, boosting herself onto the edge with her inside leg dangling. They bantered before moving out of sight, to the easy chairs. Not long after, guards scurried in and out, fetching papers and running to the lock-up. At last Ellen burst through the door, shouting. "Where's the car? He'll be at the south gate!"

Mateo ran to catch up. "How did you do it?"

"I finally got to use one of those bank checks. There was no charge for the hash."

As the taxi inched toward them, two guards in a protruding cage unshackled the shivering Malmut and ejected him. Mateo caught the little body as it hit the ground and carried the boy like an infant, laying him face-up on the back seat of the car. The bewildered imp stared upside-down at Ellen, trying for a smile. She made her own face, for the smell, and moved to the front. As they drove off Malmut choked on the bottled water Mateo offered, spraying it all over him.

Ellen turned with a grin. "Looks like you got that roommate you wanted!"

He was glad for her smile.

23

SPIDERMAN

Thursday, 9 July, 9:05 A.M.
Hotel Minza Restaurant
Rue de la Liberté
Tangier
Kingdom of Morocco

They returned to Tangier from the prison at dinnertime. Mateo bathed and shaved Malmut, dressed his wounds, fed him, and put him to bed. The youngster slept until noon and then recuperated on the balcony, surveying the city while enjoying Hotel Minzah's room service. He and Mateo joined Ellen for breakfast the next morning, taking a corner booth with Malmut in between. "The Rascal" devoured his meal and politely asked for more.

Ellen fidgeted with her cup. "I don't know what you found out yesterday, Mateo, but the people I talked to said Spanish customs will be a problem. If they catch Malmut, he'll be back in prison along with our chance at the scrolls. What about a speedboat, after dark? It's only a few miles across."

"No way," said Mateo. "The Spanish Navy tracks everything that floats. I made some calls. Our best bet is Naples. It'll take a week and it won't be cheap. I'm waiting for the green light from the boss."

Then Malmut, more animated with each calorie, interrupted.

"Forgive me, Señorita Ché, but if you speak of our return to Granada, it will not be difficult. Malmut is as the otter on the sea and can cross as always, on the Melilla ferry. It is easy to fool the harbor police, and the captain's backsheesh is reasonable—one thousand Euros. You and Señor Mateo can dance on the high deck. We can meet at the car shop after the ship docks, and from there go on to Granada."

The Americans' faces were skeptical.

"It is not for worry," the boy said. "Malmut has crossed many times. Saturday is best, when ship is crowded and Customs few. The boat docks at midnight, a good hour for shadows. Once on the seawall, Malmut is the greyhound. They cannot catch him."

It sounded simple, cheap, and according to Malmut, proven, but Ellen wasn't buying. She knew of one very tough hurdle and when Malmut didn't mention it, she spoke to Mateo in English.

"There's something our new best friend's not telling. The warden said Malmut got arrested trying to cross at Melilla, the same place he wants to go through now. It's in Spanish Morocco, and it's a fortress."

Malmut piped up. "Getting into Melilla is the easy part, Señorita, at least for Malmut!" Apparently, he knew English.

Ellen shook her head. "I've been there, Malmut. The city's double fenced, crawling with police and their dogs."

"Yes, Señorita, it is true, and it is also true that they stopped Malmut. I was lazy and tried to enter like the gecko, in the wheel well of my cousin's truck. It was on a dare after a night of fun, unwise since I have a sure way to enter."

"Sure?"

"Yes, Señorita. Like the baboon spider, Malmut climbs the great wall."

"The great wall? What wall?" Ellen asked.

"The Roman seawall," Malmut said, "to the north. The police do not watch there—they know that all who climb will die."

"Tell us more," Mateo prompted.

"In height, one hundred meters," Malmut answered. "The low stones are slimy as camel snot and covered with moss, thick as the boar's coat. The trick is working fingers and toes into seams. The Romans set the stones tight, and from some you cannot move forward or back. Only Atlas goats have a mind for such things, and they have taught Malmut their secrets. Of course, unless one has these, he will fall."

Malmut displayed his delicate hands. The fingers were straw shaped, like a doll's, the wrists slight and flat, but his muscular forearms were sharply defined, leading to full biceps and shoulders.

He shook Mateo's hand. "Malmut will not fail, Señor," he said as he squeezed. "I have topped the wall five times."

Mateo rejected Malmut's vise-grip. "Maybe, but if you don't make six, you'll be back in jail, and we can't spring you a second time."

"No, Señor, if I slip I will be with my parents in Paradise. Malmut asks only that you return the body to my aunt in Chefchaouen. But do not be silly, Señor. The spider does not fall."

They agreed to the scheme. Ellen suggested he rest a few days but Malmut balked, so they checked out and boarded Jabi's cab for the last time.

In dark Alpine climbers, Petzl headlamp, and treaded socks, Malmut slinked from the cab into a fig grove adjacent to the massive wall. Jabi drove to a viewpoint across the narrow bay, passing a police Jeep on the way. Mateo and Ellen took seats on the lone bench. She said they should make like lovers, for the police, and told Mateo to put his arm around her. He hesitated.

"Make it look real!" she commanded.

Palming opera glasses with his outside hand, Mateo located Malmut at the base. Just then the police returned, lazily searching the shoreline with their spotlight. As the beam found them, Ellen kissed Mateo. The light went quickly away but the kiss did not.

"Sorry," she said.

"No problem," said he.

Malmut was slow in scaling the moss but climbed steadily once clear, moving like a knight on the board—two stones in one direction, one diagonally, and then the reverse. More than once he had to retreat but he moved balanced and sure until two rows from the top where he lost his lead grip and foothold at once. Dangling limp by three fingers of the lagging hand, he struggled to reach the next seam.

Ellen described the scene through the glasses. "Oh God! Mateo! Malmut's lost it. He's going to fall."

But then, swinging in ever larger arcs, Malmut gained a forward handhold. He scrambled to the top, saluted, and disappeared.

24

THE RASCAL

Friday, 10 July, 10:32 A.M.
Hotel Melilla Muelle
Avenue Martinez Catena
Melilla
Spanish Morocco

Mateo and Ellen met Malmut for breakfast at their portside hotel and learned that he'd meet the Captain of the *Tras Mediterránea* on the ferry dock that afternoon. Mateo watched from the balcony as Malmut delivered their cash to the goateed sailor.

The little convict proved to be as his townsfolk described. He'd spent his seventeenth birthday in solitary for scamming a guard and bore bruises from the event, but he was light-hearted, his spirit mending as fast as the welts. It seemed odd to Ellen.

"Aren't you bitter, Malmut, about your arrest, and the beatings?" she asked.

"Bitter? Oh, no. My trust is in Allah, and it was His will." He smiled wide. "The prophet teaches that those who accept hardship go first into heaven."

With the body of a jockey, his bulbous cranium was incongruent on the slight frame and he had a habit of toggling it as he talked, back-and-forth, back-and-forth, like a bobble-head doll. His elfish grin set and he showed off with magic: sleight of hand feints with a silver coin and flying card tricks with a deck from Hotel Minza. He bummed pocket change from Mateo to buy rainbow hacky sacks, and from then on did a juggling act worthy of Vegas.

Mateo was delighted to have Ellie back, much warmed since their tiff in Granada and apparently softened by the boy. After dinner she described him as "huggable," a comment that made Mateo's eyes roll, but if it wasn't Malmut, something had changed her, and he was grateful for the thaw.

Ellen sensed no treachery from the teenager but Mateo kept his distance. If the boy was conning them he hid it well, entertaining with folksy tales and a horde of animal metaphors. How anyone that small could eat so much was a wonder. Square meals didn't improve his memory, but he was adamant that he'd lead them straight to the scrolls. At Saturday's breakfast, Malmut described the store's owner, "Señor V", as he called him.

"Señor V is an old man, daffy as a salted mule. He mutters and speaks of things past as if they just happened. It is a Señorita who works the store, Señor V's granddaughter. She is as the ewe with her lamb, directing the old man with her eyes. Fear not, compadres. We will find the shop. Malmut remembers places like a widowed dove."

Ellen and Mateo boarded the ferry a few places in line behind Malmut. He jogged onto the crew's gangplank and disappeared. Minutes later, they spotted him on the cargo deck wearing a *Tras* jumpsuit over his street clothes and cavorting with the deckhands. Mateo's doubt eased when Ellen reminded that Malmut could have disappeared once he got over the wall.

They crossed into a squall and the bow-wash drove them inside, but the sea went flat as they made the lee of Gibraltar and the ferry docked on schedule. They saw Malmut shuttle one container and not return. Minutes later, Ellen focused the glasses on his lollipop profile, backlit by the city-shine as he scooted down the sea wall, now and then throwing a no-look wave.

After waiting most of an hour at the rendezvous, Ellen had the nerve to speak. "Malmut won't be coming, will he, Mateo?"

"I don't think so, Ellie. I'm going back to the ferry. Call if he shows up."

"Okay," she replied.

He jogged to the dock and found the bearded Captain alone at the ship's bar. The sailor pretended ignorance, so Mateo threatened.

"Tell me where to find him, Captain, or we're going to Customs' House. They won't be kind when they learn you smuggled an escaped drug trafficker. If you're lucky, your license will only be suspended."

"All right," said the Captain. "Most of them go to a safe house in the Navy quarter. They can get papers if they've got the money. Pink stucco, across from the fire station."

"And from there?" Mateo asked.

"I can't say. Most hitch with truckers. There's a depot downtown and a bigger one at Puerto Piedras. Twenty Euros gets them to Granada or Cordoba, and fifty takes them anywhere in Spain."

Mateo pressed, provoking the sailor.

"That's all I know, goddammit! What do you think I am, a travel agent? They get a one way ride and a few words of advice for their lousy hundred Euros."

25

THE DINER

Sunday, 12 July, 1:07 P.M.
Auto Europe Rentals
Avenidas Ortega y Gasset
Málaga,
Spain

Mr. Smith's sleepless agents were glum and embarrassed by Malmut's betrayal. For Ellen it was her second trusting blunder in as many weeks, and as they searched for Malmut she scolded herself. It was years since Mateo had been duped, but his pride was equally dented. More galling for both was the thought that Malmut would head straight for the scrolls.

After searching the Málaga hotel, they remembered the ferry captain's tip and turned to the highways. Ellen said they'd need two cars to cover both routes to Granada, so she rented a BMW. With the engine running in the rental lot, she stiff-armed the wheel as Mateo leaned in through the driver's window.

"We'll catch him before he gets to Granada," she said.

"I hope so," Mateo answered.

"Good luck!" Ellen said.

Mateo popped inside for a longer, softer kiss.

"Sorry," he said.

"No problem," said she.

He drove to the truck stop while Ellen headed downtown and soon called from the Repsol station. "Malmut was just here. He hooked up with a trucker, but the gas guy couldn't say which highway they took."

"Well, they're only two," Ellen said, "and it's Sunday. They'll stop for dinner. Hang on!"

He heard the sound of rustling paper. "Okay. The Michelin map shows two plazas on route 92, and three on the coast highway, the A15. They'll have the standard layout, with a restaurant in the middle. Do you think we have time?"

"Yeah," Mateo said. "The truck is loaded, with steel wire the attendant said, a flatbed with blue cab. You take the coast road and I'll do Piedras. Leave money with the cashiers and promise them more so they'll call if they see him."

"Got it!" she said.

Spanish tastes are delicate and long-refined, and the roving truckers keen gastronomes. They debate food as much as sport and can give lectures on table wine. Ellen knew that highway plazas serve the main meal, "la comida," in midafternoon during siesta. On Sundays it includes an extra course, served on linen tablecloths with matching napkins, two forks, and china. It's a weekly ritual for the men of the road, and she was betting that Malmut would be with them.

Her last chance was at the Del Moro exit, just south of Granada. She spotted the blue truck and its steel from the off ramp. Peeking in from the foyer, she spied Malmut in the middle of the dining square, plain as a poppy in wheat. Immediately she phoned Mateo, donned her scarf and sunglasses, and then slinked into the bar to surveil overtop a mimosa.

Mateo screeched up as Malmut's meal ended. The Rascal was nonchalant when he saw the glowering Mateo at the register, greeting him like an old friend. He turned to his driver and thanked him, saying he'd be going on with his buddy. The guy laughed when Malmut asked for a refund.

As Ellen approached, Malmut answered her glare with a timid smile.

"Would you believe," he began.

"No!" they shouted in unison.

Flanking their captive with arms locked in his, they walked three abreast to Mateo's sedan. He tossed the boy into the back seat and cuffed his ankle to its frame. The bazaar shops were closing by the time they returned her car, so all slept at her place. Before turning in, Mateo reported to Parkinson while Ellen studied her grids. Malmut went quick to sleep on the kitchen rug, cuffed arm and leg to the pipes.

26

THE SEEKERS

Monday, 13 July, 9:45 A.M.
Café de Valor
Granada
Spain

The threesome marched in step toward Emilio's café, again with Malmut locked in between. Mateo carried a FedEx package in his free hand as he scanned the streetscape through his shades. Malmut sought eye contact, cheerfully greeting every glance before introducing himself to Emilio and charming him with a Bedouin riddle.

Mateo led to a back table. He hooked Malmut's shirt and pulled the teen to him. "Listen, you little thief! No more Mister Nice. I'm the fastest Indian on the planet, so don't try to run. If you do, I'll activate this." He ripped open the mailer and dumped its contents on the table. "Do you know what this is, Malmut? It came overnight, from Anchorage—it's a shock collar for sled dogs— heavy duty and fully charged. It'll crank enough juice to fry a small chicken."

Mateo yanked Malmut's pant leg high, positioned the electrodes behind his knee, and secured it with a plastic lock.

He demonstrated. "This is what it feels like when the dial's on 'one.'"

Malmut jerked as it discharged.

Mateo glared. "Now watch, Malmut. I'm turning it up, to *ten*. If I flip it on now, it'll cook your puny calf like a hunk of kebab. Then I'll scrape you up and really hurt you."

"Señor Mateo, there is no need," Malmut said. "You are the lion, and Malmut the lamb."

Mateo erupted. "Enough of your zoo-time bullshit! Do you understand?"

"Si Señor, comprendo!"

All morning they wandered, down one twisting lane and up the next, with Malmut a few steps out front. Ellen and Mateo faked nonchalance as they lagged on each side, tracking the globe-head like hounds on scent. Twice Malmut declared they were close, but then said no.

Mateo called Ellen aside. "I think he's scamming us again. It's his body language. He either doesn't know where it is, or he's saving it for himself. I have to talk some sense into the little crook, and I'd rather do it alone."

"Are you going to hurt him?" Ellen asked.

"Only if I have to," he said, shaking his head. "I hate to admit it, but I can't stay mad at the little shit. He's only gonna give it up one way, though, and sooner's better than later."

Ellen glanced at the beaming Malmut and then back to the strongman. "All right, I suppose we have to. I need something at the pharmacy. Is twenty minutes enough?"

"Plenty," he said, pointing to his left. "We'll be in that café."

She returned to find them at a curbside table with Malmut's head bowed and the big man grinning. He waved her close.

"It's in the old royalist neighborhood, above the bazaar, near the top of the hill in the part they call

Terraza del Rey—a senile old storekeeper, like he's been saying—Valenzuela's the name. It's a mom and pop joint, ten minutes from here by the Mirador stairs. Let's go."

Malmut tugged on Mateo's coat.

"We are partners now!" he declared.

They quickstepped with Malmut smiling and Mateo's jaw clenched. Ellen stared down, rehearsing her spiel for the bookshop. As they passed the Ayuntamiento, Mateo yanked both by their forearms.

"Quick! This way!" he shouted.

They sprinted down an alley with Malmut struggling to keep up, two strides for one of Mateo's. Ascending to the top of a narrow staircase, the Apache wheeled right, down a curving block and through the open doors of a fruit market. Gasping as they staggered to the back, all squatted behind a stack of melons. A few minutes later Mateo returned to the entrance and signaled for them to join him.

With eyes combing the street, he spoke softly to Ellen.

"Didn't you see them? The little Turk just found us, and your boyfriend was tailing you when you came back from the pharmacy. We've got to get to that bookstore."

With an angry frown Ellen grabbed Mateo's lapels and pulled him to her, at the same time grinding her stubby heel into the face of his Gucci. "Listen here, Chief! Don't mention the 'boyfriend' thing again or I'll make tapas out of your little red huevos!"

"Yes, ma'am," he squeaked.

Mateo gimped through the entrance and motioned for them to follow. There was no sign of either badman when they reached Calle La Posada. Ellen spotted the marquee. *Libreria Valenzuela—Books Used and New."*

"There it is! I told you I'd find it!" declared Malmut.

They reached the bookstore's alcove and realized it was closed for siesta. Knocking produced no result, so they crossed at the corner and ducked into a Galician restaurant. Taking a window table with a clear view of the store, they tried to stay cool. There would be at least a two hour wait.

27

THE FINDERS

Monday, 13 July, 4:34 P.M.
Valenzuela's Bookstore
Marquez & La Posada Streets
Granada
Spain

At 4:30, a young woman with a shuffling old man clinging to her arm passed by the restaurant window. They crossed the street and opened Valenzuela's bookstore. The trio was quick to follow. A dainty tinker's chime attached to the doorframe announced their arrival. They found the smiling woman behind the counter and Valenzuela mumbling at his dusting bench. Mateo moved behind a rack in the front window, peeping out as he disengaged his pistol's safety.

The young lady greeted. "How may I serve you?"

Ellen was precise. "Good evening. We understand you may have some artifacts for sale." She gestured toward Malmut. "My friend purchased a prayer book here some time ago. It's been helpful in my work at the University, and he tells me there were two leather bags with the book. Do you still have them?"

Maria Luisa could tell that Valenzuela understood Ellen's query, so she winked and triggered the show. He shouldered his dust cloth and rasped around the bench to face Ellen. All at once his convex spine inverted, both shoulders snapped square, and the eyes went young.

"May I show you a title?" he asked.

Ellen sensed his state and twinkled back. "Yes. The old leather bags, please."

"Follow me!" Valenzuela commanded.

Mateo and Malmut watched them disappear into the maze. They weaved a crooked path through the towering stacks and arrived at the far wall. Valenzuela dragged a ladder to the bookcase, opened the top shelf, dusted the saddlebags, and handed them down. The acrostics told Ellen she had the Quelle scrolls, triggering an epinephrine rush. The bookseller climbed down, pivoted like a corporal, and bowed graciously.

"I believe these are what you requested, Señorita!"

They worked their way back, each clutching a bag out front. Mateo's eyes swelled when they emerged. They placed the saddlebags on the bench and as Ellen extracted a scroll, it fractured, sending a small flake to the floor. She retrieved it and tested with Parkinson's vials. The sea green color exactly matched and the lacy lines appeared.

Ellen addressed Valenzuela. "These are what we'd hoped for. How much do you ask?"

The old guy wilted and retreated to his station, again mumbling and attuned only to Maria Luisa's next signal. She stepped in between.

"Yes, Señorita. One thousand Euros, each."

Ellen gave her standard reply. "That's a little more than I can pay."

"Very well," said Maria. "Seventeen-hundred fifty, but no less, and at that price I must ask for currency. Of course, in this circumstance, the purchase will be without receipt and ineligible for return."

Ellen scavenged through her handbag but found less than eight hundred Euros. She called to Mateo. He abandoned his lookout to make up all but two hundred.

Ellen appealed to Maria. "We have a little less than sixteen hundred here. Will you take that? If not, I have a bank check."

The woman looked sideways. "I'm afraid not a check, but I'll hold the merchandise until you complete the payment. There's an ATM in the cantina next door."

Ellen and Mateo grimaced as Malmut wedged between them, opening his billfold and adding two one-hundred Euro notes to the pile. "This will meet your price, Señorita," he declared.

After checking the sum, Maria fetched containers for the bags: corrugated wine boxes, sturdy and with handholds on each side. The women cushioned the saddlebags with crumpled newspapers and force-folded the tops. Malmut offered to carry one, but Mateo refused. He scooped a box under each arm and was turning for the door when the tinker bell chimed.

28

KAMAL KUNDAK

Monday, 13 July, 5:09 P.M.
Valenzuela's Bookstore
Marquez & La Posada Streets
Granada
Spain

In barged a dwarfish man in soiled seersucker and straw Fedora, his gleaming revolver searching for targets. Its laser sight found Mateo's forehead as he barked in pigeon Spanish.

"No die if do what Kundak say. If no do, Kundak with five bullets. You. Moroccan. Big man gun to floor!"

Malmut obeyed.

"Now kick to Kundak."

The gun skipped across the tiles to Kundak's feet and he booted it into the corner. He was gripping his revolver with both hands, assault style, its glowing orange dot jiggling between Mateo's eyes. The Apache could only glare.

Kundak screamed his second order. "You, big man. Boxes to Moroccan!"

The little Turk's shouting aroused Valenzuela. *Another customer?* the old man wondered. Mistaking his granddaughter's anxious squinting for their signal, he shouldered the dust cloth and shuffled up to the gunman. Kundak shouted for him to stop, alternately aiming the weapon at Valenzuela and Mateo, but the old guy kept coming.

Face to face, Valenzuela snapped to attention, blocking Kundak's view.

"May I show you a title?" he asked, grinning down.

The little Turk didn't dally. Dropping his right hand to the belt, he drew the blade and drove it into Valenzuela's groin, drawing him near as he stabbed. Valenzuela croaked and collapsed against him as Mateo swept his arms forward, hurling both boxes at the little man. The gun discharged into the stacks and Mateo struck, pinning the small man against the door as the revolver fired again. Then, with a single slashing blow, he crushed Kundak's larynx.

Ellen was kneeling beside Maria, trying to compress Valenzuela's gushing wound, but it pulsed around her fingers, spraying both women. Mateo retrieved his weapon and snatched the boxes as the purple-faced Kundak gurgled. Peeping out the window, he shouted.

"We gotta go! Kundak's bound to have called Adivar!"

Ellen was thumbing her cellphone with her free hand—061, the ambulance number.

Mateo shouted again. "Ellie! We have to get out of here!"

As Malmut ogled and Maria screamed, Ellen answered without looking. "I can't leave the old man, Mateo. Look. The squirting only stops when I press on it. The woman can't do it. She's freaked out. Take the scrolls to Emilio's. I'll meet you there as soon as the paramedics get here."

"But Ellie!"

"Do as I say, Mateo. Go! I'll be there, I promise.

29

ARTAN ADIVAR

Tuesday, 14 July, 12:02 A.M.
Café de Valor
Granada
Spain

They loitered in the window booth like expectant fathers outside a delivery room. Mateo slumped into the cushion as he pondered the mysteries of a toothpick while Malmut juggled his sacs in a high arc from the edge of his seat, asking incessantly as to when Ellen would arrive.

Emilio approached to clear their third coffees. "I am sorry to say it is time to close," he announced, "but you gentlemen are welcome to stay until I tidy up."

Emilio was uneasy. He'd suspected since they arrived that something was amiss with his dear Rubia. After dousing the patio candles and flipping the window sign to CLOSED, he finally had to ask. "And where is our beautiful Rubia this evening?"

Mateo could only shrug. "Ellie's in a fix, Emilio. She asked us to wait here. Sorry for the inconvenience."

Emilio crossed his arms. "In that case, we will all wait."

Mateo's constant calls to Ellen went unanswered. A cop had picked up the bookstore phone, and he worried that the police had her. Mateo was sure that the little Turk was dead and knew that the stabbing of the well-known merchant would be treated as a major crime. He could only hope that the police got a straight story from Valenzuela's granddaughter. When he inquired at the Emergency ward, the nurse reported the old man alive, but knew nothing of Ellen.

A few minutes after midnight, her ringtone finally sounded. In his haste to answer Mateo fumbled the cellphone, sending it over the edge of the table. Malmut dove like a goalie and made the save. From his back, he tossed the ringing cell to Mateo.

He tapped it on. "Ellie. Thank God! Where are you?"

"… Mister Barefoot, I presume." It was a man's deep voice, in English, with an odd British accent.

"Who *is* this?" Mateo demanded.

"Your beautiful friend is with us, Mister Barefoot, and I'm sorry to say, she's in an awkward state. Her lovely dress is splattered in blood, the makeup badly smeared, and she's in a foul mood. All the woman can do is curse, in several languages. Rather unladylike, I'm afraid."

Mateo shuddered. "Talk, Adivar!"

"Very well," said Adivar. "We each possess what the other desires. Perhaps you would consider a trade."

"How do you know I want her back?" asked Mateo. "I got what I came for."

"Please do not play me for a fool, Mister Barefoot. I have seen how you look at her."

"Talk!" demanded Mateo.

"Are you familiar with the tourist viewpoint to the south of the city, the one called 'Suspiro del Moro'? It's not far from the autovia."

"No," Mateo lied.

"You'll find it to the east of the Del Moro exit, well up the mountain, perhaps four or five kilometers."

"Go on."

"There are signs for the tourists marked 'Monumento del Moro.' They're easy to follow, but be alert on your approach. The lookout slopes away from the road and can be difficult to see. When you come upon the large boulders on the right, slow down. It's directly across."

Adivar paused.

"What else?" Mateo asked through gritted teeth.

"Listen carefully, Mister Barefoot. We shall meet there before dawn to affect the exchange. There's a large sculpture below the road: a life-sized statue of a mounted man atop a stone wall at the edge of a precipice. Three benches face the statue. The woman and I shall be waiting at the far bench when you arrive. You will place the scrolls on the middle bench and then take your seat at the closest. Once you are seated, you may not stand. I shall inspect the artifacts and if satisfied, will release the girl. I shall then call for my associates and take my leave. After that, you must not depart until the sun has fully risen."

"Is that it?" Mateo asked.

Adivar answered with commands. "Come alone and bring only the antiquities. Should you be so foolish as to attempt deceit, the woman will die before your eyes." Again he paused. "I shall repeat. Leave your weapons behind!"

"How do I know she's alive?" Mateo asked.

"One moment," Adivar said.

There was a long wait. At last Ellen came to the phone, screeching.

"Mateo! Don't do it! Don't give them up!"

He heard a scuffle and Ellen's shrieked curses, then another profane voice, and finally a sharp slap.

Adivar returned. "Unfortunately, the girl is hysterical. Too many history-mysteries, perhaps. I assure you ... what is your Christian name?"

"Mateo."

"Yes, I assure you, Mateo, I am a businessman, quite averse to violence. We need only conclude our bargain to avoid conflict. It would be wasted effort—bodies to dispose of, and so on—not at all worth the risk, and distasteful to a gentleman of my station."

"If you hurt her!" Mateo shouted.

"Please, there is no reason," Adivar responded.

"What about your little friend, Kundak? Don't you miss him?" Mateo asked.

Adivar hesitated. "Oh, yes, the Cypriot. For that, I can only thank you. You spared me an unpleasant chore. The man was becoming an embarrassing encumbrance, much too prone to violent behaviour. Dreadful. Not at all my style. And thanks to you, my share will be that much larger. How do you Americans say? 'No hard feelings'?"

"What time?" asked Mateo.

"One hour before dawn. A little after six o'clock. There will be no tourists then, and any lovers should be gone. Remember, no weapons."

"Okay. Six A.M. Suspiro Monument. Bags on the middle bench. No guns. We leave at sunup."

"Precisely," Adivar said. "I'm sure all will pass in an orderly fashion. I'm aware that this is unpleasant for you, Mister Barefoot. No one likes to lose, and you have my professional sympathy. You've been a worthy adversary, but in the end you will have the woman and we will have the scrolls. A satisfactory exchange, I believe."

Mateo hung up. At once he ordered Malmut to put his foot on the bench. He sliced the plastic tie from the shock collar. Malmut didn't move.

"You're free to go, Malmut. Good Luck."

"But what of Señorita Ché?" Malmut asked. "She is in danger. Malmut must help. Please, Señor!"

"She's my problem. Get going!"

"No, Señor, please. I am now in her service!"

Mateo glared down with a foul frown causing Malmut to plod away. He turned at the door. "Please, Señor Mateo. You must allow me to help Jefé Ché. I have shamed my good name and that of my father. I must redeem our honor."

"Go. Now!" Mateo bellowed.

Malmut disappeared into the street.

Emilio approached. "Qué pasa, Señor? What of my Rubia? What can I do?"

Mateo laid a soft hand on his shoulder. "Don't worry, Emilio, she'll be all right, I promise. But you *can* help."

A short time later Mateo emerged from the café lugging the wine boxes. He didn't bother to look for a tail—he knew one was there.

30

THE COMANCHE

Tuesday, 14 July, 2:52 A.M.
Moor's Mountain
Granada Province
Spain

Mateo resembled a grocery clerk as he hurried down the sidewalk, leaning back with arms extended and peering over the boxes stacked under his chin. Wasting not a minute when he got to his flat, he turned on every light, gathered what he'd need, and then hustled down the service stairs to the basement with a pack on his back and a box in each hand. Sneaking into the adjacent garage, he loaded his operational vehicle, a high-suspension Rubicon, one he knew his rivals had never seen. Speeding through the empty streets, he intended to be at the monument well ahead of Adivar.

Mateo struggled to remember the lookout. With no traffic, the Rubicon exited the autovia fifteen minutes later and climbed the narrow byway, more suited to a roadster than the top heavy four-wheeler. Snaking like a curled ribbon along the edge of the steep incline, there were sharp curves every hundred meters and no guard rails. He found the viewpoint as Adivar described: at the apex of a hairpin turn that sloped away from the mountain, across from a pile of giant boulders and at the edge of a perpendicular drop-off. Mateo eased onto the gravel, concealed behind the vehicle's tinted glass.

He took mental snapshots through the windshield. It was an ordinary Spanish turnout, save the pleasing view of Granada's twinkling cityscape set against the opposing mountain chain. A banana-shaped acre strung along the convex curve, the historic site was simply constructed with its parking lot at road level and broad steps leading to a grassy overview two meters below. Sightseers were protected from falling off the cliff by a wide stone wall that formed the base of the life-sized statue at its center. The wooden benches Adivar talked about could barely be seen from the road but were in plain sight from the bouldered heights above, the place where Mateo suspected an assassin was lurking. The sole focus of the lower wall was the metal caliph, Boabdil himself, on horseback and gazing back at Granada as he issued his perpetual sigh.

Mateo leaned forward to glance up at the boulders. *The sniper may already be there,* he thought, *and I don't want to tip him off.* Acting like a tourist who'd stopped for a peek, he backed out and continued up the mountain, exiting onto a goat track four curves and a kilometer beyond.

Mateo painted his face and slipped a Gilley suit over his street clothes. After pulling on a black balaclava, he assembled his rifle and scope but cursed when he discovered the silencer missing. In its place he slipped an old friend into the Gilley's rump pouch— the Comanche long-knife he'd carried since his man-dance—one he could throw to five meters. His last task was to calibrate his DEA Starscope, night binoculars that in near darkness could find any target, and they came with an infrared mode.

Mateo climbed well above the boulders and then bellied down the mountain, peeking with the glasses every meter. It took most of two hours but then, in the infrared, he identified the glowing forms of two men crouching at the base of a huge rock. Switching to the visible spectrum, he watched as they sat shoulder to shoulder against the stone with arms across their chests, legs folded up, and trunks forward. They were trying to keep warm. Propped against the rock on each side of the men were long rifles, one a bolt-action with scope—*a Mauser*, Mateo thought, deadly at short range for even the average marksman. The other profile was easy to make—*a British .303*, the snipers' best friend.

31

BOABDIL'S RETURN

Tuesday, 14 July, 6:04 A.M.
Moor's Monument
Granada Province
Spain

A black Citroen pulled into the viewpoint's empty parking lot at six sharp. Adivar's driver emerged and signaled up to the boulders with three short bursts of his flashlight. He received two long flashes in return. Seconds later, the big Turk emerged from the front passenger door and Ellen was shoved out the back, skinning her knees on the volcanic gravel. Adivar yanked Ellen to her feet and dragged her down the stairs to the far bench where they sat side by side, as if to enjoy the view.

He turned to shout at his men. "All right, you apes! Get down the mountain and wait for my call. Park precisely where I showed you, and no smoking!"

Nothing happened at the agreed time. At first the Turk made light of it, but he grew ever more testy, and at the end of a tedious hour, angry. At last, he stood and drew his gun.

"Your muscle-bound hero seems to have forsaken you, my dear, and diverted me at the same time. I misjudged his cleverness as well as his feelings for you—unfortunate for both of us. It appears that the scrolls were worth more to him than your little love affair. No offense, Miss Shea, but I can't blame him.

Money can bring women, but not often the reverse. It depends which a man values more, I suppose. Oh well, you must be heartbroken, no doubt the reason you'll be taking a lover's leap." He smirked as he waved his Beretta at the stone wall. "What a pity. But such are the perils of romance."

"Mateo did the right thing," she snarled. "The scrolls are more important than..."

Again he gestured with the weapon and herded her toward the wall, now visible in the growing light. He punched his cellphone and shouted. "The American did not come! He's not as soft as I thought. We'll kill him later as New York ordered, but the girl is now useless. I shall dispose of her here, and with great pleasure. It's the least I can do for my beloved Kundak. Bring the car! We must precede Barefoot to the airport."

Adivar aimed his weapon. "Get up on the ledge, Miss Shea."

She didn't move.

"Get up there," he commanded, "or I'll shoot you here. My men will be happy to toss your body over."

She crawled up. Once more Adivar waved the gun.

"Jump!" he shouted.

Ellen peeked into the blackness.

"Jump, or I'll shoot!" he bellowed, pointing the weapon.

Then Adivar's eyes went to the mountain. "Did you hear that?"

"Hear what, Adivar?"

"Listen, he whispered. "From up there."

Both squinted into the dawn. Adivar ordered Ellen back to the bench and then climbed on it, one hand to his ear. She took a tiny step backward. He put the gun to her temple. "No, Miss Shea. Come here, in front, where I can see you!"

Then both detected a thin voice. Soon they understood what the man was yelling.

"It's me, I'm coming! I'm coming! Wait!" the voice screamed.

A burly profile appeared against the pink sky, scurrying down the road with a cube in each hand. As he reached the parking lot they could hear him clearly, and then, screeching tires from the downhill side— Adivar's men had arrived.

Adivar stepped off the bench as the car fishtailed on the gravel, its high beams spotlighting Mateo. Three men boiled out, two with handguns drawn and tracking the Apache as he crossed the top of the lot. Adivar took aim from below. Mateo leaped to the grassy lower level and then jumped again, onto the dew-slickened wall. He slow-stepped toward Boabdil's statue before turning to face them with legs wide and boxes dangling.

Glints of sunlight ricocheted from the bronze figure as Mateo cursed at Adivar.

"You son of a bitch. You said no weapons, that this was a business deal."

"Simply a precaution, my dear man. We had no idea who you were. I just now recalled my associates. We thought you weren't coming. You're quite late, you know. And what the devil are you doing on foot?"

Mateo raged. "It's your fault, Adivar! You picked a lousy spot. You can't even see this place from the road. I drove right by, and when I realized I went too far, I tried to turn around, but it's too narrow. My car's hung up in the ditch."

"I see. Curious," said the Turk.

"Yeah, and I'm curious as to how you want these scrolls," Mateo goaded. "Together, or in a thousand pieces, scattered all over this mountain?" He shuffled backward, looking between his legs into the chasm as he balanced on his toes, with arches and heels over the edge.

"Go ahead, boys!" he taunted. "Shoot, and I'll do a back flip. The scrolls'll be confetti. Won't be worth much then, will they, Adivar?"

The Turk ordered his men back. "Don't be foolish, Barefoot. We can still close the deal."

"How?" asked Mateo.

"Yes, let me think... First, we shall disarm ourselves."

He tossed his Beretta over the wall and ordered his henchmen to do the same. They obeyed after a second cursed command.

Adivar spoke evenly. "Now, Mister Barefoot, you are in no danger, but there is nowhere to go. In exchange for the scrolls, we shall release the woman and give you the keys to our automobile. We can call for another when you're gone. Now please, place the boxes next to the statue and step down. Leave the auto at Plaza Nueva with the keys inside."

Mateo's brow flexed. "All right, but keep your distance."

Ellen accepted the keys from the driver, demanded her cellphone from Adivar, and then ran to the wall, pleading up at Mateo.

"We can't do this!" she screamed.

"We have to," said Mateo. "I can't take them all."

Adivar smirked as his men stretched forward with chests protruding and fists clenched. Mateo gently placed the wine boxes against the statue and hopped down. With the ignition key at the ready, he took Ellen's hand and they walked backward, past the benches to the foot of the stairs. Glancing at each other, they turned and rushed up the steps as the goons cheated forward, shouting at the bouldered mountainside and waving their arms.

They screamed in Turkish and Spanish. "Now! Do it now! Shoot them! Kill them!"

The dead men in the rocks did not respond. Mateo threw the Citroen into reverse and it jerked onto the pavement as the thugs latched onto the passenger handles, pounding on the windows when Mateo jammed it into drive. He shed them on the first curve.

As they sped down the mountain, the sulking Ellen looked to Mateo.

"How could you? How could you give them the scrolls?" she bawled.

Before he could answer, the muffled thunder of a massive explosion came from behind. She whirled around to look through the rear window at where they'd just been and was astonished to see a fireball rising inside a small mushroom cloud. Again she turned to the Apache.

"I didn't," he said.

32

EL GUAPO

Tuesday, 14 July, 7:28 A.M.
Road 1492
Granada Province
Spain

The sedan's tires shrieked through the swirling downhill turns, clinging to the asphalt of the outside lane as they carried Mateo and Ellen toward the autovia.

Mateo described what happened the night before. "Emilio's got the saddlebags. I gave them to him in the restaurant last night. I knew they'd be watching my place and couldn't take a chance on leaving them there, so I carried the empty boxes home as decoys and then stuffed them with every explosive I could find, booby trapped in tandem so both would detonate if either was opened. There was a lot of C4 in those boxes." He glanced at Ellen and chuckled. "Boabdil may have made it back to Granada after all."

She was too distracted for his joke. With the Rubicon in high gear, Mateo took her hand and told more. "Something I can't figure, though. I knew we could trust Emilio. He was really worried about you, and said he'd do whatever he could. When I asked him to take care of the things in the boxes, he was ready."

Her eyebrows rose. "And?"

"And then we went to the kitchen so no one could see us from the street, but when I unpacked the boxes,

Emilio got spooked, really spooked. He kept hollering 'Las alforas!' 'The saddlebags!' over and over. He thanked me four or five times, asking where we found them and if we found anything with them. I didn't know what the hell he was talking about, but there was no time to ask. Adivar's driver was watching the place, and I wanted him to follow the decoys. Anyway, the scrolls'll be safe with Emilio. He said he'd take them home."

She stared into the oncoming headlights. "Should we go to his apartment or the café? The café, I guess. It'll be open by the time we get there."

"Yeah, as soon as we ditch Adivar's car, but we have to watch out for more bad guys. His boss in New York won't give up, and there's no telling what El Guapo and the holy shitters are up to."

She squeezed his hand. "Okay, but I have to shower and change."

Ellen and Mateo hurried from her place to the café but as they turned the corner onto Calle Zacatín, they ran into a crowd. An ambulance was double parked in front of the restaurant, its amber lights pulsing with an attendant in the bay.

"I don't like this," Ellen whispered. "Let's get in there."

Mateo seized her arm and drew her into a passageway.

"Think about it, Ellie. The police are looking for a couple, and you're too easy to I.D. I'll check things out from the bodega across the street. We can meet at Amador's chocolate shop when I find out what's going on. You have to go."

Ellen knew he was right. "Okay. Get there as fast as you can."

Mateo crossed the street and found a vantage point inside the store, in time to see a second medic wheel Emilio to the ambulance, his head wrapped in gauze, one arm in a sling, and his son Rafael on the other. They fast-loaded and sped off with siren whooping. As the onlookers dispersed Mateo moved forward, but then felt a hard object press into his back.

"Don't move," a voice screeched from behind.

In a blink, Mateo wheeled around and swept the object away, coiling into a striking position with his long knife unsheathed. He thrust the blood-caked blade forward, but then jerked back. It was the smiling Malmut with marking pen in hand.

"Partner!" Rascal exclaimed.

Mateo exploded. "You little shit! What the hell are you doing? I could've stuck you. I *should've* stuck you. What's going on? What happened to Emilio?"

"It is not to worry, Señor Mateo, Detective Adjani is on duty. Is the boss with you? Is she all right? I must speak with Señorita Ché."

"She's all right," Mateo barked as he lowered the steel.

"Please take me to her," Malmut said.

Mateo responded by putting an arm around the teen and dragging him from the shop, down the walkway and into a deep alcove. Lifting Malmut by his jacket, he hooked the back of his belt over the protruding door knocker, hanging him like a piñata at eye level.

"What happened to Emilio?" he demanded. "Tell me!"

The boy looked away. "Malmut can only speak with jefe Ché, and no other. He is guilty as the burping dog and must ask her forgiveness."

Barefoot was losing control. He seized Malmut's jaw and drew the knife. Snarling as he touched its tip to the base of the boy's nose, he jabbed to the bone. The cut was small but deep, and it bled briskly.

"You little bastard..." Mateo growled. "That'll give you an idea of what's about to happen. I'll fillet you like a trout, right here, unless you tell me what you know."

The Moroccan choked on the blood. "Malmut is sorry as the pregnant sow, Señor, but he must speak with the Señorita and recover his honor. I have shamed my family and can no longer be the lone raven. Please, Señor Mateo. It is only she who can forgive Malmut."

Exasperated and without options, Mateo put the sharp edge to Malmut's throat.

"Okay, but if you cross me, *this* is where I'll cut the next time."

Mateo sheathed the knife, unhooked Malmut, and offered him a handkerchief but kept a falcon's grip on his forearm all the way to the chocolate shop. Peering between pyramids of bonbons, he saw Ellen staring back. She rushed into the street, alarmed by Mateo's expression and Malmut's bloody lip.

"What happened?"

"Ask your 'huggable' little friend here," Mateo answered. "He'll only talk to you."

"Okay, but we have to get out of sight. The police were just here. I had to hide in the rest room. Let's go to Hannigan's."

Mateo reported what he'd seen on the way.

She gasped. "Was Emilio conscious?"

"I don't know," Mateo said. "It didn't look like it."

She turned to Malmut. "What happened to your mouth?"

"It is nothing, boss. Less than I deserve."

They found a secluded booth in the back of the empty bar. Mateo wedged Malmut on the inside as Ellen leaned across.

"All right, Spider-man, talk!" Mateo commanded.

Malmut looked only at Ellen. "I did as Señor Mateo asked last night and went into the street from Café Valor, but feared for you, so I hid in the shadows. I wanted to make up for what I did. If Malmut had taken you to the bookstore—"

"Never mind that, Malmut, just tell us what happened," she said.

"Yes, jefe! I saw Señor Mateo take the boxes from the café and watched Adivar's man, the Puerto Rican, cross the corner and follow him. I was watching them and did not see that tall American coming, the one Señor Mateo calls 'El Guapo.' He threw me to the ground and then entered the café. I could see him through the window talking with Señor Emilio, but I didn't stay. I had to warn Señor Mateo."

Malmut turned to Mateo, pleading candor with his eyes.

"I caught up to you and the Puertoriqueño on Calle Reyes. We watched you go up to your room, but after a while, when you didn't come out, I went home. The man was still sitting on the bus bench, smoking a cigarette and looking at your window."

Mateo's upper lip curled. "What about Emilio? Did you just happen to be there this morning?"

"I came at the opening hour," Malmut said, "to learn of Señorita Ché, but the café was still closed, with customers looking in through the glass. One woman screamed and another called the police."

Ellen interrupted. "And you don't know what happened?"

"No, boss, I swear," he said, daubing his wound, "in the name of the prophets. Malmut is in your service now, loyal as the desert hound."

"And the scrolls?" Mateo asked. "Who has the scrolls?"

"Why, you have them, Señor. I saw you carry them home. Have you lost them?"

33

DOCTOR BAREFOOT

Tuesday, 14 July, 10:11 A.M.
Hannigan & Son's Irish Pub
Cetti Meriem
Granada
Spain

The men gawked at Ellen and worried. Seated silent and still, she breathed in sighs, head propped on elbows and hands over eyes. The news of Emilio and loss of the scrolls seemed too much.

At last she unmasked, staring between them and thinking aloud. "No sense going back to the café. If they connect Emilio to Valenzuela they'll be watching him, but we have to take a chance. He's the only one who knows what happened to the scrolls. Let's find out where he is."

They worked the phones and learned that Emilio was in the trauma ward of Virgen hospital, on the same floor as old man Valenzuela.

"Let's go," Mateo said.

"Okay," Ellen answered. "But what about Howard and the Whitcolmbs? If they've got the scrolls, they'll head for home. We have to find them."

"You're right. One of us has to get to the airport," said Mateo.

Malmut piped up. "I will follow the jackals' trail while you and Señorita Ché visit Señor Emilio. Malmut has learned much to be a detective from you, Señor Mateo. It is my new profession."

Mateo's eyes went to the rafters, but Ellen ignored him. "Listen closely, Malmut. Go to the observation deck. You can see all the gates from there. If you see 'El Guapo' or the brothers, call us. And be smart. Get the flight number and destination. Understand?"

"Yes, boss, I understand. I will take the fast taxi."

She handed Malmut her phone and showed how to speed dial Mateo's.

The Apache held his tongue until Malmut was out the door.

"This is nuts," he said. "If Malmut gets the scrolls, he'll steal 'em."

"Maybe not," she answered. "This time he seemed … different. But it doesn't matter—he's the lesser evil—Malmut'll be a lot easier to catch than Howard and the Whitcolmbs."

Mateo entered the medical center via the ambulance dock, snatching a white coat as he passed through. It was two sizes small and the I.D. badge wasn't close, but he flipped the plastic and wore it unbuttoned. Plopping down at a nursing station, he asked for help. Emilio was in 433.

Mateo stood on the threshold of Emilio's room but couldn't see him for the hovering visitors. There were no cops. He ordered a nurse to clear the room so that he could examine the patient and she jumped to the task. Meanwhile, he summoned Ellen. Emilio's wife was the last to leave the room, quizzing the nurse as they exited. The handsome woman walked up to Mateo.

"Doctor, please. Tell me of my Chori's injuries. Will there be surgery? Will the arm be straight? And that ugly thing on his forehead. Will that go away?"

The phony doctor responded. "His injuries? Yes, that's what I'm about to evaluate, Señora. Please take a seat in the waiting area."

Mateo moved to the bedside and drew the curtain behind. Supine and with head elevated, a cast covered one arm and an I.V. dripped on the other. Emilio's face was grotesque, with the left eye swollen shut and a crescent of stitches above his puffy nose. Most alarming was a deep purple goose egg high on his brow.

Emilio extended his free hand.

"Señor! It is you. You are a doctor? I did not know."

Mateo leaned over the rail. "I'm sorry I got you into this mess, Emilio. I didn't know this would happen."

He winked his good eye. "I understand, Mateo. You were defending your beloved. And I'm so grateful that you tried to return our bags. But you must tell me—do you know what's become of our other things? Did you find an old red book with the bags? And what of Rubia, our precious Rubia? Is she all right?"

34

CHORI RODRIGUEZ de SALAZAR

Tuesday, 14 July, 12:23 P.M.
Room 433, Hospital Virgen de las Nieves
Granada
Spain

The curtain rollers rattled when Ellen popped through.

"I'm fine, Uncle Emilio," she said, faking a smile. "Fine."

Ellen was shocked at her friend's appearance and perplexed by Mateo's woeful look.

Emilio's smile was crooked. "Rubia. Praise God. How wonderful to see you. I was so afraid. Mateo would tell me nothing last night."

Balancing on the bedrail, she leaned in to kiss him. "Dear Emilio, I'm so sorry. Are you in pain?"

"Perhaps a little, Rubia. It is as God wills, but please tell me. Where did you find our saddlebags? Was there an old book with them? Light red, with numbers on the cover?"

Her brow folded as she stood upright. She looked to Mateo hoping for an explanation, but he could only match her baffled look.

"*Your* saddlebags, Emilio? Yours?" she asked.

Emilio had only questions. "And how did you know they were ours? I don't remember showing them to you. They never left the shelves, and you were so understanding, about women in the prayer room, I mean. But more important, Rubia—what about Paco's book—the book of sayings? Do you have it? My son needs it to get well."

Nothing he said made sense. She asked again. "Uh, the bags are yours?"

"Yes, of course," said Emilio. "They've been with my family since the Christmas revolt, handed down through my grandfather, Capitán Zegrí, the hero of Guadalajara. The bags were among his things in our prayer room, things we brought from Bubión when my father died. They were stolen after the Atocha bombings. But the bags don't matter. What's important is the book. Do you have it? We would do anything to find it!"

Still tongue-tied, she could only stare.

Mateo spoke for her. "Only the bags, Señor Emilio. We had only the bags, and only for a little while."

Emilio explained why Hakkam's book was so important to his autistic son. It was a fantastic development for Ellen, too much of a coincidence to comprehend.

Mateo cut him short. "What happened last night, Emilio? Who's got the bags?"

"It was an American," Emilio said. "At least he had that annoying American accent, but he looked like a Swede: a tall young man, with bright hair, lean and with eyes of glass. The minute you left with the boxes, he entered through the CLOSED sign. He was well mannered at first, asking about you and Rubia. I told him how happy I was that you returned my bags. He demanded to see them and when I refused for his rudeness, he went mad, calling me a Muslim devil and shouting in English, about God and angels, saying he would send me to hell. Then he butted his head against mine." He pointed at the lump. "That's all I remember. The next thing I knew it was morning and Rafael was spritzing me."

"And the bags?" Mateo asked.

"Gone," Emilio said. "Rafael could not find them. They were in plain sight, on the drying table in the dish room where we opened the boxes. Rafael would have seen them if they were there."

Ellen signaled to Mateo with a head wag. They said warm goodbyes and promised a quick return. As they neared the door, Emilio called her back.

Taking her hand, he spoke through tears. "Rubia. You are as my daughter, you know. Please find Paco's book. It means all the world to Graciela and me. It will bring our little boy back."

"I'll do my best, Emilio," she whispered. "My very best."

35

THE CRUSADERS

Tuesday, 14 July, 2:32 P.M.
South Parking Structure
Virgen Hospital
Granada
Spain

Ellen's ringtone sounded as they exited the hospital parking lot.

"Si!" Mateo answered.

"It is Detective Adjani who speaks, on duty. I look through the glass to the Iberia gates and see three Crusaders. They sit close, like winter crows. Only El Guapo speaks, wagging his finger at the others who look back with the eyes of lambs. All carry green bags. Wait... Yes, they are boarding. Hurry!"

Mateo relayed Malmut's comments to Ellen before handing the phone across. They were twenty minutes from Lorca airport.

Ellen barked. "Malmut! Get the flight number and destination. Write down what they're wearing, every detail. We'll be there soon. Meet us at the parking entrance."

"Yes, boss. Detective Adjani is in your service."

Ellen dialed Iberia. She booked two seats on the next flight to Madrid, two to Barcelona, and two more to London's Heathrow. All but one would depart within the hour. She knew that every connecting flight to the U.S. went through those airports, and hoped to intercept the CREPT boys as they changed planes. Madrid was the best bet, then Barcelona, but by booking all three they could follow whichever route the churchboys took.

Malmut was pacing the curb when they pulled up, jittery but with every detail. The college boys were running a shell game, he said. Hendershot and his canvas bag took the Madrid flight but the Whitcolmb brothers went separate ways, each with an identical backpack. The boy Malmut described as a "milking pig," no doubt Leon, was boarding a flight to Barcelona, and "the talking peacock," for sure Jasper, was waiting for his plane to London. Malmut recited each flight number and described their dress and bags as all dashed toward the kiosks.

Mateo shouted sideways. "There're only two of us. I'll go for Hendershot in Madrid, and you can follow one of the brothers, but which one? We'll have to let one go."

She answered as they reached the kiosk. "The scrolls could be anywhere. Maybe they overnighted them, but I don't think they'd risk it, and for sure they wouldn't put them in their checked bags. They've got to be in those carry-ons."

Mateo responded as the machine spit out their boarding passes. "All the scrolls in one bag, maybe, or split in half, or thirds. Anything's possible, but Hendershot's the best bet."

"You're right. You follow Howard to Madrid," Ellen said. "I'll go for Leon in Barcelona. Parkinson's got contacts in London, so we'll ask him to get people on Jasper. At least we'll have a two-out-of-three chance." She looked down at the boy. "If only Malmut had a passport, he could trail Jasper to Heathrow."

As if on cue, Malmut reached into his jacket. "Which you think best, Jefé? To me the Portuguese would most serve."

"Son of a bitch," whined Mateo.

Malmut displayed three passports: Portuguese, Moroccan, and Romanian. All looked legit, but he was right: the purple Portuguese credential was worn and filled with validations. Quickly they bought a seat for Malmut on Jasper's London-bound plane.

Mateo's flight was called as they passed through security. The big man yelled across the detector. "We're just an hour behind, Ellie! If Hendershot doesn't have the scrolls, he'll tell me who does, and I'll call!"

"Okay, same for me," she said. "And we'll get Malmut a phone."

The Rascal chimed in. "I'll pick one up on the way."

Mateo's second boarding call came as they cleared inspection. He pulled Malmut to him by the collar.

"This is your chance to make detective, Malmut," he said with a frown. "The 'peacock' is Jasper, Jasper Whitcolmb, and he's your mark. Stay close, but don't let him see you. Steal the bag if you can but if not, stay on him day and night. If you get it, go to a safe place and call." He paused. "Now, listen. We'll give you a big reward if you bag the scrolls, I promise—but I promise you something else—if you skip, I'll find you, anywhere on earth, no matter how long it takes, I'll find you and then I'll skin you, like a mink. Do you know *that* animal, Malmut?"

"Yes, Señor, but if Allah wills it, Malmut will not fail. It is his honor to prove."

Mateo patted Malmut's cheek before sprinting down the corridor, shaking off a smile as he ran.

Ellen looked about, hoping to get Malmut a phone and spending money, but her flight was boarding and there was a line at the ATM.

"I have only a few Euros, but you can have them," she told Malmut.

"No, boss, I have money from the ferry and will share." He gave her a one hundred Euro note.

She wrote Jasper's name and their cellphone numbers on his ticket. "Get a phone when you get to London," she said. "Text or call right away."

"Yes, Boss."

As they hurried in opposite directions, Ellen shouted over her shoulder. "I believe in you, Malmut!"

"Thank you, Boss! I do, too!"

36

SARGENT MENDOZA

Tuesday, 14 July, 5:47 P.M.
Security Center
Terminal 4, Barajas Airport
Madrid
Spain

The largest terminal in Madrid's airport is an architectural gem, known to Madrileños as "Te Cuatro." It houses all of Air Iberia's operations, dozens of flights every hour. Mateo knew that Hendershot had to make his connection there and that he'd have to be quick if he wanted to intercept him, so he headed for the Security Center in Te Cuatro's basement and flashed his DEA badge at the duty sergeant.

"Yes, Agent Barefoot. Welcome. I am Officer Mendoza, here to serve you."

Mateo told his fiction. "I'm tailing a drugs-for-arms dealer. He just arrived from Granada."

"Yes, sir. How may we assist you?" asked Mendoza.

"Do you have a database for international passengers?"

"Yes, if you have a name, but we must search the airlines' manifests. We've made great progress since the ETA bombing," said Mendoza.

He invited Mateo behind his desk.

"H-e-n-d-e-r-s-h-o-t, H-o-w-a-r-d." Mateo spelled. "Iberia, from Granada."

Mateo leaned in from behind with one hand on Mendoza's chair back and the other on his desk. Moments later, the officer highlighted his find.

"Aqui. Hendershot, Howard. American national. Flight 1326, Lorca to Barajas. One checked bag, connecting to Iberia flight 71. Departs 1955 hours for Kennedy airport, Gate F 17. You have plenty of time, Officer Barefoot."

Mateo slapped Mendoza on the back.

"We'll impound the checked bag," the cop said. "How many men do you require, Señor?"

"Oh, no. I'll make the collar," Mateo said. "We're not sure who his handlers are, and they can't know we have him. Could be al Qaeda, ISIS, or even ETA. But I'll need a place for interrogation. It could get a little rough."

Mendoza's eyes swelled. "ETA? ... A little rough? Yes, sometimes it is the only way. We have soundproof quarters on each causeway. Of course, you must be accompanied by our officers at all times. We must follow regulations."

"Sure," Mateo replied. "Regulations."

The sergeant punched his intercom. "Ortega! Gallegos! To duty!" he shouted.

Two baby-faced cops, their hard bodies stretching crisp tan uniforms, burst through a side door and jerked to attention.

Mendoza charged them with their task. "This agent requires assistance with an arrest in F Concourse, Number 17. You will back up and then escort the perpetrator to the quiet room in that quarter. I will instruct Corporal Garcia to meet you there. Secure the perimeter during the detention and allow no gawkers or cameras. Understood?"

They snapped heels and shouted in unison. "Yes, Sergeant!"

37

LEON WHITMORE

Tuesday, 14 July, 5:14 P.M.
Terminal B, Concourse 4
Prat International Airport
Barcelona
Spain

Ellen took Mateo's call as she deplaned in Barcelona. He was on his way to Howard's departure gate with the young policemen in tow.

He hurried his words. "Ellie. I'm in Te Cuatro. Hendershot's headed for JFK. I bet the brothers are going there too. I'd check those flights first. Leon should be easy to make. Chunky, with sandy hair and granny glasses. Malmut said baggy jeans and a blue Polo."

"I remember," Ellen said. "I'll call when I know something. Good luck!"

Ellen had no badge or other pretense of authority and she'd never seen the man she was after, but she thought he'd stick out, especially with the green carry-on. Scanning the departures monitor, she found one JFK flight. Sure enough, when she went to that gate she spied a tubby kid dressed as Malmut described waiting in an adjacent gelato line. The bag was on his shoulder.

She'd dreamed up her con on the flight from Granada and it was time to find a cop. Returning to the central corridor, she saw two officers strolling in tandem, hands clasped on their rumps and eyes hunting. Slipping between kiosks, she yanked a shirttail, sloshed her eyes with Visine, and rushed up from behind.

Ellen bawled in her best Madrileña accent. "Señores! Help me, please. I've been violated, and robbed."

The cops about-faced. "Señorita, what happened?" asked the tall one.

She pointed. "I was over there, waiting for my flight. A man reached from behind and grabbed my breasts." She illustrated. "When I covered myself, he snatched my bag and ran. It happened just now. He's plump, in jeans and blue shirt. My bag is green canvas with brown trim."

Off they ran, one cop yapping into his shoulder radio. She watched the arrest and then approached as they spread the cursing Leon on the floor.

"Oh, thank you, officers. You're so brave!" she exclaimed. "And my bag?"

They handed it to her. Leon felt a boot on his back when he objected. She laid the backpack on a chair and rifled through it as if to check that her things were there. There were snacks, veterinary magazines, and a Kindle, but no scrolls.

One officer led Leon away as the other guided Ellen on his arm. "We must report, Señorita. An interview is required, and there are forms to sign."

"Yes," Ellen said, "but I can't miss my flight."

"We'll be as quick as we can," said the cop, "but must follow procedure."

38

CORPORAL GARCIA

Tuesday, 14 July, 7:35 P.M.
Quiet Room, Terminal 4, Concourse F
Barajas Airport
Madrid
Spain

Mateo figured that Howard Hendershot would protrude above the Spaniards in the boarding area, but there was no sign of the tall man as he approached Gate 17. Facing the wall and pretending to text, he was afraid he'd been made when the boarding calls came—still no sign of Hendershot—but with the final announcement Howard and his green bag appeared. The Apache queued behind.

Howard glanced around and recognized Mateo. He glared and then walked straight to Officer Gallegos, pleading as he gestured toward Mateo. The policemen escorted him down the concourse, shaking their heads as if to understand. Reaching the corridor's hub, they turned sharply left where a third officer with corporal's stripes was waiting. He showed all three through an unmarked door. Gallegos emerged to stand guard and allowed Mateo to pass.

The trap was sprung, but the yarn Mateo concocted for the sergeant had one too many details.

"Officer Barefoot, Señor. I am Corporal Garcia, at your service. Ortega is preparing your prisoner for interrogation. Sergeant Mendoza told me to tell you that he has contacted your agency as well as the ETA task force. Their men will arrive shortly."

Mateo went queasy. When he'd mentioned ETA, the archenemy of Spanish lawmen, Sergeant Mendoza alerted his superiors. All he could do was play cool.

"Thank you, Officer Garcia. Did you find anything in the perp's carry-on?"

"You may look for yourself," Garcia answered.

Mateo opened the green bag and found the same as Ellen—personal effects.

"How about the checked bag?" Mateo asked.

"The usual. No contraband." the cop said.

Ortega emerged from the interrogation room and declared the prisoner ready. Before entering, Mateo made an appeal. "I may have to be hard on this guy, if you know what I mean."

"Yes," Garcia said. "If you must. These animals can only be dealt with in kind. But please, leave as few marks as possible, and none on the face or neck. There will be photos."

Mateo entered the square room. With padded walls and ceiling, a rectangular mirror filled the far wall, a fisheye camera hung in the near corner, and a metal table was bolted in the center with chairs tucked beneath. Mateo knew he had only minutes to extract the truth before the real authorities showed up. The smirking Howard leaned against the table, naked and with wrists cuffed behind. Mateo dragged him to the wall by the curlies, compressing his neck with a forearm. Taking Howard's scrotum in the other hand, he fingered the testicles as a boy does marbles.

"I'll bust both of 'em if I have to," Mateo growled.

Howard laughed in his face. "You don't know who you're dealin' with, Geronimo. An' you're bluffin'—this izzin' Texas." He looked to the mirror. "They won't let you..."

"Y'don't think so?" Mateo said. "Let's see."

He squeezed the lower gonad. The tall man grimaced.

"Go ahead, Hendershot. Holler and see if they come. They know you're ETA!"

"What?" said Howard, eyes popping.

"E-T-A!" Mateo shouted in Spanish. "E-T-A!"

Both men knew that linking Howard to the Basque cop-killers would allow for any behavior. Mateo squeezed harder and Howard howled.

"Whadda you know, your assholiness?" Mateo mocked. "Looks like Don Quijote's not coming. How 'bout some more?" He squeezed even harder. "I'll pop this one first. They'll be no little saints coming outta you!"

"All right, Indian, all right!"

Mateo kept a crab claw on the testicle. "You have one minute to tell. Where are they?"

"Jasper's got what you want, in his bag, but it's too late, Redskin. I gave *him* the tight connection. He's over the Atlantic by now. An' don't bother tryin' to stop him. We've got six gorillas at JFK, bigger than you." He laughed. "I knew you pagans wouldn't go for Heathrow."

Mateo responded with a final squeeze that ended in a sharp popping sound as the testicle's capsule ruptured. Hendershot squealed and collapsed to the floor. "That's for Emilio," Mateo said, looking down with a sneer.

He knocked on the door and Garcia let him out.

"Impressive, Señor. Well done." said Garcia. "You were quite effective with your hand. We use a device, just as persuasive but more difficult to apply."

Mateo nodded. "Thanks, Corporal, but I've got to go. The lead's hot."

"No, sir, por favor." objected Garcia. "You must wait here. There are papers to complete, and Señor Lefevre wants to debrief you."

"Lefevre?"

"Yes, Inspector Lefevre of the ETA task force," the corporal said. "He's bringing your department representative, Señor Horton. They were unaware of your mission. Apparently you neglected to report in."

"Oh yeah, Horton." Mateo said. "I didn't have time, but this can't wait. I'll file the damned papers tomorrow."

Garcia crossed his arms and straddled the narrow hallway. "I must insist," he said. "The inspector was disturbed. It will be only minutes—he's on his way up."

Mateo faked a smile. Ortega stood behind Garcia with jaws clenched and legs equally wide. Suddenly a loud crash came from behind, and then another, and another. The interrogation room door bulged each time Hendershot rammed it. Garcia moved to quiet him and Mateo saw his chance, making a swim move on Ortega as he grabbed the doorknob. Bursting out, he collided with the arriving officials and stumbled away.

Mateo knew there'd be no escape. In seconds a string of cops was in pursuit. Determined to give Ellen the news, he dashed down the concourse, rushed to the rear of a Tapas bar and locked himself in the ladies' room before punching her number.

She answered. "Mateo?"

He shouted over the screaming woman on the toilet. "Ellie! I got to Hendershot, but he doesn't have 'em and I'm about to get busted! The scrolls are with Jasper, on the way to JFK. Have you heard from Malmut?"

"Not a word. I don't know if he got a phone," she said.

"Dammit! Let Parkinson know what's happening. Howard said there'd be six CREPT men waiting, so he'll have to have more. And tell him to get the boss to spring me."

Ellen jerked the phone away, reacting to the explosive sound of the steel ram as it shattered the rest room door. Easing it back to her ear, she heard a splash and then, nothing.

39

LEON WHITCOLMB

Tuesday, 14 July, 8:08 P.M.
Security Center
El Prat International Airport
Barcelona
Spain

Ellen phoned the professor from a toilet stall in the locker room of Barcelona Airport Security. It rang ten times before he answered.

"Paul Parkinson."

"It's Ellen Shea, Professor."

"Yes, Shea. For God's sake. What the devil's going on? We can't reach Mateo."

She recited the facts. "We're onto the scrolls. One of the CREPT boys has them and he's on his way to New York. Write this down, Professor. His name is Jasper Whitcolmb. W-h-i-t-c-o-l-m-b, Jasper. He flew to Heathrow from Granada and connected to JFK. Jasper's thin, twenty-two or three, with sandy hair. Tan slacks with a Navy sport coat and bow tie, Malmut said. The scrolls are in his carry-on: green canvas with wide leather straps. Mateo didn't say which airline, but there can't be that many flights from Heathrow at this hour." She paused. "And he said a gang of CREPT men would be waiting. Six, he said."

Parkinson interrupted. "I can't believe that you—"

She spoke over him. "Professor! We don't have time. Just get the scrolls. You can beat on me soon enough. I'll get to New York as fast as I can. As for Mateo, he's been arrested in the Madrid airport. Let Smith know right away."

"But—"

"Just get Jasper Whitcolmb—Heathrow to JFK—then Mateo." She hung up.

Ellen was shown to a chair outside the commander's office. She struggled to stay awake as she watched Leon's interrogation through the glass. He was shackled to a chair with two shouting cops circling and another rifling through his suitcase. No scrolls. As they finished, one cop thrust Leon's glowing cellphone in his face. At last they led him out the door where he swore and spit at Ellen, earning a sharp backhand from one of the cops.

The authorities had been more than kind to Ellen. A female officer was at her side from the beginning, offering everything from coffee to Valium. After an interview ending with her signature on a half-dozen oaths, Ellen was released. She dumped the green bag and booked the last middle seat on British Airways.

Her plane landed early. She called Parkinson from her taxi on the way to the Bronx. "Professor? Ellen Shea. Did you get the scrolls?"

"No, Shea, we did not. Your Jasper did not show. The airline indicates that he landed as scheduled in London, but did not connect. We're searching. Come to the library immediately. Mr. Smith requires your presence."

"About an hour, if I can get a cab," she said.

"Very well," Parkinson responded.

She phoned Monsignor Brahaney. This time he answered his cell.

"Monsignor, It's Ellen. The Quelle scrolls are in London. I need your help."

"Jesus, Mary, and Joseph!" exclaimed Monsignor. "I'll pack my things."

40

THE PROSECUTOR

Wednesday, 15 July, 4:07 P.M.
Astor Faculty Lounge
New York Public Library, Manhattan Branch
43rd Street and Fifth Avenue, New York City
USA

The mood in the lounge during Ellen's second visit was opposite the first. At least it started that way. Parkinson offered no greeting or refreshment. They sat as before, with the harsh lamp burning between them and their boss in the shadows. It was a show trial with the professor as prosecutor.

"We were deeply disappointed to learn of your failure, Miss Shea, and require details. Mateo will soon be released thanks to Mr. Smith's diplomatic associates, but we've been unable to speak with him. The airport police released the Hendershot chap when CREPT made a fuss and we followed him to the Urology Clinic in Hospital San Juan, but he slipped away. The brother you duped in Barcelona is in a wicket—he's been charged with 'bestiality'—it seems there were selfies from the zoo on his phone. As of this hour, your Jasper is at large in London. Our men are scouring the city, but it's a big haystack." Parkinson stepped to the tea table. "We require particulars, Miss Shea."

She replied with a cogent synopsis, chronologic and free of excuses. Ellen peeped toward the corner, but the boss was as still as Boabdil's statue. She expressed regret and accepted blame but was short of contrite. Her description disturbed the professor.

"Amazing! How could you?" he said, rattling his cup. "And I never thought Mateo would fail us. How could he leave the scrolls unguarded? You appear to have been an undue distraction, Miss Shea. I was afraid that might happen." He turned to the boss. "No doubt the artifacts are in the churchmen's hands. They may have already destroyed them."

Once again, he'd pushed past the pale. "Stop whining, Professor," Ellen scolded. "We have a good man on Jasper."

Parkinson's snout fibrillated. "The young Arab thief? You've got to be joking. He'll have the scrolls for himself. A fine state of affairs you've left us. If the church cartel doesn't destroy them, they'll be on the Arabian market. You can be sure the Wahhabis will have them. They're more taken with the Virgin Mary than the mackerel snappers... Not what we'd hoped for, Miss Shea. Not what we'd hoped for at all."

She trumped his clichés. "Maybe, but it's not over 'til it's over, Professor. I'll jump the next flight to London. When you hear from Mateo, send him to me. And by the way, Malmut's *Berber*, not Arab."

"See here, Miss Shea! I don't care if the bugger's from Mars. *We* shall decide what happens now. Perhaps we'll dispatch someone competent."

Ellen jumped to her feet, directing her anger to the dark corner. "Forgive me, sir, but I have to be crude." She gestured toward Parkinson. "I'm afraid the Professor's had his head up his ass for so long that the fumes have affected his brain. We're the only ones who can get the job done, I think that's clear. Do *you* want me to proceed?"

The boss didn't hesitate. "Yes. We'll arrange for accommodations in the West End. Tell the airport cabbie to take you to the Ritz in Mayfair."

With that, he stood and emerged into the glare, revealing himself as he fastened his coat.

41

STEPHEN PARISER

Wednesday, 15 July, 4:30 P.M.
Astor Faculty Lounge
New York Public Library, Manhattan Branch
42nd Street and Fifth Avenue, New York City
USA

I've seen this guy before, Ellen thought as the boss approached with his hand extended.

His eyes held hers immediately. In an Italian pinstripe and patterned silk tie, he was thickset but trim and no taller than Ellen. The thick gray hair was styled, flowing back and over petite ears. His tanned face was youthful if altered, the expression earnest and engaging, the eyes soulful and Basset Hound sweet. *On the wrong side of sixty*, she guessed.

He shook her hand as he spoke to Parkinson without looking.

"May we have a few minutes, Paul?"

A scowl spread from Parkinson's spastic nose. "But I insist—"

Pariser cut him off. "Paul... Not now."

"I'll be outside," Parkinson snarled, still scowling at Ellen as he closed the louvered doors. She Cheshire-smiled back.

The boss showed Ellen to her seat and pulled the opposing chair close, taking his seat with their knees nearly touching. Once settled, his eyes rarely left hers.

"Are you sure you want to go back to Europe, Miss Shea? You've learned the hard way how dangerous it can be. And our chances? Despite your optimism, I'm afraid they can't be that good... Forgive me, but I'm curious. You seem to be the adventuresome type, but now that you know of the risk, is it the money that drives you? The reward?"

Ellen made a face. "Gilbert and Sullivan, sir. They said it best."

"They did?" he asked, cocking his head.

"Yes sir, in *H.M.S. Pinafore.* 'Things are seldom as they seem; Skim milk masquerades as cream.'"

He chuckled. "Oh, yes. Sorry. I'm afraid I've grown callous. In my business there's no room for... Forgive me, Miss Shea."

"That's okay. I didn't mean to sass, but to answer your question? I can't stop now. We had the scrolls in our hands just hours ago and it's been such, well, such an adventure, like you say. I made you a promise in May, and I'm going to keep it. It's the Quelle, sir, and it's real."

"I see," he said. "I should've known. Mateo speaks so well of you."

She smiled small. "As for our chances? I wouldn't sell Malmut Adjani short. He's as bright as any of us and twice as resourceful. Jasper Whitcolmb won't lose him easily." She remembered Mateo's comment about the man's garrulous nature. "May I ask you the same question, sir? What's your interest in the scrolls? Are you a collector?"

He chuckled. "A collector? No, I'm not a collector. Whatever we find will end up in the Huntington Library, in San Marino, alongside the Chaucer and Gutenberg displays, I'd guess. It's where the Dead Sea Scrolls were published, just a block from my California home. I'll be able to visit whenever I like."

He rose and stepped to the coffee table. "Would you join me for tea?"

"Yes, please. Earl Grey, two sugars."

The boss served her like a butler, bending stiff from the waist with a napkin across his forearm as he stirred perfectly level teaspoons. Ellen supposed him to be like the Monsignor, immune to her charm attack, so she put it in neutral.

He blew gently over his brew before taking a taste as he slouched into the chair with elbows flexed and cradling the cup. "My name is Stephen. Stephen Pariser. May I call you Ellen?"

"I prefer 'Ellie' with friends," she said.

"Okay, Ellie. I can see why Mateo's so taken. Like my mother's Yiddish proverb, 'Charm is more than beauty.' He's told me quite a bit, you know. We like to gossip. It's my only honest vice."

He took a second sip, breathed from the belly, and launched a monologue.

"To answer your question, I'm looking for the Quelle because I'm a Jew, and being a Jew defines me, something I denied all my life, but something I now know is true. You've heard the story—penniless survivors flee to America with their baby boy, looking for a new life but all the while clinging to their old one— my parents, exactly. I grew up on the lower East side, near Bellevue, memorizing Talmud and enduring my father's soppy interpretations. I got sick of it—couldn't wait to escape New York and leave it all behind. I didn't realize then, but I was carrying it with me, buried deep inside, complex and strong as I was."

Again he sipped and smiled across. It could have been her grandfather.

"I got lucky in L.A. Everyone tells me what a whiz kid I was, but that's baloney. I was in the right place at the right time, and met just the right people. No more than that." He grinned. "Well, an ear to the public, twenty-hour days, and a dose of chutzpah had something to do with it, I suppose. We produced a lot of films, a few that made sense, and once I got control of the studio, and then the network? ... I didn't have a spiritual life in those days, unless you count my arguments with Saul Bellow." He chuckled. "In any event, I liked being a Hollywood big shot, but I didn't know happiness until I met Julia. She was my life for thirty years, the best thirty years, and I never thought it would end." He sighed and looked away. "But then she changed, Ellie, all at once it seemed, into another being—someone we didn't know—someone capable of evil. Julia destroyed our family trying to destroy me, and then ... our darling daughter took her life." His wounded eyes returned. "I was lost, Ellie, a zombie. My faith left me and I drifted, dulling the pain in the usual ways, but then, for the life of me I can't say why, the passages I'd learned as a boy popped into my head—at work, in my dreams, everywhere. It was soothing, and I began to heal... Am I boring you, Ellie? Is this too much?"

"Not at all, Stephen. Thanks so much for sharing," Ellen said.

Pariser nodded. "I took time off to study, the Gemara at first. Kept a flat in Jerusalem to be near the scholars. They're different, Ellie, Abraham's academics—Jews, Christians, and Muslims—they're dedicated, but it's strange. The longer they're at it, the more they drift away.

"Then I got hooked on Messianic scripture, from Pentateuch on. There's so much—Moses, Isaiah, David—and none of it's the same. I got curious about the men who claimed to be the Messiah. There were a lot of them, an odd lot. Don't get me wrong, Ellie, I'm no Jew-for-Jesus, but I wondered why, that among all the Messiahs, he was the one the world followed. It was obvious the answers weren't in the New Testament—it's been homogenized beyond recognition—but I wondered about the Quelle. Did you know, Ellie, that the people who made the Quelle thought of themselves as good Jews? Anyway, I've fantasized about finding it ever since. It's filled the void. And when Paul Parkinson showed me that 'Hierophant' parchment?" He shook his head. "Since then we've spared no expense, and why should we?

"Sorry for all the hot air, Ellie. It's a weakness. But this time I have an excuse: I don't run into a good listener very often."

Ellen leaned forward and took his hands. "Thank you for telling, Stephen. It's a wonderful story. Now I understand."

He called through the door for Parkinson. They discussed strategies for recovery of the scrolls and at the end Ellen turned to Pariser.

"One more thing, sir. With your permission, I'd like to have an expert with me in England. Monsignor James Brahaney."

"Good god!" shrieked Parkinson.

Pariser hushed him with a palm. "Sure, good idea. Everyone knows of the monsignor. I met him once, after his lecture at Tel Aviv University, though I doubt he'll remember. Of course, we'll cover expenses."

"Thank you, Stephen. I'll call him right now."

She fingered her cell as she hurried down the hall, chatting excitedly when she reached the priest. As before, the men stood in the doorway and watched her disappear.

Pariser quipped. "I like the girl even more now, Paul, and I'm enjoying the show. She's right, you know—she and the first American are all we've got—along with the petty thief and thorny old priest. Quite a cast you've assembled!"

Parkinson smoldered as Pariser turned with a snicker.

"And the fumes, Paul. They must be awful."

The professor's proboscis had a grand-mal seizure.

42

MONSIGNOR IN WONDERLAND

Wednesday, 15 July, 11:25 P.M.
Virgin Atlantic Queen of the Skies
Runway 4L, JFK Airport
Queens, New York
USA

The old Jesuit fiddled with his footrest, adjusted the neck cushion, and then beamed at his star student as they waited for the jetliner's doors to close. Ellen knew that particular happy face. It meant he had something to say.

"I'm surprised that asshole Parkinson didn't scuttle my trip," Monsignor said. "He doesn't like priests to begin with, and I'm afraid I've embarrassed him one too many times. The son of a bitch keeps score."

"I didn't ask his permission, Monsignor. I asked our boss, and he didn't blink."

"Oh. Did you tell the boss why you wanted me to tag along? And did you tell him about the al-Hakkam translation?"

"He knows why we need you," she answered. "But no, I couldn't tell him about the book. I wanted to, but I knew Parkinson was listening through the louvers. Stephen and I had a wonderful talk, just like Mateo said we would. I really like the guy. You would, too, Monsignor. He says he's met you, and if I didn't know better, I'd think you two came from the same cradle.

"And you were right about Parkinson. He's something else," she said. "I don't trust the S.O.B... The guy's a friggin' reptile."

"My classification exactly," said the priest as his mug changed to bothered.

"What's wrong, Monsignor?"

"It's your language, my child. It seems to become more *earthy* in my presence. I'm afraid I'm a bad influence."

"No shit!" she replied.

They laughed from below and then wisecracked over lift-off martinis before retreating to their own spaces. Still shy on sleep, Ellen dropped off when they reached altitude, dreaming of times past. Turbulence woke her at the Iceland break, interrupting a family swim in her grandfather's pond. Every day something reminded her of the man she called Granddad, the person whose wisdom mattered most. She liked to tease him, and the monsignor was his proxy that night. After asking for tea she lit the reading light, donned cotton gloves, and extracted Hakkam's book from the zip-lock in her bag. The priest was feigning sleep, his head tilted toward her with one eye slitted, but Ellen wasn't fooled. She flipped the tome open, shielding it from his view.

A few minutes later, she pretended to wake him. "Monsignor," she said, shaking his shoulder, "I'm reading the Hakkam translation. Would you like to join me?"

They leaned in to share the treasure, each with a gloved hand. For her knowledge of Arabic Ellen was mentor, and she delighted in the role reversal. Their dialog was energized and intricate, spiced with arcane banter and gentle disagreements. Then, triggered by a poignant parable and through the turbines' white noise, she confided in the priest as never before.

"You know, Monsignor, the first time I read from this book, I tried to think of others who wrote something like it. The Greeks came to mind, and a few poets. The irony made me think of Shakespeare. But I decided there was no comparison, nothing close." She paused. "We're not in the pews now, Monsignor, but it's time for my confession... I stopped thinking that Christ was divine when I was twelve, the day I discovered Darwin. I'm Catholic because it suits my family, because I'm comfortable with the rituals and inspired by the traditions, and by people like you and my mom. But I haven't believed since the sixth grade, and lately, with the news of the abuse and cover-ups?" She stared into the seatback. "The new pope's not enough."

"Go on, my dear."

"Since then I've been looking for another way, and no kidding, I think I've tried them all. For a while I thought meditation was the answer. It's all my Granddad needs, but for him the method's become the goal, I think. Not for me. I make my quiet time every day and couldn't stay sane without it, but... well, I don't think I've got the God gene, Monsignor. I don't know if I *can* believe. Maybe I'm a nonester. Maybe I don't need a religion, or maybe I need them all. But since my all-nighter with this damned little book, it's been strange. The passages are stuck in my head, like a jingle. I haven't felt this way since I was a little girl."

He gave his kindest face. "Do you think I haven't known, my dear? I was in that same place, for a long time. There're so many like us, but not all have the good fortune to be awakened as I was, and perhaps as you will be. May I suggest that you approach it ontologically?"

"Ontologically?"

"Yes. Think of the old maxim about proving a negative, Ellie—it can't be done—and it follows that one can never be sure about God. Your paradox is that as a scientist you're conditioned to seek the answer, not let it come to you. Your discipline allows for all but your soul to speak, and that's as it should be—you're a scholar, in the tradition of Erasmus and Ehrman—not a spiritualist. But reason and science don't always contradict faith and religion. Sometimes they harmonize... This time, Ellie, this one time, you have to let your mind pass into what for you is an unnatural place: a place of patience, where the immaterial can reveal itself without analysis. Perhaps you'll construct some new hypotheses, my dear. Who knows? This may be your hour as it once was mine, when the mystic begets the real. What do you have to lose? I won't presume, but this whole thing seems like one hell of a coincidence—that café owner, your friend, holding the scrolls all that time? Can that be happenstance?"

She didn't answer.

"The question for me has never been whether God exists," said the priest. "Creation tells us there has to be a greater power, or spirit, or mana—whatever the hell you call it. The tough questions are whether God is watching, and if He is, whether He intervenes or even cares to. And there's the big one: whether He wants us to be with Him at the end. We wait all our lives for that answer, and for most it never comes."

She turned to the window and looked across, at Orion. The priest feared he'd gone too far, but soon she returned, teary-eyed.

"They all think I'm so together, Monsignor, 'the steel blonde' they call me—but I'm not—it's an act, and I have to work at it, really hard sometimes ... like when my parents died. Everyone said how controlled I was, but I was acting, like always. I wish I had the easy kind of faith, Monsignor, the blind kind. The kind my granddad and Emilio have, or even that bastard Howard Hendershot. They're like children, at play with life, content with whatever it brings them because they know, or think they know, what happens after. They don't have the emptiness that comes with doubt, and they don't even have to try. I envy their peace, and their purpose, things I'm afraid I'll never have. People with that kind of faith make me jealous, and angry sometimes."

He nodded. "How do you know they don't struggle, just like you?" said the priest. "Take Mother Teresa.

Everyone thought she was a rock of faith, but she doubted every word, up to her last breath. Hell, I'm as good an example as any—some days I have to talk myself into it. Most thinkers would admit to the same. You've seen it before, Ellie, in Augustine and Saint Francis. Have you read Bonhoeffer or Kierkegaard? They said you have to doubt Jesus before you can believe, that not knowing's a necessity. The fact is that faith's not that easy for most people, and it's downright hard for the rest of us."

They returned to the book, parsing each passage as children do candy. Both wished for more time, but as the airliner descended Ellen stowed the book in her handbag. She fussed as they landed, waiting for a cellphone signal. When it came she tapped the Europhone and sure enough, what she'd hoped for was there: a text from Malmut, in English.

"with fast talk boy & green bag. bond street. no crusaders. please to call. 07477-83202."

"Yes!" she shouted.

She fingered the number. A woman answered, loud and Cockney.

"'Ello!"

"Yes, hello," Ellen said. "I'm answering a text from this number."

"'Oo's this? I don' do textin'," said the squealing voice.

"Well, I received one from this number," Ellen replied.

"Pro'ly was tha' bloody li'le san' monkey tha' stole m'phone," the lady declared. "I thaw' 'ee was cute, but 'ee was fleecin' m' mobile while we cha'ed! The Bobbies jus' give i' back. They gaw' the tea leaf a' th' West End lockup. Y'need ta' talk wi' th' coppers."

43

SERGEANT CROWNINGSHIELD

Thursday, 16 July, 12:40 P.M.
Harrison's Uniform Shop
612 Adelaide Road
London
England

The monsignor hadn't packed a collar, so they stopped at a uniform shop to trade his slacks and polo shirt for a parson's outfit, Canterbury cap included. Their intent was to spring Malmut, and Ellen wanted him to look the part. She bought him a prepaid phone while he was being fitted, and when she returned to the shop, Brahaney had donned the uniform.

"At last!" he declared when she entered, beaming as he brushed the sleeves, "I've always envied the Episcopalians. Can't wait to have sex again."

The jailhouse seemed out of place: a featureless brick box in a tony part of the city. It took ten minutes to reach the officer in charge. Monsignor held the cap to his chest as he launched his pitch with a leprechaun's grin and his mother's Irish brogue.

"Constable, m'dear sir. I'm Jim Brahaney, from St. Anne's Mission in Belfast. We're in need of yer' assistance."

"The name's Crowningshield, Vicar, *Sergeant* Crowningshield, if you please."

"Yes. God bless you, Constable!" said Monsignor. "We understand you have one of our African boys in custody. He's quite naughty, a mischievous lad, but he's no lawbreaker. We've been told there was a mix-up, something about a stolen mobile? Impossible with his weak mind, you must agree. It's his first time away from the mission, and he's as confused as a Viking in church."

"A name, please, yer Excellency," said the sergeant.

Ellen piped up. "Adjani, sir, Malmut Adjani. He just turned seventeen."

The cop looked askance at Ellen and then back to Monsignor. "Yes, yer honor, I remember the youngster. Processed 'im m'self last evenin'. Just a moment."

He disappeared through a swinging door and returned minutes later, dragging Malmut by the arm. The Rascal was drowning in gray overalls, his sleeves and pant legs rolled up and secured with rubber bands. The sergeant shooed him around.

Ellen rushed up, pretending to scold while Brahaney worked the policeman.

"Oh, bless you, Constable Crowningshield. His mother will be so relieved. She was good enough to put her trust in us, and now this has happened. I'm b'side m'self with shame. We shall be out of yer hair directly."

"Just a sec', Reverend," said the cop. "I'm afraid his mum won't be feelin' any relief just yet. Forgive me for sayin' it, but the boy's got yer eminence bamboozled. The bugger was carryin' two stolen mobiles, three forged passports, and near four hundred Euros. He may be daft, but he's smart enough to text. He's on the docket for theft and immigration violations, Monday next, and the Queen herself couldn't change that. Sorry, Vicar, but he'll be stayin' with us."

Monsignor objected. "Oh, dear! But his handicap is mental, Constable. It makes the lad act like a pack rat or cowbird—he'll grab anything shiny!"

"All the same, Father, birdbrain or not, he's with us 'til Monday. I imagine they'll release 'im to yer custody 'cause of his age, but there's none ta' be done just now. If you care to chat, I'll let him dally, but just a minute or two."

Malmut told Ellen that Jasper Whitcolmb taxied from the airport to a youth hostel in the West End, *Parley Apartments*. Straightaway he made rounds in the antique book shops on Bond and Curzon Streets. Malmut had no chance to grab the bag. He was watching Jasper through the front window of Abrams' Antiquities when he was arrested.

"Time's up!" shouted Crowningshield.

Ellen whispered in Malmut's ear as she hugged him. "Don't say a word."

The cop led him away. With yawning eyes he looked over his shoulder, straining for a smile as the door swept shut.

44

JASON WHITMORE

Thursday, 16 July, 2:25 P.M.
Adelaide Road & Stafford Street
London
England

They exited the jail in a rush.

Ellen questioned the priest as she flagged a cab. "Are you thinking what I am?"

"Yes, my dear. Your Jasper's a renegade. He'll sell the scrolls and run."

"To the hostel?"

"A good place to start," said Monsignor.

"I'll call Parkinson," she said as they ducked into the taxi. "He'll have a cow if we don't tell him right away."

Parkinson answered immediately.

"It's Ellen Shea, Professor. Good news. Put Malmut Adjani on the payroll. He's been on Jasper until a few hours ago, and there's a surprise: Jasper's on the run, alone and hawking the scrolls. He's staying at a youth hostel, *Parley Apartments*, Malmut said. We're on the way there now."

Parkinson yammered. "Yes! Excellent. I know the bloody place. Hold nothing back. Mateo's been released and is en route to London. I'll be there by morning."

"Okay," she answered. "Tell Mateo what's happening."

"What of the priest?" Parkinson asked. "Is he getting in the way?"

"The opposite!" she snapped. "He's the reason we got to Malmut and found out about Jasper."

"Complete your task, Miss Shea!" he screeched. "I shan't be as forgiving as our employer. If what you say is true, CREPT will be searching for this Jasper fellow as well. Don't—"

She hung up.

Jasper's accommodations were pleasant if run down: a post-blitz three-story apartment house converted into a youth hostel. It was cheap, communal living with common baths across from tiny bedrooms. They walked through the scruffy lobby to the registration desk with the monsignor again on point.

"Good day, young man. Could you tell me if one of my lost sheep is in house? Mr. Jasper Whitcolmb?"

The clerk found no such name, but Monsignor peered over and read upside down, noting a "Jason Whitmore" signature.

"Can you tell me of another lad? Jason Whitmore?"

The clerk's description of the bow-tied young man and his green knapsack left no doubt: Jasper was in Room 341.

"Is young Whitmore here?" asked Monsignor.

"Couldn't say, Reverend. The guests keep their keys, and he's paid 'til Sunday. Should I tell him his Vicar called?"

"Oh, no. I would very much like to surprise him," said the priest.

There was no answer when they knocked on Jasper's door. Ellen and the monsignor talked it over as they came down the stairs.

"He's out selling the scrolls," she said.

"Probably," said Monsignor. "It's almost three. I know the Bond street shops and most of their owners, so I'll get over there. You could stay here in case he comes back."

"Okay. I'll hide in this dingy lobby and call if he shows up. Is your phone working?"

"Radio check," said the priest, his arthritic fingers fumbling as he punched her number. Her cell sounded on the third try.

Ellen chose a ragged recliner facing the picture windows, recessed between the cracked plaster of a pillar and a dusty plastic plant. From that niche she could see all who walked by on the street and anyone entering the hostel. Taking a *Daily Mirror* from the rack, she settled into the lumpy chair.

45

CLYDE C. TAFT, IV

Thursday, 16 July, 5:55 P.M.
Taft & Bonham's
11215 Bond Street
London
England

London's Bond Street has no equal. In the blocks surrounding that boulevard cluster a matchless mix of fine-art shops, chic galleries, and rare book stores, all high-brow and trying for higher. A half-century before, as a doctoral candidate at Oxford College, the monsignor-to-be lived in the district, bunking above the store where he clerked. He'd returned many times to lecture in West Hall and had been the dealers' darling for decades.

But that day Monsignor Brahaney found a cold trail and his fame backfired. Greeted by admirers and old acquaintances, he had to wade through a patronizing parade of boastful introductions in each shop. He confirmed that Jasper had been through the day before, but none had seen him that day. The dealers disbelieved Jasper's pitch, especially when he refused to leave a sample, and to their displeasure he preached as he hawked the scrolls, his sanctimonious motor-mouth offending the straight laced Englishmen. All in all, he came off as a pious fraud, an opinion the monsignor was glad to reinforce.

The Jesuit was in Taft & Bonham's inner suite at closing time, forced to share single malt with the senior staff. The owner, one Clyde C. Taft IV, after an immodest toast about owning all of Monsignor's texts, described his meeting with Jasper.

"The chap was dressed like a common clerk. Argyle socks, no less," said Taft. "Thought he was from Harrods or Morley's until I heard the hillbilly accent. His presentation was as boorish as the clothes, and much too moral. I advised him to try Hyde Park." He guffawed. "And to suggest that he was toting antiquities of that caliber in a rucksack? Really. I allowed but a few minutes, suggesting he try the Piccadilly shops. He asked for directions and departed."

"Could we see if he took your advice, Clyde?" asked Monsignor. "Could you ring a colleague or two down there?"

"Very well," Taft answered. He ordered an assistant to make the calls.

Two toasts later, the man reported to his boss. "Indeed, Mister Taft, the young fellow has been rounding since morning, and sir, I must inform you: the chap's been using your name as reference."

With that news Monsignor downed the whiskey and excused himself. He tried to call Ellen on the way to Parley Apartments, but couldn't work the phone.

46

THE AVENGING ANGEL

Thursday, 16 July, 6:01 P.M.
Hallway 3 West, Parley Apartments
1066 Brook Street, Mayfair
London
England

Ellen idled in the lobby amid the other young faces as the minutes crawled by, scrutinizing all who passed. The priest had been away for three hours when she spotted a bow-tied young man scurrying down the opposite side of the street. On his back was a green bag like Leon's. She stepped to the window and saw panic on his face as he elbowed his way to the curb. *It's Jasper, all right, and he's running.*

He plunged into traffic, dodging fenders as he jaywalked, at last stumbling over the near curb in front of a braking lorry and pasting his nose against the glass, face to face and inches from Ellen. Pushing off and rushing to the entrance, he shouldered through the brass doors, gulped a huge breath, and ran for the stairs at the end of the lobby.

Ellen hurried to retrieve her phone and handbag, but turned again to the sound of horns and screeching tires. Coming fast and on the same route as Jasper was the reason for his haste. With athletic skill his reckless pursuer braved the steel gauntlet, straight-arming a Jaguar and leaping over the bonnet of a cab to land flatfooted on the sidewalk. It was Howard Hendershot, muscles taut and eyes on fire. He exploded through the entrance, looking in all directions as Ellen about-faced. Catching sight of Jasper's heels as they disappeared up the stairs, he chased. Ellen hustled after them, slowed by her short heels and skirt. She could hear Hendershot's loud rebuke as she approached the third floor landing.

"Jasper Whitcolmb! You devil! You turncoat! You thief! Why did you do it? For God's sake, why did you do it?" Howard screamed. "You're a traitor to me, to your brother, and to heaven! Your soul is damned forever! You cannot be forgiven!"

Ellen peered around the frame of the open doorway and recognized their profiles against the far window. Jasper was pinned to the wall by the taller man, his backpack wedged behind. Howard came down from his toes and touched his index finger to Jasper's nose, speaking at a much lower volume. Straining to hear, she inched into the corridor.

"You are Judas and I am the avenging angel," Howard said. "It's time you go back to hell."

She watched as Howard pressed the boy's shoulders against the pack, and the pack in turn against the wall. With elbows locked, the blonde boy bowed backward and in a blur launched his skull like a wrecking ball, butting Jasper's brow with a slushy thud. Then he cradled the unconscious boy's chin in his left hand, holding him upright. At once he drew the free hand away, measuring the distance from its heel to the base of the boy's nose with a first, second, and third practice blow. At last and with invisible speed he released the calloused hand, driving Jasper's nasal bones into his brain.

The boy slumped to the floor and seized. As the death tremors ebbed, Howard wiped his bloody palm on Jasper's coat and stripped the backpack away. The astounded Ellen inched backward as Howard inspected the pack, but again he felt her eyes on him and looked up. With no hesitation, he hooked the straps and came on the run.

Ellen kicked off her shoes and fled down the stairs, trying for the safety of the lobby. It wasn't close. Hendershot caught her on the deserted second floor landing. Grasping her forearm and using the green sack as counter-weight, he swung her body against the oak balusters and then back, into the wall, shattering the plaster and showering them with dust. He put the bag down and prepared for his second murder in as many minutes.

Dazed from the rag doll treatment, Ellen could only squirm as Hendershot forced her shoulders to the wall. He arched on his toes, arms stiff and diamond eyes ablaze, part one of his gruesome ritual.

"Ellen Shea! You she-devil! You temptress! You Papist! Why did you do it? For God's sake, why did you do it?" he shouted. "You're a traitor to me, to virtue, and to heaven! Your soul is damned forever! You cannot be forgiven!"

Then he calmed as before, descending to his heels as he touched a finger to her nose. His voice morphed to light.

"You are Jezebel and I am the avenging angel. It's time you go back to hell."

Squeezing her shoulders, he bowed cobra-like and delivered another precise head blow. She wilted limp. Identical to his last crime, with crimson cheeks and swollen pupils, he suspended Ellen's body by the chin and measured the distance to her nostrils. Once, twice, and a third time he aimed, at last releasing the immense killing power.

47

GERONIMO

Thursday, 16 July, 6:14 P.M.
Lobby Landing, Parley Apartments
1066 Brook Street, Mayfair
London
England

Slow-motion photography has documented the remarkable speed and explosive force of an expert Karate blow. The energy released can exceed that of a shotgun blast. Hendershot's precisely aimed thrust began its twenty-seven inch journey toward Ellen's nasal bridge with such power. In milliseconds the base of his hand would strike the leading tissues of her nose squarely, driving its bony bridge through the braincase to transect the frontal lobes of her cerebrum. But before the acceleration could peak, the stone-hard hand was deflected by a stronger vector, another more potent thrust, from an equally precise right angle. One hundred eighty pounds of wild-eyed Apache was behind it, redirecting Howard's blow into and through the fractured plaster.

The unconscious Ellen slithered between them onto the landing's linoleum as the free-for-all began.

Mateo had never faced such a fighter, his style balanced and brutal at once. He absorbed shots that would have dropped most men, opening gashes on both cheekbones. Mateo's skill was Brazilian jiu-jitsu, and he knew that if he could get Howard on the floor, the advantage would be his. He took a chance when Hendershot misfired with a glancing head butt, redirecting its momentum with a twisting bear hug. The big bodies cascaded in a roiling heap down the next flight of stairs, tumbling to rest in a clenched ball of sinew at the lobby landing. From there, Mateo was scorpion-like. Inside a second he locked Howard in a full-Nelson and then converted to a sleeper hold in which he could kink the carotid arteries at will. Howard knew he was about to die and tried to tap out, but Mateo's intent was clear. He began to twist.

At that moment both sets of eyes diverted upward toward Ellen's quaking cries. Lurching forward and near blinded by her bleeding forehead, she teetered on the steps and clutched the railing with one hand, diverting the oozing blood with the other to gain a brief, stinging look at the men.

"No! Mateo! Don't do it!" she cried. "Don't be like him! It's *just us* now!"

The Indian hesitated but did as she asked, in a blink relaxing the hold and cuffing his gasping foe to the corner post. He rushed to Ellen and lifted her into his arms, snaring the backpack in the same motion. Monsignor Brahaney arrived to join the lobby rats gawking up from the foot of the stairs, and as they reached the ground floor, Mateo handed the prize to the priest. He laid Ellen in the old chair, reclined it, and ordered the clerk to call for help. After mopping her forehead, he daubed the still weeping wound. Using his fingers, he combed Ellen's bloodied bangs from her face and tried to engage her eyes, but she was in some other place, fading in and out with each breath.

He turned to the fretful priest. "You should make yourself scarce, Monsignor. We wouldn't want to give them up now."

"Yes," said the priest. "I know just where to go... Take care of our Ellie. I love her, too, you know."

Brahaney exited with the green sack on his shoulder, standing aside as a bolus of Bobbies and paramedics rushed through the doors. They took charge. Mateo stepped to the window and watched as Monsignor crossed and disappeared into the Underground.

48

THE FIRST VISITOR

Friday, 17 July, 5:07 A.M.
Room 312, St. Anthony's Hospital
London Road, Sutton
London
England

Ellen's goose egg was as large as Emilio's, and she took more stitches. Her CAT scan was negative for bleeding on the brain but she was unsteady and terribly sleepy, so the doctors decided to watch her through the night. Mateo sported two shorter rows of sutures and was drowsing by her bedside when he was alerted by the familiar clacking of Parkinson's heels. He intercepted the professor in the doorway, whispering forcefully with a finger to his lips.

"Shhh. She's asleep. Not to be disturbed. Doctor's orders."

Parkinson rolled his eyes and signaled with a head wag toward the hall.

"Where are they?" demanded the professor. "Where are the bloody scrolls? And what happened to your face?"

"They're with the monsignor, but there's a problem," said Mateo.

"You're joking. You let that moldy old Jesuit have them? How could you?"

"He's the reason we got them in the first place. He and Malmut," said Mateo. "Don't worry. They're safe, and I can't think of a better watchdog."

"And what's the *problem*?" Parkinson scoffed.

"Looks like they're stolen goods."

"What?" Parkinson shouted.

Mateo schussed. "I told you to be quiet. *Stolen*, I said. I don't know the details, but they belong to a guy in Granada, someone Ellie's known for years. They were boosted from his apartment along with a bunch of other heirlooms."

Parkinson dismissed the news with a champion sneer. "Hah! That's ludicrous, but no matter. It was you Americans who made the saying trite—it's a British construct, you know."

"What the hell are you talking about, Parkinson?"

"Possession, my dear man, possession. It's nine-tenths the law. The scrolls are ours and shall remain so."

Mateo showed his teeth. "I didn't tell you *where* the monsignor is hiding."

He signaled for Parkinson to wait and then tiptoed to Ellen's bedside, adjusting her covers before returning to the hall. "Let's go to the hospital café and talk this out," Mateo said.

"There's no such thing, Barefoot. You're in England, not Texas."

"Well, let's 'take the air,' or whatever you Limeys do. She needs to rest."

They exited through Emergency and spotted a Costa Coffee across the street. White coats were arriving for the morning shift, and it quickly crowded. Collecting their cups, they moved to a high table in the front corner window, crouching on opposite stools. Mateo awaited Parkinson's opening salvo.

"Now see here, Barefoot. You're quite aware that you're contractually bound in Pariser's employ, and that you must comply with his wishes. As his surrogate, you must do as I ask. It's the law, and we shall hold you to it."

Mateo was in no mood. He leaned across the table, clenched Parkinson's tie in his fist, and drew him near. Opening wide, he expelled a moist cloud of lizard breath into Parkinson's nostrils. "You know damned well that no contract can be enforced if it crosses the criminal codes. Not even with *his* lawyers. And you're forgetting that Pariser trusts me more than you. Only one person will decide how this goes down, and she's asleep."

Mateo released him with a shove. The professor tottered backward and collapsed against the window. They launched frigid stares as he struggled upright, but before more words could pass, Parkinson's cellphone gonged and he pulled it from his vest. Mateo looked on, puzzled as the professor read the text and typed his answer. All of a sudden, he was in a hurry.

"We must talk to the bloody girl!" he shouted. "She has to be awake by now."

49

THE SECOND VISITOR

Friday, 17 July, 5:47 A.M.
Room 312, St. Anthony's Hospital
London Road, Sutton
London
England

When the men returned to Ellen's room, she was stirring but still asleep. At Mateo's direction, he and Parkinson took to chairs on either side of the bed. They dueled with frowns and scowls until Ellen was awakened by the duty nurse as she performed a neurologic check. Mateo stepped to the head of the bed when she finished and Parkinson rose on the other side. Still groggy, Ellen saw only the younger man. He took her hand.

"Do we have them, Mateo?" asked Ellen. "Do we have the scrolls?"

"Yes, Ellie. They're with Monsignor. A few got crumpled, but they're all there."

"And Malmut? Is he out of jail?"

"Not yet, but Monsignor's hired a barrister." Mateo leaned in. "Do you remember what happened yesterday, Ellie?"

Her head recoiled as visions of the murder flashed by. Staring glassy-eyed into the footboard, she recalled the horror in whispers. "Howard killed him. He killed that boy, right in front of me. There was nothing I could do. It happened so fast... He went into some kind of trance. It was creepy. He was going to do the same thing to me, Mateo. I don't know why he stopped. I was lucky."

"I know, Ellie, very lucky," said Mateo.

Parkinson couldn't resist. "I'm glad I had faith in you, Miss Shea. Well done."

Mateo grimaced as Ellen turned to the professor's baritone. "Professor Parkinson... Did Mateo tell you that we have the scrolls, and that they were stolen from my friend?"

"Yes, something to that effect," Parkinson said.

Ellen followed. "We'll have to negotiate with Emilio: Emilio Rodriguez. He's the rightful owner, and I'm not sure he'll want to sell."

Parkinson squinted. "Now see here. You don't think that after all this expense and effort, we would allow you to—"

Mateo reached across and seized the tie, yanking the lanky man over the bed, again nose to nose and arching over Ellen.

"This is a quiet zone," scolded Mateo. "Violators will be removed from the premises."

Then came a voice from the doorway. "Is there a problem, gentlemen?"

All looked to see the outline of a stooping man.

"You're not misbehaving again, are you, Paul?" the silhouette said.

Parkinson's lip curled. "Brahaney! You wretched fossil. What the devil are you doing here? And in that bloody uniform?"

"I've come t'see m'darlin', Paul. I might ask the same of you."

Mateo dragged Parkinson across the foot of the bed and on through the door. The monsignor stepped aside as he whipped the professor around and abruptly let go, slinging him face-first against the opposing wall. Parkinson stuck there like a tree frog, limbs wide with cheek and fingertips to the plaster.

"My goodness, Paul," Monsignor said as he approached. "You must have been a *very* bad boy."

Parkinson howled. "You old fool! I might have known that you'd find a way to weasel into my business. Did you give the girl an 'A' in 'Carnal Knowledge?'"

Mateo pounced, spinning Parkinson around and driving him into the wall with a forearm across his stretched neck.

Brahaney stepped close and on his toes whispered into the Englishman's ear. "You're still in the far place, aren't you, Paul, with your colleague, the Dark Prince?"

Mateo seized Parkinson's shoulders, jerked him sideward, and booted him down the hall. The professor staggered toward the nursing station, gasping with hands to his throat. Mateo led the monsignor to Ellen's bedside and gently kissed her on the cheek.

"Everything will be all right now, Ellie, I promise," Mateo whispered.

She smiled. "I know."

50

JUST US

Friday, 17 July, 1:10 P.M.
Parlor Suite 17, Ritz Hotel
150 Piccadilly
London
England

The recovering Ellen sat in a wheelchair at the foot of her bed, dressed and awaiting discharge. Her nurse arrived and read from a list of precautions before wheeling her to the elevator and hence to the taxi stand. She stared out the cab's window, straight-faced and silent all the way to the Ritz.

Uh-oh! Mateo thought. *Heaven knows what's coming...*

When they reached her hotel room, she asked him to take her to the balcony. Holding hands as they faced the jagged London skyline, Mateo eavesdropped on her stream of consciousness.

"What now?" she said softly. "Everything's changed... CREPT won't give up, and there's no telling what Adivar's New York boss will do. I have to get to Granada and explain things to Emilio. But how, without being seen?"

"I should go with you, Ellie. You're in no shape to travel alone."

"No," she said, "I'm okay, I really am, and I'll be better with another night's sleep. I have to do this on my own, Mateo."

"All right," he said. "There's an auto ferry from Portsmouth to Santander, on the north coast of Spain.

It sails every day. You can be in Granada tomorrow night if you make the right connections."

"Thanks," Ellen said. "Maybe I could use one of your disguises. Did you bring the Hawaiian shirt?" Her wit was back, along with more orders. "Tell the monsignor to sit tight, and make sure he springs Malmut. Help him all you can. When will you talk with Stephen?"

"Right away," Mateo said.

"Tell him everything," Ellen said. "Except about Hakkam's book. Not a word for now—I decided it's mine—I found it on my time and paid with my money. Tell him we'll be dealing directly with Emilio and that if he still wants the scrolls, it'll be at market price: eight-figures, I'd guess."

Mateo showed disappointment.

"What's wrong?" Ellen asked. "Do you think I'm being greedy?"

"No, that's not it at all. You're right—everything's changed—I'm done with Parkinson, and who knows, if he has anything to say, with Pariser." Mateo turned to her. "Like you said, Ellie, it's 'just us' now."

She faced him, grasping his forearms.

"Did I say that? I don't remember, but yes, it's been 'just us' for quite a while, and I like it that way, very much." She grinned. "Tell me something. Did you follow me home from Howard's place that night?"

"Sure," he answered. "Like I said, it's my job."

"Did you wonder why I stopped on the way, at that grungy apartment building on Calle Neptuno?

"Yeah..."

"It's where I lived as a student," she said. "I was paying an old debt, to my landlady."

"Oh," he whispered.

Neither apologized for their longest kiss.

They slept like spoons that night. At dawn Ellen slipped out through the hotel's service dock, chin down in a housekeeper's uniform Mateo had filched. He made sure that no one followed. She taxied to Portsmouth after picking up an outfit with a scarf big enough to cover the goose egg. The ferry made port in Cantabria that afternoon but all flights were booked, so she checked into the Casino hotel and then strolled on the strand before taking a meal and restful sleep. Ellen said hello to her old self in the morning mirror, disfigured but sure. Her connections were smooth and she landed in Granada that afternoon.

51

THE SALAZARS

Sunday, 19 July, 5:56 P.M.
Apt 203B, 44 Calle Colón
Granada
Spain

Ellen rang Emilio's bell a little before six. He buzzed her through and rushed down to the lobby. The Spaniard was alarmed by her appearance.

"Oh, dear! Rubia! What happened?"

"The same as you, Uncle Emilio. But just like you, it looks worse than it is."

They took the stairs arm in arm. Ellen smiled at the next-door neighbor ogling their matching lumps and then greeted Graciela and Raphael in the doorway. She was heartened by the familiar smell of their kitchen and the high pitched babbling of Francisco coming from the living room. Graciela led Ellen to the boy and they chanted on the carpet until called to dinner. After the meal, all returned to the sitting room for a chat, aided by a carafe of La Rioja. Ellen called to Francisco who was rocking in the corner with the cat on his lap.

"Francisco. Do you still have the radio I gave you?"

Rafael spoke up. "I'm afraid he hasn't listened since the burglary."

She tried again. "I brought you a gift. Would you like to see it?"

The kid didn't budge. His brother went to him, whispered in his ear, and then led him by the hand to

Ellen's feet where the kid squatted and began to see-saw. She retrieved a package from her traveling bag and offered it to the boy.

"How kind of you, Elena," said Graciela.

Simply wrapped in banker's tissue and tied with a thin yellow ribbon, she held it in the boy's line of sight. Coaxed to take it, he toyed with the ribbon, but when Raphael tore the paper and exposed a patch of leather, the scrawny boy's eyes centered. He squealed and ripped the paper away, revealing Hakkam's lost book. Bolting up and shouting alleluias in Rafael's face, he gave Ellen his biggest smile and then leaped into Emilio's lap, book in hand and speaking for the first time since the theft.

"Read, Papi! Read Paco's Book!"

For a moment Emilio was paralyzed, but then he hugged Paco and cried. Rafael and Graciela rushed to them, stroking the old book and joining the embrace. Again the boy demanded that his father read.

Ellen echoed his plea. "Go on, Emilio. 'Read Paco's book.'"

The father fought for composure as his silky voice flowed, turning each verse into a serenade. The boy's twitching ebbed as he tasted each word. Occasionally he repeated a phrase. Finally weary, he reached for the book and led his father to his room with the others in tow.

Paco kissed his dad on the lips. "Thank you, Papi. I love you," he said.

Emilio tried to ease the book away, but Paco held tight and they returned to the living room, wet eyed all. After refreshing their glasses Ellen asked for their attention, saying she had a second surprise. She told her story, revealing the ancient nature of their heirlooms, that the scrolls were safe with her priest, and that she'd like to negotiate a price.

"A price?" asked Emilio.

"Yes," Ellen said. "The scrolls are worth a great deal of money. We were surprised you didn't know. I'm sure you don't want to give up another family treasure, but now that the scrolls' existence is known, there are those who would have them at any cost. I'm afraid they can only bring danger to your family, Emilio, real danger."

Emilio explained. "My father said it would be disrespectful to unroll them. After he died the family talked about it, but in the end we decided to leave them alone. We had no idea they were copies of the sayings in the old book."

"Actually, Emilio, the book is a copy of the scrolls," Ellen said.

They spoke into the night, at last agreeing that Ellen would represent the family and make the best bargain. Emilio insisted that she take the customary bazaar commission, twenty percent, and he refused to approve until she accepted. Then she asked a favor.

"I made photocopies of the book when I found it, before I knew it was yours," she said. "I'd like your permission to use them in my work. We would publish the sayings through my university, first as they were originally written in al-Hakkam's Arabic, and then in every language, with the proceeds going to our Antiquities Department for future investigations. You have to know, though—the rights are worth a lot of money—and you'd be giving that away. But no one will know you have the original. I'll be sure to say it was found apart from the scrolls and that it's in a wealthy man's library. All of that will be true: you'll be a rich man from the sale of the scrolls and Paco's book will be on the prayer room shelf where it's always been."

They approved with broad smiles. "Rubia, my dear Rubia. I speak for us all," Emilio said. "Certainly, your school may publish the sayings. To be sure, we must share Paco's book with the world. It's what Grandfather

Zegrí would have wished, and my father after him. Praise God!"

"Thank you, Emilio. Thank you, all," declared Ellen. "God is the greatest."

52

THE NEW YORK BOSS

Monday, 20 July, 10:50 A.M.
Apt. 203B, 44 Calle Colón
Granada
Spain

Ellen spent the night with Emilio's family, sleeping soundly on their daybed with her cellphone silenced. After a salty morning bath and a calming chant with Paco, she reminisced with Graciela over coffee and carved fruit in their sun-splashed kitchen. Emilio and Rafael were off to work but Paco rocked on the stool between them, reading from the old book.

Ellen saw three voicemails when she activated her phone. Moving to the quiet of the living room, she listened in the order received. The first rich voice was her favorite, Monsignor Brahaney's, and the news was good.

"Hello, Ellie. Sorry you're not there. I wanted you to know that Malmut's been released to my custody and that we're safe in the Mount Street rectory. The saddlebags are secure in Barclay's vault, with keys and passwords separate. I'll wait for your call, my dear and, just a moment… Malmut wants to talk."

She'd heard Malmut in the background, pestering Monsignor for the phone. The Rascal spoke in English. "Miss Ché! I am with joy to know you are well. God be praised. I miss you very and am proud as Raisuli's lion to be on the team. Please to hurry back."

She chuckled and went on to the second message, from Mateo. He was cryptic as expected, but loud and machine-gun fast, with alarm in his voice.

"Ellie! We have to talk. The game's changed. We're at the Ritz. Call, please."

She replayed the message but still couldn't make sense of it.

The third voicemail was from Pariser as he crossed the Atlantic. The mogul addressed her excitedly. "Ellie. It's Stephen Pariser. Congratulations on your triumph. I'm ashamed to admit it, but I'd just about given up. I'll be in London by morning." He paused. "I think I understand the offering terms. There's tax timing to consider since we'll be gifting the scrolls to the Huntington, but I'm confident we can negotiate a fair price. I understand you've requested that the young Moroccan be hired. Mateo agrees. We can always use more security. And Ellie, I imagine Mateo's filled you in about Paul Parkinson. I was shocked. Don't worry, we'll see to him... That's all. Ciao!"

It was confounding. Mateo hadn't mentioned Parkinson, and there was no call from the peevish professor. *Odd*, she mused, *I thought at least one of the voicemails would've been from the professional jerk.*

Mateo answered her call on the first ring.

"Ellie! Are you okay? I've been calling every ten minutes."

"Sure, I'm okay. Why shouldn't I be?"

"It's Parkinson, Ellie. He's been on the other side all the time. In fact, he *is* the other side. I kept thinking about the cellphone he was carrying in London—cheap and disposable—the kind you'd use to avoid a trace. *He* was the one getting the coded texts!"

Ellen pondered. "What? You mean from Adivar's driver?"

"Yeah. The Puerto Rican was working for Parkinson, along with Adivar and Kundak. I told the boss what I suspected and he was skeptical, but our crew found the ciphers in his desk at the library. Adivar's messages were going straight to Parkinson, and every order back to Spain was from him. He was the Turks' New York boss and was using Pariser's money to finance the whole thing. We're looking everywhere for him. Where are you?"

"I stayed over, at Emilio's," she answered.

"That's bad. You mentioned Emilio's name in the hospital, remember? I'm sure Parkinson caught it. It won't take him long. He knows how much … You gotta get outta there, Ellie!"

"What about Emilio and his family?" she asked.

"What about 'em?"

"That means they're in danger, too," she said. "Graciela and Francisco are with me. I won't leave them alone."

"You have to think about yourself, Ellie. You won't be as lucky the second time."

"We'll see about that," she said. "We'll go somewhere and call you. Get here as fast as you can! 203B, 44 Calle Colón!"

"But Ellie!"

"Just get here, Mateo."

Loud pounding came from the foyer as she said goodbye. It wasn't knocking. Someone was trying to get in.

53

FRANCISCO de ZEGRÍ

Monday, 20 July, 11:15 A.M.
Apt. 203B, 44 Calle Colón
Granada
Spain

The hammering quickened as Ellen moved to warn Graciela. She watched as the door panel fractured and then shattered to splinters with a heel. Two men squeezed through the jagged hole. It was Parkinson, preceded by his new thug, a bulky North African in plain black jellaba. Ellen threw a candlestick at the man and fled to Paco's room, trying on the way to quick-dial Mateo, but the husky man forced the door and pinned her against a dresser as the boy cowered on his bed clutching his precious book. The brute dragged Ellen by the hair into the living room and tossed her onto the sofa. When she tried to stand, he wound up and slapped across her ear.

Paco trailed them, cursing when the man hit her. As Parkinson restrained his mother, the boy attacked the hulk with his dainty fists and was swatted aside like an insect. Instantly the runt popped up and charged again, this time attempting a tackle at the knees. Unmoved but plainly irritated, the thug used his fist. The heavy blow on Paco's neck drove him to the floor. All watched the courageous kid struggle to his haunches and crawl away, through the beaded curtain and into the prayer room.

Parkinson changed places with the brute as Graciela cringed in the corner, her eyes fixed on the curtain. He loomed over Ellen and snickered.

"Well, Shea, it seems you're bait once again, and this time you shan't escape, either with the artifacts *or* your life."

"To hell with you, Parkinson. You'll never get what you're after."

"We shall see. Love is blind, as they say, and musk the strongest attractant. May we borrow your phone?"

She looked away. Parkinson ordered his man to take it, and as the goon was presenting the cellphone it sounded with the opening trumpets of *The William Tell Overture*. The professor tapped it on but said nothing.

"Ellie? Did you get out of there?" the caller asked.

Parkinson answered. "No, my good man, she did not. But don't fret. Your precious 'Ellie' is with us. I must say, Mateo, I'm disappointed in my old roommate—such disloyalty for a red man—what's become of your code? And you must know how difficult Stephen is making my life. No matter. We shall consider the tally even, *after* you instruct the priest to give me the scrolls."

"But I just talked to her! How could you? " Mateo questioned.

"Do you think I'm bluffing, Barefoot? Please. This time you're not dealing with that fat fool, Adivar. I'll accept no Trojan horse as he did. And be assured—the girl will suffer greatly as she dies—unless you produce the scrolls. Perhaps we should give you a preview."

He aimed the phone toward Ellen and ordered his accomplice to hurt her. The man hiked his sleeves and squeezed her hand white. She whimpered.

"More!" commanded Parkinson.

Ellen yelped as the bully doubled her wrist. Parkinson signaled his approval and then taunted Mateo.

"Sufficient, my Redskin friend? I'll ask again. Do you think I'm bluffing?"

Then all looked to Graciela as she screamed. "Paco! Paco!"

She'd seen her little boy parting the curtain with the unsheathed Jambiya dagger, but the others were distracted by her cry and did not. The sixty pound child charged the black robe and drove the razor-knife through it, between the lower ribs of his heroine's assailant. The tip of its blade severed his aorta, and he exsanguinated in seconds.

As Parkinson gaped, Ellen bisected his groins with the point of her shoe. He fell to his knees as she jumped to her feet in search of the candlestick. Swinging the thick pewter with long arms, she batted him in the temple, toppling his ganglyness to the floor.

Graciela eased the dripping blade from Paco's hand and placed it on a high shelf. She cradled her boy as Ellen hogtied the unconscious professor with an extension cord. That accomplished, she retrieved the cellphone from the floor. Mateo had witnessed every sound.

"Mateo?"

"Ellie! What's happening? Are you okay?"

"I'm okay, but we need you—I need you."

"We're on the tarmac," Mateo answered. "We'll be there as fast as the jet can fly. Are you sure you're all right?"

"203B, 44 Calle Colón, on the Alcazar corner," she answered. "No need to knock."

Pariser and Barefoot arrived at sunset. They found Emilio and a homicide detective in the living room, standing aside as technicians photographed the blood-blotched carpet. Paco and Raphael cuddled behind them in the easy chair, whispering with arms entwined. Mateo asked for Ellen and was told she was resting at the neighbors'. He found her alone on their flowered terrace, reclining on a futon and staring into the pink sky. She wore a splint on her wrist and a fresh dressing on her ear.

Mateo lingered in the doorway. At last, he called softly.

"Ellie?"

Through bloodshot eyes, ghost pale, and with bruises stark in the dying sunlight, she looked at him as not before. He knelt and extended a hand. She drew him to her and they kissed twice, the first soft and sweet, the second much more.

Both could see heaven.

54

THE CELEBRITIES

Wednesday, 21 October, 2:05 P.M.
Martyr's Lawn, Fordham University
Rose Hill Campus
Bronx, New York
U.S.A.

Autumn in New York City can be magical, even in the Bronx. The sloping meadow on the southern quarter of Fordham's campus flaunted fall's colors, with all staged as the university intended. Scarlet maples and orange-tinged oaks lined the walkway to Martyr's Court, framing the celebrities against an emerald field as they posed on a captain's bench. With eyes front and elbows touching, they endured a host of flashing cameras. Stephen Pariser anchored the center, hands clasped. The monsignor and then Mateo flanked him on the right, with Ellen and Malmut on the opposite side. All but the Apache tried for photogenic smiles.

The young men resembled matching bookends, one jumbo and the other his miniature. In dark pinstripes and crimson ties, their shades and earpieces were stored for the moment. Malmut's braid was shorter but knotted like Mateo's, and he aped the big man precisely. Ellen dressed formally but down, repressing her beauty with wool and clear glasses. Monsignor squirmed in frock and collar, but the boss was at ease as he directed the scene.

The intermittent commotion of jostling journalists allowed for snippets of conversation among the bench sitters, but the man in the middle offered the only comments, his raspy voice squeezed between waves of camera clatter. "I'm sad that this is our last meeting. We must stay in touch—a yearly reunion with the scrolls in San Marino, perhaps—heaven knows, we might find another adventure." He laughed. "I've enjoyed our time together and am satisfied. The contracts we've just signed assure that the documents will be available to all scholars, and then to the public."

Another wave muddied the last of his remarks. "Congratulations on your pending appointment, Ellie. I'm sure the university is pleased and Monsignor content knowing that his department will be in such capable hands.

"And Malmut, we're happy to have you and your wildlife on board."

The imp beamed. There was a final flourish before the boss stood.

"All right, ladies and gentlemen, that'll do!" Pariser shouted. He called to his men. "It's time we accompany the scrolls to their new home. With me, now."

Mateo and Malmut donned their shades as they bracketed Pariser, the big man elbowing a swath out front and his clone en guard behind. Monsignor and Ellen strolled away arm in arm, pausing on the chapel stairs to wave at the helicopter as it banked toward them and over the painted trees.

Monsignor faced Ellen and took her hands.

"I'll be giving thanks now, in our usual spot. Would you care to join me?"

Her face flexed. At the end of a sigh, a smile broke out.

"Sure!"

EPILOGUE

THE HIEROPHANT

A.D. 2018
National Mall
Washington, D.C.
U.S.A.

The armored triaxle passing through Huntington's stone gates was licensed to haul one ton of valuables. But instead of cash cubes or steel boxes filled with gems or precious metal, the cabin guards stared down on the puniest though most valuable load they'd ever carried: two pine crates weighing thirty-nine pounds. CHP motorcycles flashed amber and blue, encircling the truck as it lumbered down the library causeway. A cloud of uniforms enveloped the vehicle at the receiving dock as the driver dismounted to muscle the doors and then pass the crates to the librarians. Stacks of papers were signed before a flock of academics dollied them to the document laboratory.

It took most of a year for Huntington's technicians to aquify, flatten, repair, and at last affix the ancient parchments inside their climate-perfect stages, and nearly as long before Papias' scrolls were formally presented to the world. Professor Shea's translations were swift, with electronic renditions of Hakkam's text released in time for Christmas. The salient preface was attributed to "J.P. Brahaney, S.J."

The great church bureaucracies responded as the monsignor predicted. Only Muslims embraced the scriptures whole. Because the science of the scrolls' substance was difficult to deny, most Christian denominations declared them documents of interest and relegated them to perpetual study. The few accepting Papias' Logia bound it as an ancillary text, all scriptural conflicts ignored. The inerrancy faction denounced the scrolls as devils' deceit and their finders agents of the Antichrist. Their scathing sermons mated Papias' collection with evolution, climate change, and other "secular myths."

Then the earthquake began, as do so many, with a trifling tremor. In the winter following Professor Shea's first publication, on a blustery mountainside inside Barón's Chapel of the Little Martyrs, a pimply preacher delivered his first homily to a dozen halfhearted parishioners who'd been lured to the service by the promise of hard cider. On the following Sunday, the small building overflowed with the curious and just convinced, and by the fourth Sabbath the teen was invited down the mountain to Órgiva's football stadium, overflowing with two thousand eager faces.

From there the speed and power of the spiritual cyclone had no precedent. In each succeeding locale the youngster's sermons were declared inspired and his delivery the most eloquent any ear could remember. His routine never varied—only the language changed— each time to a dialect that matched his audience. As he was being introduced the boy would fidget in the wings, head bobbing with eyes to the floor and fingers in his mouth. When called, he'd timidly step to the podium with text in hand and then shrink behind it until the applause ebbed. But then, as the expectant multitude came quiet, he'd open the little book, arch scarecrow tall, and blossom.

After reading a passage, the boy mesmerized each audience with a thirty-three minute homily. Dramatic and cogent, he linked one bold notion to the next, seasoning his allegory with dollops of common sense. His conclusions came in a cascading crescendo, but then, with the last word, he closed the book, deflated, and fled into the shadows. Invariably he was pursued by his look-alike companion, the same young man who'd introduced him and the one who managed his every move.

The pair hopscotched through seventeen Spanish capitols before crossing the Pyrenees, where in the same fashion and in equally matched vernaculars the boy enchanted the French nation. They progressed in that manner across the continent, presenting fresh interpretations of Papias' Logia to ever larger crowds. The youngster and his handler shunned all contact as they canvassed the capitols of Asia, Australia, and Africa. By the second year, when they landed in South America, their arrival was heralded as an historic event.

The young speaker seemed to choose his excerpts at random, reading only a line or two at one stop, but then pages at the next. Each interpretation was novel: ardent but shy of zealous, congruent but never predictable, and always hypnotic. Not every pundit favored his perspective—there were legions of detractors—but all likened him to their greatest orators. In France he was compared to Danton, at Westminster to Churchill, in Botswana to Shaka Zulu, and in Bogota to Bolivar.

The boy-preacher's last appearance filled the mall in Washington. Following his usual introduction, Professor Shea led him by the hand from behind Lincoln's statue and then took her place by his side. When the multitude quieted, he inflated and opened with his usual refrain, spoken that day in Standard General American.

"I am Francisco of Granada, disciple of Abraham, Papias, and al-Hakkam, keeper of Jesus' sayings and sayer of His teachings, come to you this day from Ottawa to tell of godly things, of things that never die."

Then he paged to the back of the little red book and for the first time in public read Papias' final passage. "And when the last supper ended, Jesus called Mary to his side and whispered. 'I will return to you when the Hierophant is taken. In the still of the last dawn you will find me...'"

The Americans answered his end-of-days sermon with a colossal roar followed by continuous applause. Then, as Francisco closed the book, his body lurched across the podium and fell limp into Ellen's arms, driven by the sniper's bullet as it mushroomed through his brain. Once again she was drenched in blood and on her knees, holding him tight and rhythmically rocking as she chanted the saints' names in the hopeless hope that he would respond.

Inspired by Francisco's insight and motivated by his martyrdom, spontaneous movements arose. One that sprouted among the nonesters of southern Germany gradually eclipsed the others and began to erode the established sects. Its followers swore themselves true to the tenets of the Logia and to any document vetted by their scholars. With only oral guidelines and no hierarchy, its goal was to be faithful to Papias' example: to collect and spread the words. Profit and professional clerics were among the few things forbidden. Their meeting houses were constructed on the Quaker model: simple buildings with concentric central amphitheaters and peripheral social quarters. Weekly gatherings were unique to each congregation, though nearly all opened with incantations and song. Discussion then followed in the Roman example: members stood to offer their interpretations and then awaited comment from their fellows. Francisco's analyses were most often referenced.

They were labeled "Bavarians" by their detractors but called themselves "Readers" and named their sole text "The Quelle." By convention, each reading house kept one copy per member. In most they were kept on shelves encircling the amphitheater, in some beneath a cross, and in others between bronzed saddlebags.

Bound in red goatskin with the acrostic fish on its cover, each frontispiece bore a single quotation.

"I am in you and in all that surrounds you. You need only my words to find the way."

omega

END

APPENDIX OF HISTORICAL CHARACTERS

1.   EUSEBIUS OF CAESAREA (263-339 CE) – Church historian, bishop, and participant at the Council of Nicaea, he was commissioned by Emperor Constantine to create a collection of accepted scripture for the churches of Constantinople. Eusebius was succeeded by Acacius of Caesarea, his brilliant single-eyed student.

2.   PAPIAS OF HIEROPOLIS (80?-155 CE) – Early Christian leader who sought out and recorded oral accounts of Christian pioneers like John the Apostle who were "spreading the words" of Jesus in the southeastern provinces of the Roman Empire. Papias called his collection "Logia," meaning "Sayings and Deeds." His Logia would have contained much of the Quelle source referenced in this novel as well as the "L" and "M" sources of Luke and Matthew, but no copy of his record is known to survive.

3.   JESUS OF NAZARETH (4BCE-29 CE) – A homeless Jewish peasant, disciple of John the Baptist, exorcist, miracle worker, and orator, this escatologic prophet was crucified by the Romans for sedition in the third decade of the modern era. Some of his followers believed that he rose from the dead and was the long predicted savior of the Jewish people, anticipating his prompt return when he would expel the Romans and establish a Jewish Kingdom. It was that promise and his message of eternal salvation that made the new religion thrive, along with its rejection of the corrupt order and its teaching of equality,

charity, and hope. As important as Jesus' deeds and lessons was their recording after his death, passed on papyrus and parchment from one community to the next. In the first centuries there were many competing Christian sects with disparate perspectives and literatures. Despite persecution, the nimble religion evolved and coalesced, separating from Judaism and allying with Rome to become the dominant faith and primary influence of western civilization. Jesus remains an essential prophet in the Islamic world, where he and his mother are greatly revered.

4. MORTON SMITH (1915-1991 CE) – A Columbia University professor who, in 1958, while researching the Greek Orthodox library of Mar Saba, discovered and photographed a mysterious letter from Bishop Clement of Alexandria. The third century letter alluded to the existence of an earlier, "more spiritual" gospel, one that contained "secrets to the Kingdom of God." The document was sequestered and supposedly misplaced. It has not been seen since 1977.

5. IGNATIUS OF ANTIOCH (40?-107? CE) – Disciple of the apostle John, companion of the pioneer Polycarp, and willing martyr, he was an avid opponent of the Gnostics and one of the first Jews to embrace the label "Christian." He taught the unequivocal divinity of Christ, advocated a hierarchy of bishops, priests, and deacons, adopted the term "catholic" to infer the universality of his religion, and advocated John of Patmos' version of Revelations.

6. CONSTANTINE THE GREAT (272-337 CE) – Roman Emperor from 306 to 337, he embraced Christianity, resulting in its legalization in

313. From then on he nurtured the church but remained ecumenical and unbaptized until his dying days. In 325, for congruent religious and political reasons, he called a meeting of bishops near his palace at Nicaea to facilitate the confederation of Christian belief. The result was a common creed.

7.   POLYCARP OF SMYRNA (69-155 CE) – Older confidant of Papias and disciple of John the Apostle, he interacted with eyewitnesses to Jesus and preserved their accounts. Polycarp was martyred as an old man, possibly alongside Papias.

8.   ORIGEN OF ALEXANDRIA (185-254 CE) – A passionate Christian scholar, ascetic, and free thinker of the third century who was forced to leave Alexandria for Caesarea in 231 where he headed a catechetical school that became a lynchpin of the growing religion. An avid collector of early Christian documents, he interpreted scripture in the liberal Greek tradition and categorized each text as acknowledged, disputed, or spurious. His methods were perpetuated by later scholars like Eusebius.

9.   PAUL (SAUL) OF TARSUS (5-67 CE) – An important, some say central, influence on the course of Christianity, he was a Roman citizen and contemporary of Jesus, though they never met. As a young man he was an avid persecutor of Christians, but after his miraculous conversion he proselytized tirelessly, especially among gentiles, utilizing Roman roads and ships to disperse his distinctive perspective of Christ. Many of Paul's beliefs were at odds with Jesus' brother James and the apostle Simon Peter, but it was his alternate version, especially as expressed in his letters, which became doctrine.

10.   THEODORE (GREGORY) THAUMATURGUS OF
      CAESAREA (240?-309 CE) – A devoted disciple
      of Origen, he became bishop of Caesarea and
      was best known as a miracle-worker. Tireless
      and ingenious in his proselytizing, he utilized
      pagan customs to convert the entire region to
      Christianity.

11.   ALEXANDER OF ALEXANDRIA (280?-328 CE) –
      Egyptian bishop and the primary opponent of a
      popular doctrine espoused by one of his Libyan
      priests, Arius, which said that Jesus was lesser
      than God the Father. Initially successful in his
      effort to defeat Arius at the Council of Nicaea, he
      was succeeded by his secretary, Athanasius, who
      continued the struggle.

12.   OSIUS OF CORDUBA (257-359? CE) – Bishop of
      Corduba, Hispania (Roman Spain) and advisor
      to Emperor Constantine, it may have been at his
      urging that the Council of Nicaea take place, and
      he may have presided. A lifelong antagonist of the
      Arian philosophy, his wisdom and integrity were
      respected by all.

13.   IRANEUS OF LUGDUNUM – (125?–202 CE)
      An influential second century bishop, he
      compiled one of the first church canons. He's
      said to have reasoned that since there were four
      elements, four winds, and four seasons, there
      should be four gospels. Iraneus championed
      those of Matthew, Mark, Luke, and John while
      advocating the destruction of others. In his
      treatise *Against Heresies* he denounced the
      Gnostics and other unorthodox sects, and in the
      same era advanced the concept of an Antichrist.

14. ATHANASIUS OF ALEXANDRIA (296?-373 CE) – Bishop Alexander's secretary at Nicaea, the assertive clergyman succeeded Alexander and continued the struggle against the Arians. In his Easter message of 367, he advocated a list of scriptures including John of Patmos' apocalypse. With little modification, that collection set the standard for the New Testament. Like Iraneus before him, he labeled competing scriptures heresy and advocated their suppression. The Nag Hammadi cache may have been hidden by monks to avoid Athanasius' censors.

15. MUGIT-AL-RUMI (680?-730? CE) – Berber warrior and fearsome lieutenant of Tariq ibn-Ziyad, he was ordered to capture Christian Visigoth Corduba in 712. He did so efficiently, by bribing the gatekeepers and annihilating the defenders after besieging them in the Church of the Martyr.

16. AL-HAKKAM II (915-976 CE) – The wise and openly gay Caliph (king) of al-Andaluz (Muslim Spain) who reigned from 961 to 976 in his magnificent capitol of Qurtubah (old Corduba). The Caliphate thrived under his tolerant rule, significantly expanding its borders and wealth. He was a booklover and patron of education who undertook the massive task of translating his half-million Greek and Latin volumes into Arabic. All but a few of those texts were later destroyed by Islamic fanatics.

17. FERNANDO III OF CASTILE (1199-1252 CE) – A successful king in Spain's fight to reclaim their lands from the Muslims (Moors), his armies liberated several cities in al-Andaluz (the Andalusia of modern Spain), including Corduba.

18.   MUHAMMAD XII (1460-1533 CE) – The twenty-second and last Nasrid ruler of al-Andaluz (Muslim Spain). Known to the Spaniards as Boabdil, he fought on both sides of the Reconquista (reconquering of Spain), in the end losing his realm to Ferdinand and Isabella. He's best known for his "last sigh," an act of regret on horseback from a viewpoint overlooking Granada as he rode toward exile in the Alpujarras Mountains. He lived there only briefly, choosing to return to his ancestral homeland in North Africa while leaving many of his belongings behind.

19.   KING FERDINAND OF ARAGON (1452-1516 CE)

20.   QUEEN ISABELLA OF CASTILE AND LEON (1451-1504 CE) – The "Catholic Monarchs" united their kingdoms and then seized the rest of southern Iberia from the Moors, creating the modern nation of Spain. Their final triumph was marked by an extravagant riverside surrender of the last Muslim stronghold, Granada. They seized that city from their old ally Muhammad XII (Boabdil) and then sent him into exile, gifting him an estate south of Granada in the Alpujarras region of the Sierra Nevada Mountains.

21.   FERNANDO DE VÁLOR (1520-1569 CE) – Known to his fellow Muslims as Aben Humeya, he led the ill-fated Morisco revolt, an uprising against the Spanish King which devolved into a guerilla war. For their disloyalty, the Morisco inhabitants of the Alpujarras were exiled and replaced by the Spanish king with settlers from the North, though one Morisco family was allowed to remain in each village to teach highland farming to the newcomers.

22.   RODRIGO ZEGRÍ (1911-1937 CE) – A composite character invented for this novel, he's depicted as a descendent of Morisco sheepherders and a soldier in the Spanish Foreign Legion. Zegrí is portrayed as a deserter from the Legion at the onset of the Spanish Civil War and a Republican hero at the Battle of Guadalajara, fighting there against the Nationalists led by his old general, Francisco Franco. In the novel, he and his descendants inherit Morisco artifacts from the era of the Christmas revolt.

23.   FRANCISCO FRANCO (1892-1975 CE) – General of the Spanish army and leader of the Nationalist (Royalist) faction against the Republicans in the Spanish Civil War, he proved to be a consummate politician, said by Adolph Hitler to be the only man who ever outsmarted him. He assumed dictatorship in 1939 and then wisely avoided joining the other fascist states that were about to be defeated in the Second World War. Franco ruled Spain ruthlessly for nearly four decades in close alliance with the Catholic Church.

24.   KING JUAN CARLOS DE BOURBON (1938-CE) – Modern King of Spain who was chosen by the dictator Francisco Franco to continue his repressive rule, he wisely and willingly gave his power to the young Spanish democracy.

25.   SIRHANE BEN ABDELMAJID FAKET (1968-2004 CE) A Tunisian Al Qaeda terrorist, he mastermind the 2004 Madrid train bombing which killed or maimed two thousand innocents. Carried out on the brink of a national election, the attack altered the course of Spain's government and its support for the American war in Iraq.

26.   BART EHRMAN (1955- CE) – A New Testament scholar, professor of biblical studies, and popular author, he was first trained in the evangelical tradition. An authoritative and commonly referenced agnostic, his books and blog have helped to introduce biblical scholarship to the public. Some of Ehrman's work has been challenged, especially by advocates of biblical inerrancy.

27.   ELAINE PAGELS (1943- CE) – A meticulous and insightful religious historian, professor, and author of popular texts explaining Gnostic, Satanic, and Apocalyptic Christian literature, she lapsed from and then returned to the Christian faith.

28.   CARLTON PEARSON (1953- CE) – A contemporary Christian pastor and disciple of Oral Roberts, he enjoyed a large fundamentalist following replete with the trappings of a modern media preacher until he declared a change in his beliefs by denying the logic of hell and inerrancy of the Bible.

APPENDIX OF HISTORICAL
REFERENCES

a. GNOSTICISM – A belief system originating around the time of Jesus which by the second century threatened mainstream Christianity. Like Greek, Egyptian, and Eastern mystics, Gnostics taught that to achieve spiritual fulfillment one must acquire knowledge (gnosis) by looking to the self and that a church was not necessary to do so. They claimed a secret oral knowledge from Jesus himself but assigned an unorthodox meaning to his acts and resurrection, believing that they were not literal. Most of the texts discovered at Nag Hammadi were Gnostic.

b. QUELLE THEORY – In the nineteenth century, scholars noted many factual differences when comparing the Christian gospels to each other. At the same time, they marked many similarities between the Gospels of Matthew and Luke, much of which seemed to come from the older Gospel of Mark. They theorized that other congruent portions of Matthew and Luke came from a second set of early documents. Thus, the "two-source hypothesis" was born. They called the theoretical second set of scriptures "Quelle," German for "Source." This second source has been referred to as "Q, Q Manuscript, Q Document, Q Gospel, Sayings Gospel, and Synoptic Sayings Source." Written in Greek and perhaps Aramaic, it represents the earliest and therefore least altered record of Jesus' sayings and stories, only some of which made it into the New Testament. Papias of Hierapolis may have documented much of the Quelle.

c.   CODEX SINIATICUS FOLIOS – In 1859, under the auspices of the Czar of Russia, Constantin Tischendorf rescued a cache of Greek folios from St. Catherine's monastery near Mount Sinai. Copies of the Old and New Testaments which may have originated in the library at Caesarea, they revealed critical differences when compared to modern Bibles, including additions to the Gospel of Mark.

d.   NAG HAMMADI TEXTS – In 1945, an Egyptian farmer found several Coptic codices buried in a jar. They were papyrus copies of Christian and other writings, largely Gnostic and likely translated from Greek. Several were unknown, including the "sayings" gospel of Thomas. Neither apocalyptic nor messianic and likely part of the Quelle, they appear to have been hidden by Pachomian monks to avoid destruction by Bishop Athanasius' censors. Their discovery ignited new interest in the concept of the Quelle.

e.   DEAD SEA SCROLLS – Between 1946 and 1956, approximately one thousand biblical and related documents were discovered in the Essene caves at Khirbet Qumran, near the shore of the Dead Sea. The originals were sequestered for decades, but photocopies were finally released in 1991 by California's Huntington Library.

f.   AL-ANDALUZ – In 711, Berber infantry and Arab cavalry from North Africa invaded Iberia in the name of Muhammad. The Spaniards called them Moors. In a few decades they created a wealthy, tolerant, and enlightened culture that thrived for hundreds of years. Al-Andaluz and its capital, Corduba, were shining islands of civilization during Europe's otherwise Dark Age.

g. HAKKAM'S LIBRARY – Al Hakkam XII, the gifted caliph of al-Andaluz (Muslim Spain), embarked on a lifelong project to translate his huge collection of Latin and Greek literature into Arabic. Tragically, after his death, the library was destroyed by a second North African invasion.

h. VULGATE - A compilation of older Latin versions of the Bible (Vetus Latina) commissioned by Pope Damasus in 382. Largely the work of St. Jerome and widely disseminated as the *Versio Vulgata*, it was later translated into European languages. Scholars have enumerated substantive differences in Jerome's work and its subsequent translations as compared to the original Latin and Greek texts.

i. THE RECONQUISTA – Beginning in Northwest Spain and under the banner of Saint James, the Spaniards slowly reclaimed their country from the Muslims whom they called Moors. Their struggle culminated in 1492 with the elaborate surrender of Granada by Muhammad XII (Boabdil) to King Ferdinand and Queen Isabella.

j. THE MORISCO REVOLT – In 1568, descendants of the Moors called Moriscos attempted to reclaim the Alpujarras region from Spain. On Christmas Eve, they launched a guerilla war by seizing several mountain villages. The revolt was crushed after its leader, Aben Humeya (Fernando de Válor) was assassinated by his rivals.

k. THE SPANISH CIVIL WAR – In 1931, Spanish reformers ousted the conservatives (Royalists) and founded the Second Republic, an ineffective democracy that proved unable to govern. Five years later the same conservatives, calling themselves Nationalists, recalled General Franco from Africa to lead them against the Republic. His merciless campaigns triumphed in 1939. As vicious as any war of the twentieth century, the conflict haunts Spain to this day.

1.   MADRID BOMBINGS – On March 11, 2004, Al Qaeda operatives bombed several commuter trains in and around Madrid's Atocha Station. Nearly two hundred died and eighteen-hundred were injured in the cold hearted assault. The attack led to a change of government and ended Spain's support for the American war in Iraq.

RELATED TEXTS

Christ Actually, James Carrol, Viking Adult (2014)

Waking Up: A Guide to Spirituality Without Religion, S. Harris, Simon & Schuster (2014)

How Jesus Became God, Bart Ehrman, HarperOne (2014)

Jesus: The Human Face of God, Jay Parini, New Harvest (2013)

Christian Beginnings, Geza Vermes, Yale Press (2013)

Christianity After Religion, Diane Butler Bass, HarperOne (2013)

Zealot: The Life and Times of Jesus of Nazareth, Reza Azlan, Radom House (2013)

Bad Religion: How We Became a Nation of Heretics, Ross Douthat, Free Press (2013)

Canon Revisited, Michael J. Kruger, Crossway (2012)

The Power of Parable, J. Crossan, Harper Collins (2012)

Revelations, Elaine Pagels, Penguin (2012)

Through the Eye of a Needle, Peter Brown, Princeton Press (2012)

Francis of Assisi: A New Biography, Augustine Thompson, Cornell Press (2012)

Did Jesus Exist, Bart Ehrman, HarperOne (2012)

Heaven in the American Imagination, Gary Scott Smith, Oxford Press (2011)

Forged, Bart Ehrman, HarperOne (2011)

A Concise History of Spain, Wm. & Caria Philips, Cambridge Univ. Press (2010)

Last Steps: The Late Writings of Leo Tolstoy, Jay Parini, Penguin (2009)

A New History of Early Christianity, Charles Freeman, Yale Press (2009)

Jesus Interrupted, Bart Ehrman, HarperOne (2009)

The Gospel of Inclusion, Carlton Pearson, Atria Books (2008)

Surprised by Hope: Rethinking Heaven, N.T. Wright, HarperOne, (2008)

A Marginal Jew, Volumes 3,2,1, John P. Meier, Doubleday (2007, 2001, 1994)

Jesus for the Non-Religious, John Shelby Spong, Harper (2007)

Eusebius: The Church History, per Paul Maier, Kregel Academic (2007)

El Documento Q, Cesar Vidal, Grupo Planeta (2005)

Misquoting Jesus, Bart Ehrman, HarperOne (2005)

No god but God, Reza Azlan, Random House (2005)

The Gnostic Gospels of Jesus, Marvin Meyer, Harper Collins (2005)

Gallo Rojo, Gallo Negro, La Guerra Civil, Daniel Muchnik, Grupo Editorial (2004)

Beyond Belief, The Secret Gospel of Thomas, Elaine Pagels, Random House (2004)

Jesus: Apocalyptic Prophet, Bart Ehrman, Oxford U. Press, (2001)

The Essential Kierkegaard, Hong, Hong, and Hong, Princeton Press (2000)

The Case for Christ, Lee Strobel, Zondervan (1998)

The New Spaniards, John Hooper, Penguin (1995)

Jesus under Fire, J.P. Moreland & Michael Wilkins, Zondervan (1995)

The Lost Gospel: The Book of Q and Christian Origins, B. Mack, HarperOne (1994)

The Complete Gospels, Annotated Version, Robert J. Miller, Macmillan (1994)

A History of God, Karen Armstrong, Ballantine Books (1993)

Jesus, A Life, A.N. Wilson, W.W. Norton (1992)

The Historical Jesus: A Jewish Peasant, J. Crossan, Harper Collins (1991)

The Library of al-Hakkam, David Wasserstein, Ter Lugt Press (1991)

The Koran, Revised Translation, N.J. Dawood, Penguin Classics (1989)

Iberia, James Michener, Ballantine Books (1984)

The Gnostic Gospels, Elaine Pagels, Random House (1979)

Clement of Alexandria, The Secret Gospel of Mark, Morton Smith, Harvard Press (1973)

A Textual Commentary on the Greek New Testament, Bruce Metzger, Stuttgart (1971)

The Source, James Michener, Ballantine Books (1965)

Julian, Gore Vidal, Little, Brown & Co. (1964)

Mere Christianity, C.S. Lewis, Geoffrey Bles (1952)

The True Believer: The Nature of Mass Movements, Eric Hoffer, Harper Bros. (1951)

The Westminster Study Edition of the Holy Bible, Westminster Press (1948)

The Story of Civilization, vol. III, Caesar and Christ, Durant, Simon & Schuster (1944)

Discipleship, Dietrich Bonhoeffer, Munchen (1937)

Orthodoxy and Heresy in Earliest Christianity, Walter Bauer, Sigler Press (1934)

The Lost Books of the Bible, Solomon Schepps, Testament (1928)

A Commentary on the Holy Bible, J.R. Dummelow, MacMillan (1927)

The Golden Bough, James Fraser, Touchstone (1922)

Where We Got the Bible, Henry G. Graham, B. Herder Books (1911)

Quest of the Historical Jesus, Albert Schweitzer, Fortress Press (1906)

The Life and Morals of Jesus of Nazareth, Thomas Jefferson, National Museum (1904)

The Varieties of Religious Experience, William James, Touchstone (1902)

A Plain Introduction to Criticism of the New Testament, F. Scrivener, Bell & Sons (1894)

Life of Jesus, Critically Examined, David Strauss per Marian Evans, Blanchard (1846)

An Inquiry Concerning the Origin of Christianity, Charles C. Hennell, T. Allman (1838)

The Decline and Fall of the Roman Empire, Gibbon, Strahan, and Cadell (1789)

ABOUT THE AUTHOR

Joel Benner Keats is a retired medical school professor whose lifelong fascinations with science, history, and religion intersect in his novels. A Catholic altar boy steeped in evangelism as a teen, his exposure to Eastern, Native American, Muslim, and Jewish traditions allows for a kaleidoscope of historical and spiritual perspectives.